BULLET
CATCHER

BULLET CATCHER

JOAQUIN LOWE

HOT
KEY
BOOKS

First published in Great Britain in 2016 by Hot Key Books
80-81 Wimpole St, London W1G 9RE
www.hotkeybooks.com

A CIP catalogue record for this book is available from the British Library.

ISBN: 978-1-4714-0506-8
Also available as an ebook

1

This book is typeset in 10.5 Berling LT Std using Atomik ePublisher
Printed and bound by Clays Ltd, St Ives Plc

www.hotkeybooks.com

Hot Key Books is an imprint of Bonnier Publishing Fiction,
a Bonnier Publishing company
www.bonnierpublishingfiction.co.uk
www.bonnierpublishing.co.uk

For Paloma and Emiliano
And sibling rivalry

"We're catching bullets with our heads and hearts and all the darkest parts of us . . ."

From the song 'Bullets,' by Tunng

PART I

Chapter One

It's late at night when the memory comes for me, like it always seems to when the relief of sleep seems ready to draw me under. The fire. I recall it as a heat on my face, a deep, quickened voice that might be my father's, my brother's skinny arms around me, the glass of the windows blowing out, explosions that for the longest time I thought were fireworks. But they were gunshots; I know that now. The curtains going up like they were made to burn, like kindling. The thick smell of smoke. Then darkness.

All I can do is lie on my cot in the corner of the washroom, the same room where I've spent all day washing dishes in the back of the bar, and wait for the memory to burn itself out. The room is small and square. The sand oozes up between the splintery floorboards. There's the washbasin where I spend most of the day, and there's my beaten up writing desk in the corner, buried in books bought or stolen from traveling sellers.

Memory is a monster, far worse than anything lurking under a bed. I stare at the ceiling while my memories threaten to swallow me whole. I rub my eyes, slap my cheeks, anything to fight it off. But it's no good. So I close my eyes and I dig

3

down deep into the past, trying my best to remember the good times in between all the bad.

I think of my brother, Nikko. I think of our parents' old homestead, before the fire. I think we were happy then, but I was too young to know for sure. So young that when I try to imagine my parents' faces the image is blurred like a washed-out photograph. And then there's the monster again, coming for me in the memory of the orphanage, in the glowering faces of the Brothers and Sisters who took us in.

"Immaculada Amaya Moreno!" the Sister yelled. "Get over here now!"

And there I am, peeking out from behind my brother. He was bigger than me and good to hide behind.

"Imma," I said. "Call me Imma."

The Sister grabbed me by the arm and hauled me in front of some fat old man, the latest prospective adopter. Some who came to the orphanage wore the nervous expressions of hopeful parents, but mostly they were just people looking for cheap labor. Small hands are good for watch tinkering or bullet making. Small fingers are useful for polishing the inside of shell casings.

"This one's ready for immediate adoption to a good home," the Sister said. The fat man grabbed my hands and checked my fingers. Held me by the jaw and pulled down my lip and examined my teeth and the whites of my eyes like he was buying a farm animal.

"Too skinny," he said. "She looks ready to keel over any minute."

"You'd be getting her at a significant discount," the Sister said. But the fat man just snorted and moved on down the line, examining the other orphans. I hid back behind Nikko and he put his arm around me.

Back then, Nikko didn't have much more meat on his bones than me. He was starved-looking, cheeks pasty and sucked in, his smile crooked and forced. But he was always the strong one. He had a sorry little mustache that I remember him being so proud of. Whenever I think of him walking around with his shoulders back and his chin up to show everyone his new mustache, looking like a dead caterpillar stuck to his upper lip, it makes me smile, a smile so big my dry lips split and I taste copper. It's my second favorite memory of my brother.

One day, he took me by the shoulders, stared straight into my eyes and said, "Imma, after I get out of here, I'm going to join the bullet catchers. And all the wealthy families and banks and shop owners are going to want to hire me as their bodyguard."

"What'll happen to me?" I asked, my voice small and squeaky back then.

"I'll earn enough money to get you out of here. I'll buy a whole block of apartments in a wealthy town and we'll live like royalty." And I believed him. I was so proud of the person he was going to be that my eyes would cloud over and I'd smile big, probably the biggest I've ever smiled, a smile that showed off all my missing baby teeth. Nikko was a dreamer. That's my favorite memory of him.

I was nine the last time I ever saw Nikko. He had just turned fifteen, and he was proud of every one of those years. The night of his birthday, I helped him tie bed sheets together for a rope to climb down from the window of our dormitory up on the third floor. We slept in a large room, overflowing with rusty iron bunk beds and the sounds and smells of hundreds of orphaned children sleeping. He flung the bleached white sheets out the window and the full moon made them glow. It was so bright I could see for miles into the desert. Nikko grabbed me by the shoulders the way he always did when he was excited and said, "I can't take you with me now. You'll slow me down and we'll get caught. But I'll come back for you."

"Promise me," I said, my voice breaking.

He looked at me and said, "I promise." And I believed that too, even though I cried as he slipped through the window and down the bed sheets.

I waited for him by that window every evening for three years but I never saw my brother again. One day, Dmitri came looking for cheap labor and took me away to Sand. He put me to work behind the washbasin the day after we rolled into town. For years I had to hold back tears, believing that when Nikko finally rode back to the orphanage, head up, his shoulders square and strong, a bullet catcher, he'd find me gone and not know where to look.

It's been six years since then. I'm as old as Nikko was the day he hugged me and escaped into the desert. I'm fifteen and I know better than to cry. I don't think he ever returned to the orphanage. I think he died the very day he escaped. If not from the heat, then by marauders. Or maybe he was hunted down by coyotes, picked over by vultures. At the orphanage, I saw flu and hunger take many children before I was adopted. At least when Nikko died it was under the big sky of the desert and not in the orphanage infirmary. In the end, death is a kind of escape.

And again the monster rears its head and I know there will be no fighting it off tonight. My eyes burn, I'm so tired, and I can tell I'm no longer smiling because it hurts to smile, and I don't feel anything anymore.

Chapter Two

I toss and turn for hours until I'm completely tangled up in blankets. No, there won't be any sleep tonight. I untangle myself, pull on a shirt, trousers, and shrug into my old frock coat. Stuffing my pockets with bullets, I grab my gun and head out into the desert to practice my aim.

In the Southland everyone has a gun, and I'm no exception. Though I've never shown it to anyone. It's not exactly a gun someone can be proud of. It's a lady's pistol, tiny so to fit under a bustier or corset or harnessed to a thigh, concealed under a dress. The space between the trigger and finger guard is so narrow most men wouldn't be able to squeeze the trigger with their fat, stubby fingers. It's low caliber and completely inaccurate, but it's mine. And like its owner, it's a little odd. It has four barrels and holds four bullets: a barrel for every shot. Or that's the way it's supposed to work.

When I bought the gun off a traveling merchant who'd stopped one afternoon to wet his whistle in the saloon, it was in piss-poor shape, rusted tight and clogged with sand.

It took me a while—lots of nights poking around under the lamp, the oil burning low and casting flickering shadows along the walls of my room—but I managed in the end to get it apart. I cleaned and oiled it. Salvaged parts. I got one barrel working. It's a one-shooter. Which is a little scary, having only one bullet between life and death. But it's better than nothing.

Overhead, the moon glows like a second sun, casting silver light that makes long shadows down Main Street. In Sand, Main Street is little more than a dirt track that runs between the ramshackle rows of storefronts. Potholes. Horse dung. Unspent bullets glittering like pennies in the gutters. Out here, where every little thing is precious, where water is a luxury, bullets are cheap. I pull my coat close against the cold desert night.

Just outside the town limits a rusted old sign, swinging on its hinges, reads:

WELCOME TO SAND: POPULATION 500

Maybe once upon a time. Half those people must be buried in that mound of dirt we call a cemetery. Little more than rotten wood crosses surrounded by chicken wire to keep out the coyotes.

I walk into the desert that goes on forever, golden and featureless, so that if you look in the right direction, away from the mountains in the south, you can see the curvature of the earth. Terrifying, that openness. At least, before you get used to it. After all, it's no more frightening than a man with a gun. They both promise the infinite. But the gun will send you there faster.

The only things that manage to grow all the way out here are cacti and scrub brush, brown and thorny. I make my way out here most nights to practice my aim on the cacti, which in the half-light of the moon can resemble a person. They're skinny and bent like all the people out here.

When we were young, Nikko and I would play gunslingers and bullet catchers. I would pretend to chase Nikko around, firing make-believe bullets from the tip of my finger. Nikko always played the bullet catcher. He'd pantomime snatching the bullets from thin air. He'd catch an invisible bullet in his teeth. He'd take my imaginary bullets and bend them back at me, like a real bullet catcher would. And for my part, I'd always make sure he got me, if not through the heart, then the gut. I'd stagger and moan and collapse. Dead.

These nights, when I practice my aim, I always imagine the reedy figures of the cacti as a pack of menacing gunslingers come to get me. I draw a bead on one and fire. There's the bang of the gun, the sulfur smell of smoke, the ping of the shell, the dry sound like wind through brush as the bullet takes a chunk out of the cactus. I have to reload after every shot and I miss a few times, but in the end, I get them all. I only stop when my pockets are empty of bullets. My hand buzzes with the spent energy of the pistol. The moon has started to descend down the far side of night.

Sand is an old mining town and those who live here are the fevered few still clinging to the dream of striking it rich. We have every kind here: silver and gold miners. Coal. Metal ore. But the only ones who seem to turn any kind of profit, besides the tavern keepers and merchants, are the water miners. Glorified well diggers, really. But then again, way out here, they have to dig deeper than any of the other miners.

And water is the rarest and most essential of all the things hidden beneath our feet.

Walking home, I pass the miners heading out to their claims. Many of them are on foot, dragging the toes of their boots in the soft sand. But some have horses and wagons to carry their gear. There's even a motorized buggy or two, coughing dark exhaust in the colorless dusk. I lower my eyes and pull my coat tight around me. It's no good being a girl out here all by yourself, but I'm small and in the early morning there is just enough darkness to sneak back unnoticed. In town the streets are waking to life. I hurry along the boardwalk, duck down the alley beside Dmitri's, and slip in through the back door. In my room I undress and collapse onto my cot. There are still a couple hours before I need to be up. I close my eyes and drift into a short and empty sleep.

The next day breaks like a fever over the low rooftops. Dmitri wakes me with a slap, points to the dishes already stacked in the washbasin from the breakfast shift and says, "Get your ass in gear."

I pull on my clothes, go outside and fill a bucket with sand from the alley. At the washbasin, I scoop up some of the sand with a cloth and start scratching the flecks of food from the plates. What people don't know about sand, because it's so small, is that sand is hard, unbreakable. It's already broken down as much as it's going to get. Sand will grind you down and bury you. So, yes, sand is good for washing dishes. Good thing, because clean water that doesn't taste and smell like lead or snakebite or piss is hard to come by in this town. Water that hasn't been recycled a hundred times over is a luxury.

Glamorous work, washing dishes, but good work for a girl. Respectable compared to the other girls, who fancy themselves older than they are because of the clothes they wear, the things they do for a few silver.

And so the day goes. I clean and stack the dishes. They pile up again. There are days when you just can't get out from under all the dirty dishes. Sand is light on people but heavy on drunks. And snakebite is the drink of choice. They distill it from the green slime found in the leaves of the nightsnake succulent, which has no problem growing all over the Southland. The green alcohol smells like the stuff the old drunken doctor at the end of town uses to clean gunshot wounds, and it doesn't taste much better. The destitute arrive in the morning and don't leave until Dmitri kicks them out at closing time. They buy their snakebite on credit and pay it off collecting rewards on bounties or by doing odd jobs they pick up in the saloon.

In the afternoon, before the miners return, there's a lull. I drop the rag in the basin and go out back, into the narrow alley between the saloon and the sundry shop that sells dried jerky and pathetic strips of dried fruit that grow who-knows-where. There's not a single tree of any kind in Sand. At the end of the alley, I hug the wall and peer out down both ends of the street. This time of day, when the sun is just starting to sink, no one walks the streets unless they have to. It's hottest in the afternoon, when the sun is orange and purple, like an angry wound. There's not much to venture outside for anyway. Besides the sundry and general store, there's the dead-broke bank, the jail that houses only drunks sleeping one off, and the stables with their spindly, useless horses. If you aren't a miner, odds are you wait out the heat of day in Dmitri's or the cathouse at the end of town.

The sun never shines into the narrow alley, so it's always a few degrees cooler than everywhere else. Pressing my back against the wall, I sit in the soft sand and rest my eyes. Dmitri's is hot and stifling, thick with sweat and cigar smoke. The alley is an icebox by comparison. I like to come out here when I have a break or if there's a tussle in the bar. But drunks take to stumbling down here after Dmitri's kicked them out, and since the drunks are easy marks, the alley is sure to have at least one villain: at best a pickpocket, at worst someone feeling murderous. So I rest in the coolness of the alley with my eyes half open.

There's a commotion from the street. Popping to my feet, I wrap my hand around the handle of my little gun, tucked into my waistband. It's hot and cold at the same time. It makes me feel brave being out here all by myself. A few men have emerged from the saloon, swaying back and forth. They sing off-key, and can't quite agree on the song. Despite their good humor, I don't trust them, not in a place like Sand. Ducking back into the shadow of the alley, I hold my breath and wait for them to pass. They walk by and don't notice me. I let out my breath.

"Imma, you scoundrel! Where the devil are you?" Dmitri yells from the back door of the saloon. Cursing, I skulk back to the washroom to tackle another stack of dishes, reeking of bad cooking and stale snakebite.

* * *

The rhythm of washing can be hypnotizing. It has the power to grind down your thoughts the way time and the weather grind down a mountain. My mind empties. Only when the sun sinks low in the sky and light slants into my eyes are the glasses, spider-webbed with scratches, clean and stacked chin high.

Stretching my back, I step away from the washbasin. Resting against the doorframe between the bar and my room, I watch the barflies, the men in big hats playing cards for pennies, the lonely gunslingers passing through town on their way to someplace else, spinning their guns on their fingers for the girls turning tricks. That's when The Stranger appears. He pushes through the batwing doors, looking like a tornado the way the sand spins around him, the way his brown, threadbare coat billows around his thin body.

All eyes turn on The Stranger. The saloon goes dead silent. Not for long, just enough for the old hinges on the swinging doors to creak twice, like two crickets exchanging hellos. Then the noise starts up again, voices each louder than the next, the clack of boot heels on the old wood floor, the clatter of drinks. I watch, absently working the sand into a dirty glass with my rag.

The Stranger crosses the saloon and sidles up to the bar. He holds up two fingers. Even from where I'm watching, I can make out his calluses and scars, dusty mountain ranges running every which way across his skin. Dmitri pours him two fingers of snakebite.

In the Southland there's an unspoken rule that when you settle down for a drink in a saloon you put your gun on the table. It's a sort of peace offering. It says, 'I'm not here to make

14

trouble. I'm just here to drink.' And it establishes the pecking order in places like this. The person with the biggest gun is boss. But The Stranger doesn't have a gun. He doesn't seem to have any peace to offer.

I press myself closer to the doorframe, making myself invisible. Easy when you're small, skinny like a knife. The Stranger's eyes flick from his drink to me, fixing me with a stare that pierces me to the core. In this mercury-popping heat, my heart freezes. No one sees me. Not when I don't want them to. I'm the unnoticeable girl. It's my power. It's a good power. But The Stranger sees me. From under the wide brim of his hat, his eyes peer out like the moon on a bright day: white and pale blue and almost invisible. His eyes bore into me, then he lifts his drink, sips, and like that I'm forgotten.

"Imma! What do you think you're doing!" Dmitri hollers over the din of the saloon. His voice shakes the glasses on the bar. Everyone looks up at the sound of his voice. His is a voice that commands attention, everyone's but The Stranger's. He doesn't move a muscle.

And then Dmitri's standing over me. He grabs the glass from my hands and holds it up to the light.

"You press too hard," he says. "You're ruining my glasses."

"They're cheap glasses."

"Cheap!" he yells. "Cheap! I'll show you! I can ruin cheap things too!" He swipes me across the face with the back of his hand. He hits me hard enough that his expensive straw hat falls off his head. It staggers me, drops me to my knees. He raises his hand to hit me again, but stops, picks up his hat, dusts it off, and goes back out to tend bar.

15

I shake away stars, pull myself up and look at my reflection in the pint glass, at the bruise developing blue and yellow across my cheek. But it doesn't hurt. No one can hurt me—I just bruise easy. It's another one of my secret powers: fast-developing bruises. Once anyone sees the yellow-purple blotches developing they always let up. I pick up my rag and press the sand in harder.

From the other end of the saloon comes the screech of chairs pushed back quickly, the clatter of a table overturning. I leave the washbasin to peek into the bar. Cards flutter through the air like dying lightning bugs. Guns draw, a hammer cocks.

"You trying to cheat me?" says a grizzled man with revolvers like cannons.

"You the cheat," the other man yells back. His eyes are yellow, his skin pallid from too much snakebite. "I earned that silver fair and square!" His guns lie on the ground, amongst the spilled over cards and scattered silver. He hadn't been quick enough to grab them when the other man upturned the table.

"Either way, you ain't walking out with it." The grizzled man aims his guns meaningfully at the yellow-eyed man's chest.

The other man's eyes flick to his guns on the floor, and he says in a calmer tone, "Fair 'nough. Long as I get to walk out at all."

The grizzled man backs off, lowers his guns. The yellow-eyed man seizes his moment, dives for his guns, and pops up shooting. The grizzled man is faster than he looks. He dives behind the upturned table, unloading his irons as he falls. Everyone hits the deck. Glasses of snakebite explode. A man jerks back as a bullet passes through his cheek and out the top of his head. He crumples to the ground. And then the yellow-eyed man

16

is lying on the floor, bleeding from the mouth and the bullet hole in his chest. He wheezes, reaches for his gun. It slipped from his grasp as he fell and now lies just out of reach. But the grizzled man stands, dusts himself off, walks over to the injured man, steps on his wrist, applies pressure until something pops. The yellow-eyed man lets out a strangled gasp.

"Better luck next time," the grizzled man says, and finishes him off with a shot to the heart.

Then the saloon is full of the sound of chairs and tables being righted, lowered voices cursing, thanking whatever creator they pray to that they made it through another firefight. And then I notice The Stranger. During the fight, he hadn't moved. Not a muscle. He just sat there, looking through the mirror on the other side of the bar, now cracked with bullet holes. The glass is riddled with bullets on either side of The Stranger, but the glass before him is unbroken, as though the bullets didn't dare approach.

That's when I work out what he is: a bullet catcher.

And I'm not the only one who's worked it out. Things have just started calming down when a man comes up behind The Stranger and grabs him by the shoulder. He's tall, broad as a barn. His face is dark with three scars on each cheek that travel from his nose to his ears. At first I think he's just snakebit, but his eyes are narrowed and serious, and he stands straight and sober.

"I know you, Bullet Catcher," he says.

For a time the Bullet Catcher doesn't say a word, doesn't move. Then, calmly, he picks up his drink, finishes it in a single gulp, and says, "There are no more bullet catchers." He speaks in the voice of the desert: that stillness right before the wind picks up and blows everything to hell. If you're caught up in one of those sandstorms you're as good as dead. You end up looking like a pincushion, full of a million little holes. The sand gets going so fast it goes right through you. The sand doesn't care if you're made of flesh or stone.

The Bullet Catcher stands and drops some silver on the bar. He looks the scarred man up and down and says, "I'll be moving on, then." He tips his cap and, just like that, walks out of the bar. The only sounds are his boots across the floor, the rusty hinges singing as the doors swing open and closed. All I can do is watch, my head peeking up just above the counter, my palms gripping the bar, sticky with spilled snakebite.

I turn to look back into my little room, at my meager belongings, my sorry life. I think of Nikko, the way I let him go so easily because I was sure he would come back for me. But in this life you can't wait around for anyone. If you want something you have to take it. I learned that the hard way. And right now, all I want is to be out of here. I want to be free of Dmitri and his adoption papers like chains, shackling me to this washbasin. I want to be free like Nikko was, even if that freedom only lasted a night and a day.

All eyes are on the scarred man, waiting to see what he'll do. I dive back into my little washroom. I grab what food I have—a couple handfuls of dried meat and fruit—empty the yellow water from the recycler into a skin, and throw everything into a pack. I untie my apron and pull on my coat. I stow my gun in the coat's breast pocket, fill my other pockets with bullets, and sling the pack over my shoulder. It takes only a minute to pack everything I own, besides my books, which are too heavy to carry. In the end, my escape is easy. Maybe I had been planning it all along. Maybe I was just looking for my chance. Nikko ran away from the orphanage to chase the bullet catchers. Now I am going to chase one of my own. I give my sorry little room one last glance and smile at the thought that I'll never see it again. And then I run back out into the saloon.

The scarred man stands by the bar, looking like his girl stood him up. Finally, he sticks his thumbs in his belt and marches out the door. Everyone rushes after him. And there's Dmitri's big straw hat hanging on a peg behind the bar. Grabbing it, I pull it low over my head and blend into the crowd. I'm the unnoticeable girl again, a good foot shorter than the next shortest person.

The townsfolk line Main Street. The Bullet Catcher's back is to everyone as he walks away. The scarred man ambles to the center of the street and squares himself to the Bullet Catcher, his hands on the butts of his pistols. When the Bullet Catcher is nearly to the end of the street the scarred man takes off his long, dark duster and drops it in the dirt. He has two of the biggest, shiniest revolvers I've ever seen. The townsfolk see them too and gasp. But I know better. When something's shiny it means it damn never gets any use. All of a sudden this guy doesn't seem so big or bad. He stands with his legs apart. His fingers tickle the handles of his shooters.

"Turn and face me, Bullet Catcher!"

But the Bullet Catcher just keeps on walking. Drops of sweat, big as marbles, develop on the scarred man's forehead. He has to do something. The Bullet Catcher is nearly out of range.

Pushing through the crowd, I duck into the alley and run down the side street, fast as I can, trying to catch up with the Bullet Catcher. I turn the corner of the last building as the shots ring out, two loud bangs that turn the air white. The bullets must be as big as cannonballs to make a noise like that. Fire into the air with those guns and you could make craters in the moon. I hit the ground. It's instinct. Stray bullets are a problem in towns like Sand. You think that there's so much open space and so few people that the odds of getting hit by a stray bullet must be damn near impossible, but it always seems a few folk a year kick the bucket that way. I look up through the dirt, puffed up in a cloud around me from when I hit the ground, and watch the Bullet Catcher spin, his hands a blur. He moves so fast I think I may be imagining it, because a moment later he's just walking off again on that line out of town, like nothing in the world can break his stride. Picking myself up, I run out into the street. The man with scars on his cheeks lies on his back, like he's making an angel in the dirt. His two shiny revolvers glitter at his sides. They won't be there for long. As soon as the townsfolk get over the shock of seeing someone bend a bullet, they'll descend on the fallen man like vultures, whether he's dead or not.

Ahead of me is the open desert, hot and merciless. Behind me is Sand. I don't turn back; I don't say goodbye. The Bullet Catcher carves a straight line through the desert, walking toward the distant mountains.

And I follow.

Chapter Three

The Southland is a largely unmapped expanse of desert, pin-marked now and again by one- and two-horse towns, and very rarely the occasional market city, places where the spokes of trade routes converge. But Sand is miles from anywhere else, and I don't know what lies to the south, if anything.

At first, when Sand became nothing but a speck behind me — never has its name seemed more fitting—I took to counting my steps. I counted for hours before I realized I was looking at my feet instead of the Bullet Catcher. I thought for sure when I looked up he'd be long gone and that I'd be lost in no man's land, where there is nothing but cacti and lizards that flick out their tongues like they're telling jokes about you. But when I looked up he was still there, a skinny, black figure on the pan of the desert, shimmering in that way that's both magical and terrifying.

I've been tracking the Bullet Catcher for three days and my water is long gone. So is my food. I began by walking in the footsteps of the Bullet Catcher, matching his long strides, drinking when he drank, eating when he ate, sleeping when he slept. But now, without water or food, all I do is walk and sleep and bake under the sun. Dmitri's stolen hat is my only shade. My skin is burned and cracked, and covered in sand. I thought catching up to the Bullet Catcher would be a matter of hours, not days. I was planning on sneaking up on him the first night, when he'd fallen asleep around his campfire, but how do you sneak up on somebody when you can't catch him? When there's nothing to hide behind?

The wind picks up, but it doesn't cool me down. It's a gust from the devil's backside. The sand stings my skin like a million horseflies. The wind fills my eyes and nose and mouth with sand. I've stopped sweating, and it's not getting any cooler, so that has to be a bad sign. Next will be the lightheadedness, then the hallucinations. Up ahead, the Bullet Catcher goes in and out of focus. And then he's gone. I stop and blink dumbly at the spot on the horizon where he'd just been. But he doesn't reappear. I look behind me, at my footprints receding into the north. If I turned around, I would never make it back to town. The wind picks up again and blows away my footsteps, like I'd never been there at all. And I realize, with a sense of doom, that I have no choice but to soldier on after the Bullet Catcher.

Night falls a few hours later. The setting sun takes all the heat with it, and the air is freezing and dry. The moonlight turns the sand and rocks a brilliant silver. Off to the east, a lightning storm crackles. Rain falls in dark sheets. I can smell it, but it's miles from me. Too far to walk in the wrong direction. It feels like a joke at my expense. But when I look back to the south there's a shadow, too large to be a person, looming in the middle distance. The light of the gibbous moon describes the edges of what might be a shack or tent. Could it be the Bullet Catcher, stopped for the night? Or is it a hallucination? I always imagined I'd see an oasis or a wagon train coming out of the distance, something like from the stories I've heard about travelers in the desert. Maybe if you have a bad imagination, you have boring hallucinations. My brother always said I was too much of a realist, even as a kid. He dreamed big enough for the two of us anyway.

It is a shack, much larger than it had seemed from a distance. I put my eye to one of the knotholes in the wall and inside I can just make out what looks like a pile of rags. Then the rags shift. It's a person, standing beside a small cast iron pot, sitting atop a cooking plate, stirring and tasting the contents. Circling the shack, I find the door. It's latched from the inside. I have no idea who this person is, living so far from anywhere else. He's probably mad. Marauders and outlaws are common throughout the Southland. And I've even heard of cannibals living wild in the dunes and caves, who prey on travelers. I draw my pistol, check that it's loaded. My hand hesitates an inch from the door, but I have no choice. I knock. I wait. I put my ear to the door, but hear nothing. I knock again and the door swings open. I stumble back in surprise and land on my butt. The gun drops from my hand and goes off. The bullet sings into the night air, harmless.

The figure stands hunched in the doorway, looking at me. I reach for the gun, but the figure makes a sideways shuffle in my direction and I scramble back. He picks up the gun and tucks it in his waistband. But he doesn't move to attack me. He just stands there, hunched and a little askew. Then he reaches out a hand that's gray and scaled. A leper's hand.

"You look thirsty, child." It's a woman's voice, sweet and parched. I take her hand and she lifts me to my feet. She's surprisingly strong. Because she's stooped she's much shorter than me. She wears a headscarf and a patch over her left eye. She looks up at me with one jet black eye, and says, "Come, come." She retreats into her shack, waving for me to follow.

The wind howls outside. It's cold out there, but inside it's surprisingly warm, despite the wind whistling through the knotholes in the slat walls. There's a square table in the center of the room. Two unlit candles, held fast by melted wax, stand on the tabletop with a quiet crank-powered gramophone. There's a four-poster bed on the other side of the room, bowed slightly in the middle by a heavy mattress and piles of blankets and quilts. There's a tear in the mattress and the swept dirt floor is littered, here and there, with bird feathers. Gilt picture frames hang a little askew from nails on the walls, filled with charcoal and pencil sketches. An open box of pencils and charcoal sticks tell that the artist is my host. Beside the bed is a small table with two tintype photographs, from which the ghostly eyes of a well-dressed family look out into the room. A mother, father, and their daughter. The warm air is filled with a hum that's familiar, but takes me a moment to place. It's a generator, humming away somewhere outside, probably for the icebox and the small electric cooking plate. Near me, there is a hole in the earthen floor, encircled with stones. A rope is coiled to one side, attached to a bucket. A small well.

The leper pushes a battered tin mug into my hands and motions me to drink. She lights the candles and gives the gramophone a couple cranks. Soft orchestral music drifts from the horn, filling the room. She looks back at me and again motions with her hand for me to drink. "It's only water," she says. I drink, watching as she pulls blankets and quilts from the bed and arranges them into a makeshift sleeping spot on the floor.

"Sit, sit," she says, pulling out the single chair for me, before returning to her cooking.

"Why are you helping me?" I ask, taking a seat.

She shrugs. "Maybe I'm not. Maybe I'm only going to fatten you up to eat you." She half turns and studies me as she says this, her one eye rolling in its socket. There's a moment of tense silence, but then she starts laughing quietly to herself. She stirs the contents of the pot, her body quaking. "The thing is, I've already eaten so many children today that I've grown bored of it. Maybe tomorrow." She motions for the mug. I finish the water and hand it back to her. She ladles broth into the mug and returns it to me. I take it in both hands, holding it close to my chest for the warmth. The broth steams and smells like earth. I sip. It tastes healing, herbal. Where could she have gotten vegetables and herbs? For that matter, where did she get all this stuff? And how did it end up out here? She must sense my astonishment, because she sidles up to the other side of the table, places a chipped porcelain soup dish, steaming with broth, before her, and says, "There are many travelers and caravans come through this part, willing to trade all manner of things for some water and a little direction. But I am unused to people staying long enough where I need two sets of dishes. I apologize for only having the mug for you to eat from. This is a home, after all. Not a camp."

25

"No, it's great, really. And the soup tastes mighty fine."

She nods approvingly, dips her spoon into her dish, and then, seeming to notice her rags for the first time, shrugs them off like a heavy coat, revealing simple but clean farmer's clothes beneath: cotton trousers and a plaid shirt, cut and sewn neatly at the shoulder where her left arm would have been. She pulls off her headscarf and thick black hair falls over half her face. She's the girl from the photograph on the nightstand. Same hair, same high cheeks, same dark, intense eye, shining out. She's beautiful, younger than I thought. She might not even be thirty. It's only her affliction that makes her look old. She folds her costume of rags into a neat bundle on the floor by her feet. She flashes a coy smile, showing off straight white teeth, and says, "I didn't know who you were or what you wanted. With strangers, best to look the part that's expected of you." She settles back in front of her food and says, "So, what's your name then?"

"Imma."

After a few moments of silence she says, "Mine's Endd, since you're so kind as to ask."

"Sorry. I'm just—"

"You are never too hungry to forget your manners. Your parents should have taught you better."

"You're right. They should have," I say, not wanting to explain why they didn't.

She stares at me, stirring her soup with her spoon. "I see," she says. "I should have known when I first set eyes on you. You are all alone." She takes out my gun and holds it up to the light. "What a sad little thing," she says, examining the gun.

"It's good enough for me."

She nods. "So you are hunting the Bullet Catcher. And when you kill him you will have fame and glory and a hundred boys begging for your hand. And you'll never be alone again. Have I guessed your plan?"

Despite her hospitality, anger rises up in me at her words. "No. You're wrong, as a matter of fact. I'm following the Bullet Catcher so he'll train me. And I could never kill anyone."

"Then why do you need this?" she says, holding up the gun. The candle flame makes the tarnished metal glow orange and angry.

"For protection."

She snorts. "It's a good liar who can convince even herself."

"You don't know what it's like in the towns, how bad it can get. Living all the way out here, you don't need protection."

She holds out her arm, covered in scaled flesh and lesions. Her flesh looks like eroded earth. "You're right," she says. "I have no idea how bad things can get. Do you think it was my choice to live out here all alone? Or do you think I might have been driven from my home, from the town I was born in and raised, once my body began to wither?"

I swallow, draw my knees up on the chair, and wrap my arms around them. I look down at the toes of my boots. "I'm sorry," I say.

"Good," she says. "You should be."

That night, I sleep on the makeshift bed Endd's made for me. The wind howls, furious, outside, rattling the frames on the wall. Endd sleeps quietly on her big bed. Before retiring, she'd gone outside and switched off the generator. Now, without the constant hum from the machine, with my ear close to the ground, the sound of water, stirred by the moon overhead and the gentle turning of the Earth, comes up out of the well, filling the room, sending me to sleep.

When I wake, Endd is gone, and for a brief moment I think she might have been a ghost. But then I hear her shuffling around outside. She hums to herself, something that sounds like a nursery rhyme. I stand and stretch and when I reach for my pack it's heavier than I remembered. Endd has refilled my skin with water, and there are a few dry vegetables, too.

Outside, Endd is running a rake through the dirt where the stems of vegetables struggle out of the earth like miniature scarecrows. When she sees me emerge from the shack, she shuffles over, using the rake as a cane.

She looks like she's about to say something, but I stop her. "I want to apologize again for last night. What I said—well, it was a terrible thing to say. I'm sorry."

She nods. There's a look on her face that's something like satisfaction. "What you said last night, you said out of youth, not malice. I'm old enough to know the difference." Then she reaches into her pocket and produces a small glass vial, stoppered with a cork. She puts it in my hand and says, "For your sunburns. I was too angry last night to give it to you."

"I can't thank you enough," I say. "I think you saved my life."

"I did save your life and you should be thankful," she says. "And I don't get by out here by giving this stuff away." Her words are stern but she's smiling again.

I turn the vial over in my hand. It's full of a thick transparent goop. I store it in my bag and I repeat the question I asked last night: "Why are you helping me?"

She tilts her head to the side and shrugs her shoulders. "Because it was within my power to do so. And because when I offered you my hand you took it."

"But it wasn't kindness that made me take your hand. You were my only hope, and besides, I knew from books that I wasn't in danger of catching."

She smiles a big smile. "You don't give yourself enough credit. Ignorance keeps you mean. Learning makes you kind." Then she shuffles around so she's standing beside me. "Now," she says, pointing a gnarled finger toward the mountain range. "The Bullet Catcher makes his home high up in the mountains. It's at least three days from here, maybe four, on your young legs."

And then I remember what Endd said last night, about me hunting the Bullet Catcher. I had been too flustered in the moment to understand. "You know him? You know the Bullet Catcher?"

"He stops here for water when he travels north from the mountain. Sometimes he talks. Sometimes he doesn't. I know him well enough to know that he won't train you. But he might not kill you either, so that is something."

"How can you be sure he won't train me?"

She shrugs. "Nothing is for sure. I am only telling you the odds. He does not like people. And he has not taken on a new apprentice in some years."

I weigh my pack in my hand, heavy now with food and water. If Endd is right, I'm halfway. With the new supplies, I could make it back to Sand. I could beg Dmitri for forgiveness. He probably wouldn't beat me too badly. He hardly ever did. He'd probably let me go back to washing dishes. Endd looks at me like she can hear what I'm thinking.

"The road home is tinged with regret and the road forward is full of the unknown," she says. "They are both difficult roads to walk. But then again, on these legs I've never walked a road that wasn't difficult."

I look off toward the mountains. "I can't turn back now," I say, pulling the pack over my shoulders.

"Sure you can," she says. "That's just inexperience talking."

"No. It's not that." I'm thinking of Nikko. I'm thinking of all those nights waiting by the window of the orphanage, staring so long into the desert that my eyes burned. "It's my brother. If he were here in my place, I don't think he would have turned back."

Endd nods. "That's it then," she says. "No one is ever truly alone." We shake hands and I thank her again, knowing no matter what I say it will never be enough.

Before we part, she returns my gun and says, "As long as you carry this you are in danger of using it."

"That's what I hope anyone who tries to hurt me will think." And then I press on south, toward the mountains.

Late in the afternoon of the third day from Endd's shack, I'm still on the trail of the Bullet Catcher. I finished the water last night. The salve Endd gave me soothed my burns, but I've run out of medicine and the sun is so hot it burns my skin through my clothes. All my supplies are gone and I'm going to die out here. I thought it would be more frightening, dying, but after so many days walking, after so much hunger and thirst, it's a release. It would be easy. I could just lie down, right here, and let the sand cover me like a blanket. But my legs, clumsy as they've become, keep stumbling forward on their own. I'm not frightened and I'm not sorry. Not even a little bit. Nikko and I shared this fate, six years apart. We both walked into the desert, and we will both have died out here, under the wide-open sky. At this moment, I feel closer to him than I have in years. Maybe that's what Endd meant when she said that none of us are ever truly alone.

The sun finally sets. For about the length of two breaths, everything is perfect. The wind is cool, the sand doesn't sting, the piercing blue sky turns dark and colorless. Then the temperature drops. Drops through the floor. It locks my knees and brings new pain to my sunburns. The cold splits my lips, and I lick them to get that little bit of moisture. I'm thinking about Nikko, thinking that soon I'll lie down and fall asleep and when I wake he will be there with me, and then I stumble over something soft but firm and fall face first into the dirt.

I roll over on my back, fairly certain I'm not dead. Everything hurts too much. My skin is fried, my mouth is full of sand, my legs and feet throb. The cold night air has one hand on my heart. Hell has to be less of an ordeal than this. But the view! The view in heaven can't be any better. In heaven you look down on everything, and it all must seem so small, so insignificant. How can something insignificant be as beautiful as looking up at the limitless dome of the night sky in the middle of the desert?

When we were kids, before we went to live with the Brothers and Sisters, Nikko and I would stretch a sheet over our heads and poke it full of pinholes. Above the sheet, we'd hang candles that would flicker and cast light through the pinholes. It was like sleeping under the real desert sky only better, because it was warm and Nikko was there, and there were no snakes. When a bit of the colored candle wax dripped onto the sheet, it would expand slowly in a small violet or pink or blue circle.

Nikko would point and say, "Look, those are stars exploding."

Tonight, as I gaze up, all but unable to move from the pain and cold, the sky looks much like those warm, safe nights of my childhood with my brother. It's a million miles away in every sense, but it doesn't matter. The feeling of my lips, splitting wide open again, tells me I'm smiling.

I don't feel the cold anymore, and at first I think it's the memories warming my skin and bones, but then something clicks in my mind. It's hypothermia that makes me feel warm. If I fall asleep now, I won't wake. And because I know Nikko must have fought on until his last breath, I roll onto my side and try to get to my feet. That's when I see it, the thing I tripped over. A desert fox lies on its side. Its black eyes stare right into mine. Its tongue hangs from its mouth. At first I think it's dead, but then I see its stomach rising and falling like a bellows. A large hunting knife sticks out of the ground by the fox. I grab the knife and pull myself up. There's a word carved into the ground.

DRINK.

I've heard travelers tell stories about the desert thirst, the horses and dogs whose blood they drank to walk just a few more miles, to make it just one more day. Heaving, I pull the knife free from the cold ground. I tumble backwards onto my back. Holding the blade up to my eyes, it catches all the light of the moon and stars.

I crawl toward the fox. It doesn't move. Its breathing quickens. The angle of its back tells me it's broken. I run my hand through its fur as if it were a dog, and its breathing slows. It looks at me with knowing eyes. Then, tracing the line of its neck, I find the artery and make the cut. The blood makes a slash across my face. When I press my lips to the fox's neck and drink, the blood is thick and warm and thaws me from the inside out. It's gamey like bad meat, but it's good all the same, and I drink until the nausea is too much and my stomach lurches. When I pull away, the fox is still looking at me, but its eyes are empty now. I'm sorry and grateful all at once.

I fall onto my back and when sleep comes I don't fight it. The blood doesn't quench thirst like water. After drinking the blood I feel inches closer to death, but resolved to live. I've drunk blood. I can do anything. I'm the vampire girl. I crawl close to the fox and press myself against it. It's still warm. That's how sleep takes me, with blood on my face, holding close to the fading warmth.

Chapter Four

The fox has begun to stink. I wake to the sight of vultures overhead, flying in tight circles that I think are meant for me. But I'm not ready, I'll fight them off with my knife, I'll tear at their feathers, and I'll keep one to eat. I'll eat it raw, I don't need a fire.

I'm the vampire girl. And I'm going to live.

The foul black birds with their burned faces land a few feet away. They hop and skulk toward the fox. They peck and tear at the flesh, oblivious to me.

Getting to my feet, my legs are stronger than I anticipated. The desert stretches behind me. Before me, the mountains loom close enough that I can make out trees, basking in the shade of the high peaks, just below a steep snowline. I'm so close to the mountain that promises animals to hunt, wood to make a fire, shelter, and, of course, the Bullet Catcher that I can't believe I'd ever thought of giving up.

It's early, but the desert is already blindingly bright. It's difficult to tell the earth from the sky, and at first I mistake the figure as a shadow, before realizing that there's nothing there to cast it. It's a free-floating shadow, a nightshade, a ghost. It's

34

the Bullet Catcher. He stands in the distance, watching me. Then he turns and starts walking.

It had been the Bullet Catcher who left me the fox and the instructions to drink its blood. He knows I'm following him, and for whatever reason he's helping me. I kick away the vultures and cut a few pieces of drying flesh from the fox. I stuff the raw meat into my pack. The knife, I tuck into my belt. And then I follow the Bullet Catcher into the very end of the desert.

That afternoon, the sky is sharp blue and piercing. I take a strip of the raw fox meat from my pack. I eat the whole strip and suck the congealing blood from my fingers.

As I eat, I think of Nikko. He was tough and ingenious. He could be mean as hell, but never to me. That's why I looked up to him. That, and he was so much taller than me. While I was busy making myself small so I could fit into any shadow or hiding place, Nikko puffed out his chest and made a name for himself: troublemaker, dirt kicker, sinner. That's what the Brothers and Sisters called him.

Nikko once made me a music box. It only played three notes, but it was the only music I'd heard since before the orphanage. He showed it to me in theology class, winding it up and cupping his hands around it so the Sister couldn't see it. Before he could give it to me, the Sister came over and rapped his knuckles with a switch. He returned nothing but a snarky smile. She pulled him from the lesson by his hair, dragging his heels along the floorboards of the schoolhouse. I watched through the wavy glass of the windows as they dragged him into the yard, tied him to a post, and whipped him until his shirt tore to ribbons—yellow from dust, red from blood. I think Nikko had smiled at the Sister so she would forget the music box. I hid it in my desk so no one would see it.

That night was the first time he ran away. He didn't tell me he was going to do it. I don't think he'd planned it. He just ran. When I discovered he was missing, I found one of the Sisters and asked, "Have you seen my brother? Will you look for him, please? I'm worried."

"One less mouth to feed," the Sister said and gave me the back of her hand for speaking out of turn. I went back to the dormitory, took out the music box from where I'd hidden it under my pillow, wound it up, and cried. I was certain he was dead. The next day he came back on his own, starving, panting from thirst.

When Nikko ran away for good he had a plan: he was going to join the bullet catchers. He squirrelled away food and water under a loose floorboard by his bed. But the bullet catchers didn't just agree to train any skinny kid with a sob story. You had to be special. And Nikko was special. The music box was just one thing he made. He was always taking apart anything he could get his hands on. Clocks, small engines, the orphanage's boiler and water recycler, they all met with the sharp end of Nikko's screwdriver, and they all revealed their secrets to him. He was always making me little clockwork toys out of scrap: little marching soldiers, or a dog that opened and closed its mouth like it was yapping, a bird that would raise and lower its wings. He made his own sun-powered engine. It didn't do much; it only lit a light bulb. But to see his eyes shine! He was a genius at gizmos and mechanics.

The thing was, no one but the bullet catchers knew the secret to catching bullets. Some said it was to do with the planet's magnetic poles or black magic. Some of the more snakebitten drunks said that it was all done with mirrors. Others speculated that even the bullet catchers didn't know how they did it, that each one of them carried a slip of paper with one piece of the secret written on it—maybe no more than a word or letter—that to learn the whole thing you had to find every bullet catcher and put the secret together.

But Nikko didn't care about the secret.

Instead, he made a glove that he said could catch bullets. He only showed it to me once—he was afraid of the Brothers and Sisters finding it. Late one night, we went out behind the schoolhouse, one of his hands around my wrist, the other clutching a canvas bag. We crouched in the shadow made by the steeple, rising up between the moon and us, and he produced his invention. It was made from an old glove, the kind wranglers use to grip their lassos. Across the back, brass barbs arched like jumping spider legs. Thin coils of brass were molded in tight spirals around the fingertips.

"With this," he said in a whisper, "I'll be able to catch bullets as well as any bullet catcher. When I show the bullet catchers this, they'll have to let me in."

I couldn't say anything. I was awestruck.

He flipped a switch and the glove hummed, low and nearly inaudible, but full of power, like the quiet sound the planet makes if you have your ear to it in the middle of a desert night with no one around, when there are no animals howling or plants growing their spindly roots.

The mountain is not so far now. For whatever reason, the Bullet Catcher keeps within sight, slowing when I begin to slow, speeding up to pull me along. I think about Nikko, reduced to a set of bleached bones somewhere out in the desert. The bullet-catching glove he invented rusting away in his pack. Or maybe that's all gone now, his bones carried away by grateful coyotes, his pack stolen away by salvagers. Because, now that I've nearly done what he only attempted, I know that if he had lived, if he had found the bullet catchers, he would have come back for me. He would not have left me all alone for so long if he had lived. What will I say to the Bullet Catcher when I finally catch up to him? If I could only figure out what Nikko would have said, I almost feel I could keep him alive, in some small way. I'd pick up where he left off, and I'd feel close to him all over again, like I did last night, when I'd been close to death.

Near evening, I follow the Bullet Catcher into the huge, crooked shadow of the mountain. The shade cuts a dark, jagged scar in the desert and freezes my sun-drenched skin. At the foot of the mountain, tired-looking shrubs with dull flowers and spiny petals peek out through the shale. Midway up, where the earth turns from sand to stone, pine trees make a dense, green ring around the steep mountainside. Higher up, the trees turn sparse. The sight of snow, whitening the mountain peaks, makes my teeth chatter. If I close my eyes

I can hear the wings of small birds fluttering from brush to brush, the sound of a weak stream running through the crags that make paths and switchbacks up the mountain. It's into one of those switchbacks that the Bullet Catcher disappears: one moment there, then gone. He's the disappearing old man and I'm the unnoticeable girl.

The memory of last night, when I was so close to dying, when I drank the blood of the desert fox, fills me with strength, reminds me I can do anything. I grind my teeth to keep them from chattering, and follow the Bullet Catcher up the mountain.

The Bullet Catcher makes no footprints. He doesn't break a single branch. He doesn't make a sound. There's no hope in tracking him, so when the path comes to a fork I take my best guess and just keep heading up. Every now and then I come to a dead end of fallen trees or unscalable boulders and I have to double back to the last turning.

Night is falling when the ground flattens out and the trees open up into a small clearing. At one end of the clearing stands a tent made from canvas and animal hide, nestled in the shadow of a low cliff face. The canvas walls are propped up with wood poles tall enough so you don't have to duck through the flap. Away from the tent, a line stretches between two trees, bowed with hanging clothes. Iron cookware sits in the grass in a neat stack. And there's the Bullet Catcher, sitting in an old rocking chair, feeding dry grass and twigs into fresh embers. He pokes at the small fire and rocks slowly in his chair. He takes a piece of charcoal and puts it to the end of a pipe, puffing quickly to light the tobacco.

He leans back in his chair and smokes. From where I crouch, behind a wide, stout pine tree on the edge of the clearing, I suddenly think that maybe he isn't what I thought he was, that maybe he isn't a bullet catcher, because from here he looks like any other wizened old man, made small and bent by time. His gaze is far off: that look old people get when they're looking at something far back in the folds of memory.

He gives his pipe a puff and says, "Come out from behind that tree, young lady."

I swear I can see the words *young lady* spelled out in his tobacco smoke as he exhales. My heart seizes, but there's nothing else to do but what he says. I want to appear confident, strong, but I'm so tired. After a week in the desert, and the last hours hiking up the mountain, I'm covered head to foot in sand, blood, and pine needles. I smell only a little better than the corpse of the desert fox. The Bullet Cather watches as I step into the open and approach the fire.

"So, you lived," he says. His voice is soft and slow. His voice puts me at ease, but when he looks at me with those piercing blue-white eyes, those dead man's eyes, my spine goes rigid.

I nod my head, and eke out, "I did, sir."

"I'll have my knife back, then," he grunts, reaching out his hand. I take the knife from my belt and hand it back to him. He studies it in the light of the fire. It's dirty, stained with blood. Pouring clear water over it from a skin, he cleans the knife meticulously, wicking away the water and blood with long steady swipes of a cloth.

"You can stay here by the fire till morning," he says, not looking at me. "Then you'll go home. There's another town down the other side of the mountain, a bit closer than Sand, if you prefer."

I edge closer to the fire. As soon as I feel the warmth on my skin, I realize how cold I am, how thin the air is high above the desert. The fire is hungry for the air. There seems precious little left for me. My starved legs buckle. But it's warm near the fire and I don't care that my lungs huff and puff and won't take in the air. I could die right here. I made it.

I want to tell him why I followed him. I want to tell him that it wasn't just to get away from Sand—although that would be reason enough. I want to tell him about Nikko, and I want to ask if he knew him. I want to ask if he knows what happened to him. I found a bullet catcher. I made it through the desert. Suddenly it doesn't seem so crazy to think that, all those years ago, Nikko might have made it too.

I want to demand he train me, to make me a bullet catcher, like Nikko would have. I want him to tell me the secret to walking forever in the desert. I want to know how to catch bullets with my hands and toes and teeth. But the fire is so warm, and I'm afraid that if I say anything he'll chase me away and make me sleep in the woods, with the coyotes and wolves. So I don't say anything. I lie by the fire, in the dirt, not bothering to sit up or straighten out. The heat of the fire envelops me, and I drift into a dark, dreamless sleep.

The next morning, the Bullet Catcher doesn't nudge me awake. He kicks hard.

"Up," he says, already walking away, a towel over one shoulder and a tin mug with a toothbrush sticking out the top in his hand.

Rubbing my side, I feel the bruise developing already. I whisper a few curses in his direction as I shrug off a blanket. I didn't have a blanket when I fell asleep. I watch the Bullet Catcher disappear down the path. Who is this person who would leave me a knife and food in the desert, who would cover me with a blanket, but kicks me in the morning and pushes me out of his camp? Folding the blanket, I place it on the Bullet Catcher's rocking chair and follow him out of the clearing.

The path weaves through the sparse trees, down a small bluff that ends at the edge of a lake. A lake! An actual body of water. It's like discovering that Nikko and my parents are still alive and they've just been waiting until I was old enough to tell me. I imagine Nikko and my parents emerging from the lake, their smiles so bright they reflect off the water. I imagine them taking me in their arms and inviting me into the water with them. Below the surface is where life really starts. Everything to this point was just to prepare me, to toughen my skin, to make me waterproof. But then I snap out of it and look for the Bullet Catcher.

He's sitting in the water, on a rock just below the surface. His back is to me, tanned brown and zigzagged with scars. His skin is a map: scars like roads and rivers that lead to his pelvis and shoulders. Taking a rock covered in little dimples, he rubs his skin in tight circles, scratching away the dirt and sweat and dead skin.

His thinness is amazing. Under all his clothes, with his broad, scarecrow shoulders, he seemed so much larger, so much stronger. He could be a hundred years old or a thousand. He's the ageless man.

Then I backtrack through the trees. I want to be waiting, like a good student on the first day of class. When he returns he's fully clothed, his coat slung over those wide shoulders, making him look broad and strong again. His shadow goes on forever, and all the courage I built up down on the lake's edge, when he looked so skinny and vulnerable, disappears.

He doesn't look surprised to see me. Without a word, he drops his bathing gear by his tent, strides across the camp, grabs me by the back of my neck, turns me around, and marches me to the edge of the clearing. With a push, he banishes me to the wilderness. He throws my pack after me. I don't protest or struggle because there's no time. It's over in seconds. One moment I'm staring at him as he walks back into camp, and the next I'm on my butt, watching him walk away.

Sitting in the nest of pine needles, I want so badly to leave. Haven't I already accomplished something just by escaping Sand? Isn't it enough that I found the Bullet Catcher? That I even spoke to him? I made it farther than Nikko. I could start again in that new town on the other side of the mountain. Maybe it's better. Maybe it sits by a river, and everyone has water and fresh food and fat cattle. Or maybe it's just like Sand, and I'll end up exactly where I started, with nothing but the desert in my lungs, a bruise on my side, and fox blood churning in my stomach for souvenirs.

In my pack I still have a hunk of flesh I cut from the desert fox, its blood turned to jelly. When I take it out, my hand is sticky with the thickened blood. The bruise on my side suddenly feels like a challenge. My fingertips are red with blood. I rake them down my face. War paint. I am the warrior girl. I stand and march back into the Bullet Catcher's camp. Warriors don't run away; they keep fighting until they can't draw breath. Warriors don't go to town and wash dishes; warriors fight back.

The Bullet Catcher is at the clothesline, unhanging each item and folding it carefully, setting the folded clothes in a basket by his feet. Even this mundane activity is full of focus. Hearing me, he turns slowly and regards me. His look stops me dead. Then he turns back, finishes folding the shirt he has in his hands, and picks up his hat from where it sits by the basket. He turns and puts it on. His face is relaxed and expressionless. He doesn't move. Does he expect me to act first?

I reach into my breast pocket and wrap my hand around my gun. It's warm from being nestled close to my body. I draw the gun and point it at the Bullet Catcher. I hold it loosely, my arm bent. I'm just showing it to him, I'm not really aiming. My legs should still ache from the miles I walked through the desert, but they don't. Even though I haven't had enough to drink, or enough hours of sleep, my mind feels sharp, my trigger finger quick. The Bullet Catcher straightens his back, spreads his feet into a ready stance. He relaxes his hands at his sides and shakes them out to get the blood flowing.

"I didn't come here to fight you!" I call across the clearing.

"A gun is not a threat, young lady. It's a promise."

Looking down at the gun in my hand, I feel suddenly foolish. Shaking away the feeling, I point it again at the Bullet Catcher and say, "I've come to train as a bullet catcher."

"There are no bullet catchers. You're about five years late."

"I saw you in Sand. You killed that man with his own bullet."

44

"You've been too long in the desert. Your mind's playing tricks on you."

I remember what Endd told me, that the Bullet Catcher wouldn't train me. But I've come too far to take no for an answer. And Nikko wouldn't have stood for no either. I thrust the gun forward and say, "I'm not asking, Bullet Catcher!"

"I see," he says, his voice calm. He stares down the barrel of my gun. He doesn't care that the gun is small, old, mostly broken. He respects the gun. He takes nothing for granted. "There are two paths open to you now, young lady, and one is fast closing. You can either pocket that gun and walk out on your own two feet, or I can come over there and take it from you." He pauses a moment, then adds, "It will hurt."

"I'm not dropping it!"

The Bullet Catcher doesn't say anything else. He marches toward me, his eyes cold.

"Stop! I'll shoot!" I scream. I take a step back and my feet tangle.

He reaches out and grabs the gun. I curl around it and rip it back from his hands. My momentum sends me tumbling backwards, and as I reach out my left hand to break my fall, I throw out my right arm for balance and the gun goes off in my hand.

The trees, surrounding us on all sides, swallow up the report of the gun. For a moment, there's only the smoke leaking from the barrel. The smell of exploded gunpowder.

The bullet catcher moves gracefully. He flicks his wrists. He pivots. I hit the ground with a thud, knocking the air out of me. I try to scramble to my feet, but there's no strength in my arms, my lungs won't fill with air, and when I lift my hands in front of my face, they're covered in blood.

I don't have to look down to see where the bullet hit me. I know it's bad, bad enough to take the feeling out of my hands so that I drop my gun. The last thing I see, before everything goes black, is the shadow of the Bullet Catcher crossing over me like the moon in front of the sun, turning day to night.

Chapter Five

It's raining when I come to. I smell the rain before I open my eyes. I hear the rain in my dream that is not a dream, but a memory of rain. Nikko and I play in the mud that minutes before was burned desert. Our parents sit on the porch, Father for once not grumbling about the crop withering in the sun. Mother comes down the porch steps to play with us, muddying the hem of her skirt. Father smokes and smiles a little.

I try to stay in that memory of home. The image of my mother and father is sharper than ever before. My mother wears a crooked smile because in that moment she's truly happy, but she can't forget the sadness of the empty desert. It's a hard life out there. So she smiles with half her mouth and frowns with the other. Father is stoic, strong, square-shouldered, and looks like I remember Nikko looking, only all grown up, and with eyes that are deep set and dark and tired.

When I manage to sit up, I'm not looking at the shabby warmth of the old homestead, but into the clearing, from inside the Bullet Catcher's tent. The rain putters on the canvas roof. The air smells of pine needles and sap.

I am stiff all over, and my chest is dressed in bandages, clean and bright white except for the perfect red circle just above my right collarbone. My right arm is wrapped too, tied to my body so I can't move it. Besides the stiffness, there isn't much pain, though I'm wrapped so tight I have to breathe through my stomach.

This is my first rainstorm since childhood, and despite everything, I can't force down that deep, long forgotten wonder that used to accompany all new things. On my hands and knees I crawl out into the rain. I lie on my back in the mud. I close my eyes and open my mouth, and drink in the cool rainwater. It is the cleanest, coldest water I've ever tasted. It's the most water I've ever drunk at one time, and even though it hasn't been so long since I was shot, I feel vital in a way I never have before.

I lie there and drink until my belly is full and I can't drink anymore. Then I just lie there and let the cool rain pitter-patter on my sunburned skin. When I open my eyes the Bullet Catcher is standing over me, looking down.

"Only children and pigs play in the mud," he says.

"It's raining." It's all I can think to say to the man who put a bullet in me. Who then dressed my wounds—it could only have been him—and let me rest in his camp while I healed. If I were keeping score that would make it twice he's saved my life and once he's tried to kill me. Does that mean he doesn't want me to die or that he owes me one? The wound pulses with new pain, like it recognizes the man who made it.

The Bullet Catcher looks up at the sky, as though to confirm the fact that it's raining. He grunts and ducks into the tent. I lie in the mud, afraid to move until he says, "If you stay out in the cold your wound will become infected and you will die of fever."

Only when I'm out of the rain do I start shivering. The Bullet Catcher points a bony finger to a quilt and I wrap it around my shoulders.

"You're muddy," he says. "When you're healthy enough, before you leave, you will go down to the lake and wash the quilt and your dressings."

A drunk at Dmitri's once told me, "You don't know what kind of person you are until you've been shot and lived. After that you either jump at any loud noise or you become brave in the face of anything." All I know is that right now I'm not afraid of the Bullet Catcher. And I'm not leaving.

"No."

The Bullet Catcher sits and crosses his legs. He grinds his jaw that's crisscrossed with scars. His face is nothing but skin pulled tight across a skull. He looks like Death himself.

"Only a poor guest does not clean up after themself."

A poor guest? I clear my throat and say, "What I mean is, I'm not leaving."

"That is not up for discussion. You will heal and you will leave, or you will catch infection and die, and I will bury you with all the others who have come to kill me over the years. Those are the only two paths that lie before you."

"I didn't come to kill you."

The Bullet Catcher pulls a blanket off a large chest in the corner. He opens the chest and it is full of guns, some large and gleaming, like those of the gunslinger the Bullet Catcher killed in Sand, some old and rusted, some blood-splattered.

49

My gun sits on top, small and pathetic-looking. How many guns does the Bullet Catcher keep in this chest? How many people are buried out there, anonymous in the cold ground?

He picks up my gun and weighs it in his hand. His fingers are so long, and the gun so small, it looks like a toy. Then he tosses it to me. Its weight tells me the chamber is empty.

"There's only one reason to draw a gun, young lady. To kill someone. Next time, keep it in your pocket."

I look down at the gun in my hand, then back at the chest of dead men's shooters. "Why didn't you kill me?"

"You are young and foolish," he says, closing and putting away the chest. "But someday, you may be old and wise." A shadow crosses his face as he pulls the blanket over the chest, and he says, "It is always difficult killing the young."

The look on his face tells me not to pursue. Instead, I say, "I came here to learn from you."

"Yet you pulled your gun on me," he says, looking at me sideways. "You must be very confused."

I lie on my back, pull the quilt tight around me, and close my eyes. "I can't go back to Sand," I say. "I'd rather be dead."

"There are many towns in the Southland," The Bullet Catcher says. "You do not have to live in Sand."

Propping myself up on my elbows, I look at him, then the rain, still pouring down. "It's not about where I live. It's about what I want to do. I want to be a bullet catcher. It promises more. It means more. And it meant something to my brother." I look back at the Bullet Catcher, who says nothing. "My brother's name was Nikko. It was his dream to be a bullet catcher."

"You are in the habit of living other people's dreams?"

"We're brother and sister. We had the same blood. You could have drawn blood from both of us and held it up to the light and you wouldn't have been able tell the difference. Our dreams are the same." It's difficult talking this much, putting into words things that were only feelings before. The bullet wound throbs and makes me lightheaded.

The Bullet Catcher raises an eyebrow as if to say 'calm yourself.'

I breathe out the pain and when I speak again I take all the emotion out of my voice, doing my best to mimic the Bullet Catcher's voice that is flat and calm. "My brother, Nikko," I say. "He was very smart. Could build anything. He was strong." I look at my hands that are cupped as if I were holding the memory of him in them.

The Bullet Catcher lets out a sigh and says, "And he looked like you, only much taller. You're Immaculada, then."

My face grows hot at the sound of my name. "Imma," I say. "Call me Imma." And then the gears start to turn, slowly because not in my wildest dreams did I expect the Bullet Catcher to know Nikko, not really, let alone to know my name. I blurt out, "You know my brother!"

The Bullet Catcher looks out at the rain, coming down harder than before, turning the clearing to slurry. "I *knew* him," he says, finally. "It *was* a dream of his to become a bullet catcher. But he was undisciplined, angry. He wasn't interested in training. It was too painful for him." The Bullet Catcher is silent for a time, just looking at the rain. "In the end, the training killed him," he says.

The air goes out of me. The canvas, pitter-pattering with rain, turns into a kaleidoscope of color. I lie back down and close my eyes. The sound of rain surrounds and envelops me.

I hope that it comes down so hard that it floods this place. I want the water to carry us down the mountain and throw us against boulders and trees until all our bones are broken and we are nothing but blood and torn skin and mud. I've been living with his death for six years, but now, after this brief moment of hope, it's like he's died all over again.

"He spoke of you often," the Bullet Catcher says beyond the sound of rain, his voice almost apologetic. Perhaps he says more, but his voice is indistinguishable from the rain, a white noise through which nothing else can penetrate.

I sleep without realizing it. There are no benefits to this kind of sleep, full of so much blackness. When I open my eyes the rain has stopped, but the smell of it hangs in the air, crisp and clean and earthy. The sun shines through the canvas, making the air golden and warm. The Bullet Catcher is outside, fixing his firepit, drying his rocking chair.

"You passed out," the Bullet Catcher says when I join him. I nod.

"Your wound is bad. It's nothing to be ashamed of."

"You don't have to make excuses for me."

He nods and says, "I see."

"How can I help?"

"The best thing for you is rest. You will heal quicker. Then you will leave. Same as before."

I want to ask him how Nikko died, but all I can get out is: "I'd like to help. To thank you for your time."

The Bullet Catcher scans his camp, half destroyed by the rain, before resting his gaze on me. His eyes are soft, almost kind.

"There is much to do. It will be hard work in your condition. But the rain will have made the lake cool and fresh. Hard work is seldom without reward."

We sweep away the mud with heavy branches tied together into brooms. Pine needles pepper the clearing with fragrant green bristles. We take the clothes that were hung on the line when the rain came and wring them out and re-wash them so they don't turn musty. We find everything that the mud carried down the hill, boxes of supplies, clothes, equipment, and haul it back up to camp. I carry only the lightest of things because of my wound. The Bullet Catcher strips to the waist, showing off his canvas of scars, and carries the heaviest things as easily as any pack mule.

We scatter the ruined food around the perimeter of camp so the foxes and wolves and coyotes will come. The Bullet Catcher says the hunting will be good. He makes traps, pitfalls, and snares, using the ruined food for bait, and I watch. When we walk back to camp, I review how he made the traps so next time I'll be able to set them myself.

"Don't you use a rifle to hunt?" I ask.

"There's no need," he says. "We will let the animals hunt themselves."

The Bullet Catcher doesn't rest. He moves slowly, but constantly. Over the months that I spend with him, healing from my gunshot wound, I become his shadow. When he wakes before the sun, I'm right behind him. When he goes into the woods to check the traps, I'm there, asking questions. I'm there when he skins the fur from the wolves that fell into the traps. I help as he hangs the hides in the sun to dry. Later, he tells me, he will make blankets from the hide. He cuts the meat from the bone in a way that draws hardly any blood. He saves the bones and shows me how to suck the marrow from them. He salts and preserves the meat. Nothing of the animal goes to waste.

There are no seasons in the desert. The weather changes from hot to not quite as hot and then back again. Up on the mountain, fall slowly turns to winter. When the dawn breaks, brisk, with only the promise of light, I go down to the lake to bathe. I find a large smooth rock just beneath the surface of the water and sit. The thin film of ice breaks away as I disturb the water, so cold that I want to jump out and run for my clothes, run back to camp and burn down the whole forest for the heat. So I take a large flat rock and balance it on my lap to keep me anchored. Like the Bullet Catcher, I find a small dimpled rock and scratch the dirt from my skin in little circles.

The skin where the bullet pierced me is pink and rough, but it's finally closed. It still hurts when I breathe deeply, but the pain is only an echo of its former self. I pass my fingers over the scar, regretting how fast it's healed. Every day, I've examined the wound in the Bullet Catcher's old, cracked hand mirror he uses for shaving and ticked off the days in my mind. Soon he will force me out.

Still shivering, but clean and refreshed from the mountain lake at sunrise, I start a fire and boil water for coffee. The Bullet Catcher gives a curt nod as he heads down to the lake for his turn. When he comes back he pours two mugs of coffee and hands me one.

"Thank you."

He sips, sits in his chair, pulls out his pipe and begins cleaning the bowl with a handkerchief. "Your wound has healed," he says. "You are healthy enough to make it to town." He packs the bowl with tobacco, lights it, and puffs zeroes into the air.

"It still hurts when I breathe and the skin is still raw." I pull my shirt down one shoulder to reveal the spot above the collarbone where the bullet passed through.

He raises his hand to stop me and says, "You will have food enough and water to make it down the mountain and across the desert. You helped with the hunting and preserving. You have earned your share."

"I have earned more than that." My face is hot despite the cool mountain morning and the icy lake water soaked into my pores.

He puffs calmly on his pipe and says, "You are young and without ties. I offer you enough food and water to get to town. From there you can go any direction you wish. You could even go north, out of the desert, for as few ties as you have to the Southland."

"You talk like it's a blessing to be untethered, to be an orphan."

"There are blessings and misfortunes to every walk of life. The orphan is lonely, but weightless, and can fly anywhere. A person from a large family is tied to others, but also to the ground, and finds it difficult to travel."

"And if I tie myself to you?"

"Then you will be like a balloon tied to the wrist of a child, compelled to follow wherever he wanders. But that is not the life for you." He had been watching the smoky zeroes as they

55

floated skyward and unraveled, but now he looks at me and says grimly, "Your brother came to understand that, but too late."

"This is the life I want. And you've been teaching me whether you realize it or not." I take a deep breath and say, "I've learned to trap and clean wounds. I've learned to build a fire. I've learned so much."

The Bullet Catcher studies me with narrowed eyes. He lets smoke curl up out of his nose. Then he taps the spent tobacco from his pipe into the dying fire, rises, and strides purposefully to his tent. When he emerges he's carrying one of the large silver revolvers from his chest of trophies.

"Stand," he says. He points to the far side of the clearing. I stand and go to where he points. He counts out the paces to the other side of the clearing—maybe twenty-five yards away—and faces me. "Have you ever heard of the merchant's curse?" he asks.

I shake my head.

"The merchant's curse is to get everything you ever wanted."

"Doesn't sound like much of a curse," I say.

The Bullet Catcher sighs and says, "Very well. This is the first test that all bullet catchers face: I will fire this bullet at your heart. I won't miss. To live you must dodge the bullet."

"But how do I dodge bullets? You have to tell me first!"

"This is the way it has always been. This has always been the first test. It is the test I took. It is the test your brother took. Everything that comes after this is perfection and amplification. This is what you wanted."

My heart threatens to break out of my chest. I'm not the bullet-catching girl. I'm the dishwashing girl. Is this how Nikko died? Did he make it out of the orphanage and across the burning plane of the desert, only to die on his first day? Is this what following in his footsteps means?

"Please!" I call across the clearing. "Give me something!"

He points the gun at me. "I will give you two things," he says. "The first is advice. It is good to fear the bullet, to fear the gun, to fear the person holding the gun, because all these things aim to kill you. Do not confuse good sense with cowardice. The second thing I will give you is the means to prove yourself." He hesitates a moment, peering at me over the gunsight.

He squeezes the trigger.

I always imagined that a bullet catcher could slow and speed up time at will, that he has time to think how he will direct the bullet. Will he skip it across the ground like a stone across water or will he deflect it back to its shooter? Will he aim for the shooter's gun to disarm him or will he hit his heart to kill him? But I'm a dishwasher, not a bullet catcher. Time does not slow for my sake, and there's no time to think.

But in that moment the Bullet Catcher gives me before he pulls the trigger, something occurs to me. He's given me a hint. He's told me where he's aiming. 'Your heart,' he said. And then he pulls the trigger and there's no time to move out of the way. For a split second I *think* I see the bullet. But it's less than a blur. Without thinking, I swat at it, like trying to swat gnats out of the air. Then everything goes white and all I feel is the air slam from my lungs as I hit the ground.

The first time the Bullet Catcher shot me didn't hurt at all. In shock, my body shut down and refused to feel anything. This time my body knows the deal. My lungs won't take in air and my mouth can't find the shape to scream. But my body screams. It screams in the voice of a million nerve endings firing.

The world spins back into focus. I'm on my back. Above me, the tops of the trees are green teeth, the blue sky a gaping mouth. The sounds of the forest and my beating heart echo in my ears. The Bullet Catcher's footsteps crunch over the pine needles, closing in on me. Maybe he'll put me down like a horse with a broken leg. Maybe, even though I'm alive, I've failed, and he'll kill me anyway. The pain is everywhere and I don't know where I'm shot.

The Bullet Catcher kneels down beside me, blocking out the sun. His shadow is a cooling balm on my wound. He takes my hand in his and opens it. There, in a small pool of dark blood, is the bullet.

He pulls me to my feet, and for a moment I have to lean against him to steady myself. My legs are woozy as the adrenaline evaporates. He's still holding my hand in his, studying it, like a fortune teller might the lines on my palm, reading the future.

"This will leave a good scar," he says. "It is important that the first scar is good."

"This is the second one," I remind him, feeling like I'm going to pass out.

"This is your first as a bullet catcher's apprentice."

Chapter Six

We build a tent for me, just like the Bullet Catcher's. It's small, but big enough. During the day, I keep the flap tied open and it feels like the whole mountainside is an extension of my tent, another room. We fill the tent with a bedroll made of canvas and stuffed with feathers from the birds that nest on the mountain and rugs made from the furs of wolves and bears. The Bullet Catcher gives me a small chest for my clothes. He brings out one of the chairs from his tent and sets it around the fire, beside his own rocking chair. He gives me some of his old clothes and we hem them in together. I've been sewing and hemming my own clothes for as long as I can remember, but the Bullet Catcher is fast and his stitching is straight and strong.

We sit around the fire sewing the last of the clothes he donated to me. He watches my work out of the corner of his eye.

"Pull that stitch and try again," he says, his hands never stopping their work.

I let out a long sigh and pull the stitch. "I've never known a man who was so good with a needle and thread. It's not very manly."

"That is an old lie told by incapable men," he says. He makes me pull my stitches and start over many times. By the end, my hands are cramped and the spot on my palm where I caught the bullet is sore. The Bullet Catcher holds up the shirts and trousers, examining the stitches. He folds them and hands them back to me with a solemn nod.

"Fine work," he says, and because we've been working all day, and because I know he wouldn't say it unless he meant it, his words make me light on my feet.

We wake every day before dawn. The squirrels and wood mice are still asleep; the foxes and wolves and nocturnal creatures are still out hunting. We hunt with them for a time. The Bullet Catcher leads, his steps silent and light so as not to break twigs and hoarfrost underfoot. I'm his shaky, half-asleep shadow trailing loudly behind him. When the light breaks and the nighttime animals bed down, we are still out, tracking through the woods around camp. We aren't hunting for anything in particular. The Bullet Catcher's just testing me. Each morning, I'm sore, but stronger than the previous day.

"Exhaustion is good for focus," he says all the time. And I scowl and clamp my mouth shut to keep from cursing.

We get back to camp in time to see the sunrise over the eastern peak of the mountain. Winter is in full swing. And though the sun alights the sky a bright orange-purple, it does nothing to warm the morning. When we break into the clearing the Bullet Catcher's breath is slow and even, only his flared nostrils give away any sign that we just ran for miles through the craggy mountainside. I collapse in the dirt. I'm so tired my eyes water. The dirt sticks to my face, turning my skin the same color as the earth, and I wish I could just melt into the ground and sleep for a time beneath it. I crawl to the firepit and begin arranging tinder onto the blackened remains of last night's fire.

"What are you doing?" the Bullet Catcher asks from over my shoulder.

"Building a fire for breakfast."

"Do not crawl in the dirt like an animal unless your legs have been shot out. Even then, you should do your best to stand."

I scowl into the cold campfire and struggle to my feet. "I can't feel my legs," I say. "They may as well have been shot out."

"Then it is good practice." He waits for me to finish preparing the fire and to pull out the flint before he says, "A bullet catcher bathes before they eat."

I drop the flint into the sooty dirt and can almost feel the hairs on the back of the Bullet Catcher's neck standing on end. He glares at me from over his shoulder, his eyes telling me to pick up the flint, to respect one's tools, but I'm too tired to care. I stomp past him to my tent and as I'm passing him, I spit in the dirt by his boots. He doesn't say anything. But hellfire flickers behind his eyes.

Back in camp, my hair is wet and freezing, but the Bullet Catcher has the fire burning. It warms my bones, soaked through with ice water from the lake. He's fed up with me, so he says nothing when he grabs his things and goes down to the lake for his turn to bathe.

When we eat is when we rest. Really rest. The Bullet Catcher cuts his meat slowly, eats slowly. I can tell it's one of the few things he truly relishes. I have a habit of staring at him, of studying him.

Now he catches me looking and raises an eyebrow, asking, "What?"

I often wonder what the Bullet Catcher did when the gunslingers were hunting down the bullet catchers. Maybe the gunslingers took him prisoner and tried to starve information out of him. And what about the scars on his back? They could be whip marks. They look a bit like the scars on Nikko's back, made by the Brothers and Sisters.

Since I've been caught in my studying him anyway, I work up the courage, and ask, "During the fighting, did you come up here to hide from the gunslingers?"

"No," he says. He takes a slow bite of his food. "Not at first."

"Did they torture you, the gunslingers?"

"That's enough questions for one morning," he says.

But I can't help myself. "What's your name?" I've asked it every morning for the last month. And every morning he says nothing.

We sit there and eat slowly. The wind comes through the trees. Birds chirp and beat the air with their wings. "How's my progress?" I ask finally to break the silence.

"Slow."

"But promising?"

"When you are young everything is promise."

I grumble into my coffee. "How about Nikko? Was he promising?"

"He was young," he says. Then he looks at me and seems to understand what I'm looking for. "Yes, he had promise. Like you say, he was smart."

"Like me."

The Bullet Catcher grunts. I think he might actually be teasing me in his own dried-up way.

"What was he like?" I ask, looking at the ground, drawing shapes in the dirt with the toe of my boot. "I only knew him when we were kids."

The Bullet Catcher looks up from his food for the first time and his expression grows soft. The Bullet Catcher can be surprisingly sentimental. Sometimes he will suddenly pause our training just to stare at a particular blossom on a tree or a new flower that's sprouted on the side of the path. He will crouch down and bring his face right up to it and stay that way for a long time. When he speaks of the past—the few times I've got him going—his gaze turns inward. When he tells stories he sounds both yearning for and troubled by the past.

"He was tall," the Bullet Catcher says, meeting my eyes. "He had dark hair with flecks of auburn that made it look dusty in the light, like yours. Same eyes. You remind me of him."

"But what was he like?"

A shadow flashes across his face. "He was angry." He drinks his coffee. "My turn to ask a question," he says. "Why do you want to become a bullet catcher?"

"To follow in my brother's footsteps," I answer automatically.

And now it's the Bullet Catcher's turn to study me. "One of these days," he says, "you will need a better reason." He finishes his coffee, picks up the dishes and walks down to the lake to wash them. When he comes back, his face is a brick wall and I know the time for idle talk is over.

"Your hand is healed," he says, pouring sand over the fire. "It is nearly time for your second scar."

"What do you mean?"

"Catching bullets is learned by doing. There is no other way." His look is stone. I get the feeling he's repeating words that he himself was told many years ago, when he was an apprentice. "Bullet catching is not magic. You can't wave a wand or speak an incantation and stop a bullet. Bullet catching is a discipline."

"But why do I need scars?"

"You do not need scars. If you bend or catch the bullet you will not be hurt and your skin will remain smooth and unbroken." He bends down so our faces are only a few inches from one another. I sometimes forget how tall he is. The tip of his nose nearly touches mine, and I notice that even that, his nose, is scarred in a light thin mark across the bridge. "But," he says, "I have never encountered another bullet catcher without a multitude of scars." He smiles, and it's almost apologetic. But then he turns on his heel and starts walking out of camp. We always train at the foot of the mountain.

"But I've caught a bullet already!" I yell at the Bullet Catcher's back.

"Once is luck, twice is skill," he says and disappears into the trees.

I look down at my palm, where the skin is pink and new. With my finger, I trace the scar in the shape of a circle. For a scar, it isn't ugly. Like the Bullet Catcher said, it's a good scar.

64

Something I've earned. But I can't imagine being covered head to toe in scars, like my teacher. He's so scarred he's almost deformed, like Endd. I close my hand and can still feel the heat of the bullet in my grasp. I take a deep breath and follow the Bullet Catcher down the mountain, trying not to think of the shape my second scar might take, because I know the Bullet Catcher is right: once is luck.

At the base of the mountain, where the ground becomes flat and even, the Bullet Catcher leads me through the practice steps, sequential positions, like in a martial art or dance. He shows me where to have my hands and feet. He corrects me if my stance is too narrow or wide, if my hands are too high or low. He slows me if I'm too fast, quickens me if I'm too slow. He tells me to close my eyes and focus on breathing. Or he says to keep my eyes open and imagine gunslingers in the warbling line of the desert. He quizzes me on what position I would use if they were shooting at my gut, my legs, my heart.

The positions are second nature by now, and mostly the Bullet Catcher only tweaks my posture, putting his hand on mine, shifting it a half inch or so, or he'll tap my shoulder and I know I haven't turned enough to my imaginary gunslinger, that I'm providing too large a target, or he'll nudge the back of my leg with his toe, because my stance is a little too narrow and if I had to suddenly shift my weight, I'd lose my balance. At first, we would go through the steps in slow motion, but lately we've sped things up.

The Bullet Catcher uses an unloaded gun as a prop. He points it at me, and barks, "Legs! Chest! Head!" I shift my stance to dodge his imaginary bullets. Each position has a number and a name. "First position! Parting the clouds!" I extend my arms to either side of me and flick my wrists. "Second Position! Wolf howling at the moon!" I extend my arms upward and raise my chin, looking skyward. We only practice dodging. He says nothing about catching or redirecting.

Today, in preparation for my second scar, he points the gun and mimes the recoil, but he doesn't tell me where he's aiming. I keep my eye on the subtle shifts in his aim, clear my mind, and let my muscles react.

"Visualize the bullets!" he instructs. "Even when the bullets are real," he says, "you have to visualize them. Bullets move too fast for the eye."

Finally, out of breath, I throw up my arms and double over at the waist, my hands on my knees, sucking air. The Bullet Catcher lowers his prop gun and walks over to me. He produces a skin of water, takes a swig and hands it to me. I drink greedily. I wipe away the water dribbling down my chin and say, "When you shot at me, I thought I could see the bullet. Just for a moment."

The Bullet Catcher looks up at the sky and closes his eyes. "It's possible," he says.

"Because I have promise," I say, affecting a big smile.

The Bullet Catcher opens his eyes and looks down at me. He grunts and turns his back to take up his position again, but not without giving me a small smile first. The Bullet Catcher doesn't smile like other people. It's more of a grimace, like his face hasn't moved that way in a long time and it's trying to remember how the expression goes.

We train through the day, stopping to watch the sun set behind the mountain, then we keep going. "The darkness is good for visualization," the Bullet Catcher says. "Fatigue is good for an obstinate mind."

That night, we eat dinner and wash the dishes in the lake. When we come back to camp he says, "It's time."

I look down at my hand and trace the circle of scar tissue. My heart beats loudly in my chest.

"I'm ready," I say, because I know I must face the test whether I am or not. Better to at least appear confident.

I think the Bullet Catcher might actually chuckle, ever so slightly, beneath his breath. He knows I'm lying. He's done this before. Who knows how many hotheaded kids like me he's turned into bullet catchers. How many students has he graduated? How many washed out? How many didn't survive?

'It is always difficult, killing the young . . .' That's what the Bullet Catcher said. Was he talking about his students? Was he talking about Nikko?

The Bullet Catcher produces his prop gun. He flicks open the chamber, loads a single bullet, and flicks it closed. Suddenly, the gun is huge and evil-looking, dull in the light of the moon.

The Bullet Catcher walks over to me and puts his hand on my shoulder. It's heavy and warm. Even through my clothes, I can feel the multitude of scars lining his palm. I look down at my own hand and draw the circle of my scar.

"Remember," he says, "it is good to be frightened. Fear is not the absence of courage."

My nose and cheeks burn from fear, from losing my nerve. "We've worked all day," I say. "Let's do this tomorrow."

The Bullet Catcher shakes his head gently. His hand is still on my shoulder, radiating warmth. I look up at him and he *is* smiling, like he's finally got the knack of it. His smile is small and wan, but like his hand it radiates warmth. And I understand that he's been where I am now, with his teacher's hand on his shoulder, fear running through his spine at the thought of confronting the test. The Bullet Catcher judges my every mistake, but he doesn't judge my fear.

"It's better to do it now," he says, "when you are tired and your mind is clear. Tonight you will sleep well, knowing you won't have to do this in the morning. There will be no thoughts of running away in the night when fear gets the better of you."

"How can you be so calm? How can you tell me you're going to shoot me as easily as saying you're hungry?"

He lets out a breath, looks at me. He says, "In some ways, living as long as I have hardens you. And in other ways it makes you understanding."

"What the hell's that supposed to mean? How does that help me?"

But he doesn't say anything. I knew he wouldn't. He takes his position on the other side of the clearing and I take mine, accepting my fate. The woods are two paces behind me. I imagine running away. I would run so fast that I would tear up my legs and palms pushing through the undergrowth. I would run across the desert, all the way back to Sand. The Bullet Catcher reads my expression and has nothing but sympathy. He has seen and done all this before. He has encountered many different would-be bullet catchers. Brave. Cowardly. Full of hubris or disconsolate and unaware of their potential.

"First position. Parting the clouds," he calls.

My mind is blank, but my muscles remember. They take first position, my right foot just ahead of my left, my toes slightly pigeoned, right hand up, left hand down, so they form a diagonal across my body. From first position I can adjust to wherever the Bullet Catcher aims. The Bullet Catcher doesn't use first position anymore. He says that with enough practice, the positions become more relaxed, more natural. First position is just for beginners.

"Ready," I call back, my voice shaking.

Unlike the first time, he doesn't give me any hints. He raises his gun and fires. The explosion is deafening. It explodes the Bullet Catcher's lessons in my mind. It sends all the birds in the forest into the air. I don't have time to move. I don't see the bullet, can't visualize it. It's too terrifying to imagine. The bullet only grazes my arm, but it knocks the wind out of me just the same. It sends me sprawling to the ground, clutching my arm, the blood pouring through my grip.

I squeeze my eyes shut. My legs bicycle in the dirt. There's so much blood I'm going to bleed out. Then the Bullet Catcher is standing over me. He kneels beside me and pins my shoulder to the ground to stop me writhing.

"Open your eyes, Cub," he says gently. He's never called me that before. What does it mean?

I shake my head. "You've killed me," I squeeze out.

"No. It is only your pride."

I force my eyes open and look at him. His eyes are upturned crescents, shining in the light of the moon.

"I'm sorry," I say.

"There is no reason."

"I failed."

"Where did I hit you?"

He knows where. The blood is everywhere. The question is a test. "The arm," I say. "Below the shoulder."

"What did you forget?"

"Fourth position. Sparrow on the lookout," I grunt through the pain. It's a difficult position. You need to raise one foot so only your toe touches the dirt, extend your arms out, one before you, the other backwards, and balance on the ball of your planted foot.

The Bullet Catcher nods. He reaches down and pries my fingers from the wound. "The bullet bit you hard," he says. "It will be a large scar, not as good as the first, but not bad either. The bullet did not hit you flush and you are still alive. Do not look for failure where there is progress."

The pain gives way to anger and I shake his hand from my shoulder. I get to my feet, and almost pass out from the adrenaline and loss of blood. I avoid the Bullet Catcher's gaze as I grab the med kit and sit down by the fire. I clean and stitch the wound myself. The Bullet Catcher stokes the fire to give me more light.

It takes me a long time, dressing the wound, and as the adrenaline wears off the pain and nausea comes back with added intensity. But finally, I finish.

* * *

I bed down for the night without a word to the Bullet Catcher, and he leaves me be. From my bedroll, through the canvas ceiling, I follow the bright light of the moon as it passes from one corner of the sky to the other. Despite what the Bullet Catcher said, it's hard to think of the test as anything but a failure. The first time he tested me, I caught the bullet. The second time, I panicked and failed. The Bullet Catcher was wrong. I do not sleep easy. I *do* think of running away, driven not by fear, but by the thought that it's all hopeless, that I'll never become a bullet catcher. All these years I wanted to be like my brother. I wanted to walk in his footsteps. But Nikko never became a bullet catcher.

I did learn one thing: the Bullet Catcher won't kill me. He wasn't aiming for anything but my arm.

The Bullet Catcher sees progress. I only see its absence. But I don't run away. I stay there all night, watching the passage of the moon, and by the time morning comes I'm resolved. I don't want to be a bullet catcher because of Nikko. I used to think that if I could succeed where he failed I might, in some small way, keep the flame of his life burning. But those are childish thoughts. And now I understand what the Bullet Catcher meant when he said I needed a better reason. If I'm going to become a bullet catcher, I have to do it for myself. I want to be a bullet catcher not because it's easy, but because it's hard. Because what makes it difficult makes it special.

I trace the circle on my palm. Sleep overtakes me as the birds sing in the new day. At some point the Bullet Catcher ducks his head into my tent, but he doesn't disturb me. He lets me sleep.

Chapter Seven

At the end of every month, the Bullet Catcher administers another test. And when it's over I lie under my canvas roof and think about running away, and each morning, when I finally find sleep, I'm resolved to stay. Sometimes it's because I'm too tired to run. Other times because I refuse to let the Bullet Catcher break me. And every now and then because I sense some improvement: a near dodge, a glimpse of the bullet.

I've been shot so many times I might actually be getting over my fear of it. When the Bullet Catcher puts his hand on my shoulder and says, "It's time," I don't feel anything, only gray acceptance. I follow him out to the clearing, where we count out our steps, and I take the bullet like bitter medicine. My arms have become tiger-striped with scars. I'm the tiger girl, barred, and banded, and unafraid of the hunter and his guns.

The mountain has circled back around to winter. Our breath rises like muzzle smoke in the air. I count the months in the series of scars on my arms. Eleven scars. Eleven months. Somewhere along the way, I turned sixteen. One year more than Nikko ever saw.

Back on the homestead, before my parents died, were the only years I ever celebrated my birthday. At the orphanage, such things were considered a waste. They fed us for pennies a day and celebrations would eat into their bottom line. Dmitri, for his part, never so much as asked when my birthday was, and the years I lived in Sand were passed indifferently. I was always silently thankful toward Dmitri for his indifference. The bullet catchers and gunslingers took all kinds. But otherwise, throughout the Southland, boys are prized for their strength and girls are seen as nothing but a burden. Even in a town as small as Sand, I saw enough daughters sold by their parents to pay off debts, or to lessen the load on the family, to learn that indifference is a kind of blessing. Indifference makes you lonely, but it's also a shield.

This morning, the lake is thick with ice. I break through and ease myself into the water. The peaks of the mountain range are snow-capped. While I bathe, I watch the wind blowing snow across the peaks, a white sandstorm. It distracts from the subzero water, the feeling of my skin knitting back together from my latest test.

Once of my only clear memories of my father is when he would kiss me in the middle of my forehead and call me 'his winter child.' Nikko was his summer child. I never much knew what he meant by that. But now I think I understand. Nikko was charming and outspoken. I was insular and quiet. Nikko was warm. I was cool. Though being close to Nikko warmed me by degrees. Maybe that's why I've always felt so out of place in the Southland, under the beating sun and swirling heat-stroked winds. Maybe I was meant for winter, the cold and rain.

I trudge back to camp blowing breath into my cupped hands, but the Bullet Catcher hasn't started the fire. There's no coffee brewing. Snow coats the ground, looking like confectioners' sugar. If I were still a child I would delight in the soft, fluffy flakes alighting on the ground. I would forget everything and start cartwheeling in the snow.

But not anymore.

Most mornings I think of nothing but training and the morning exercises. The small tree branches the Bullet Catcher had me carry as I shadowed him through the woods in the early days have turned to logs that I easily sling over my shoulders and run with. Despite my slow progress, my muscles have become steel ropes beneath my tiger-striped skin.

But this morning the Bullet Catcher has broken the routine. He stands before the little shed where we store the salted meat, drumming his knuckles against the open door.

I walk over to him and he says, "It will be a difficult winter and I fear that we did not catch enough game before the chill drove away the animals. A week of stores is all we have, I reckon."

"What do we do?"

"We'll have to go into town. Earn some coin. We can sell some furs, take a job or two."

"What kind of work is there for a Bullet Catcher and Cub?"

He looks at me for the first time. I expect him to be amused, hearing me use the nickname he's given me. He knows how it rankles me—probably why he calls me it. But all I see in his eyes is concern for going into town.

"Fine work for a bullet catcher, dangerous work for a Cub," he says.

We pack sleeping rolls, furs to sell, the last of our salted meat, coffee, and skins of water for the journey. For my part, I carry most of the supplies and furs. The Bullet Catcher's pack is light, with only his sleeping roll and the food. When we head out, I'm relieved to discover we're not headed toward Sand but to the town on the far side of the mountain. Although, I would have liked to see Endd again. The Bullet Catcher promises it will be hard going to get to town, and we will have to ration our remaining food if we are going to make it, but I'm excited. My excitement surprises me. Perhaps it's just cabin fever, or maybe it's that starting over is impossible without other people around to see it. Maybe everything else is just running away.

To get over the mountain we have to ascend a narrow pass that takes most of the first day. Upon summiting, and looking down on the desert basin below, I realize that the mountain is only an interruption in the desert, a scar, not a border. The desert goes on forever.

The Bullet Catcher gazes across the desert, at a point in the distance, in the direction of the town that's not even a dot on the horizon, and takes a deep, quiet breath. He produces my little gun and hands it over without looking at me. The weight tells me it's loaded. He holds out his other hand and it's full of loose bullets.

"I thought we only used guns to train," I say, stuffing my pockets with bullets.

"This isn't training any longer. Where we're going there are consequences. You must be able to protect yourself." He looks at me sidelong and says, "Of course, it is your choice to use the gun. I am only giving you the option."

We descend down the far side of the mountain, following a creek bed as it winds through a shallow, rocky canyon. It's the long way down, but not so steep. The creek is dry but the bed is dark and cold and our boots make deep impressions in the clay. Near the foot of the mountain, the clay lightens and becomes a series of dry cracks. The boulders and trees and brush dwindle and are replaced by sand, stretching for miles before us.

I hardly look up from the ground in front of me. My back is bent under the weight of everything. My eyes are fixed on the Bullet Catcher's last step. I try to walk in the imprints his boots leave in the desert sand, but his stride is too long and my legs too short. The cold mountains are behind us. Before us lies the familiar desert, blazing hot and empty.

Five days later, the town appears as a speck, framed in the half circle of the setting sun. When the town comes into view the Bullet Catcher stops so suddenly I bump into him.

"We bed down here for the night," he says. "We'll enter town tomorrow morning and look for work."

My stomach gnaws at itself. We finished our last coffee and salted meat that morning. There wasn't much, just enough. And now with the promise of food just hours away, my mouth fills with saliva. Shaking away my hunger pangs, I let down the furs and bedroll and ask, "What town is this?"

"It's name isn't important," he says, preparing a fire. "It's a town like any other."

I'm already setting up my bedroll. If I can't eat tonight, I plan on going to sleep right away. I take a mouthful of water and stretch out on my back. The sun dips below the horizon. I count the stars as they poke holes in the dark sheet of the sky and think about those childhood nights on the homestead with Nikko. My back aches from the long walk and the heavy pack strapped to my shoulders.

"So this carrying most of the weight has been some sort of lesson, then."

"Of course." Then he looks at me and flashes his almost-smile and says, "Also, I didn't want to carry the furs. They're heavy."

My eyes don't want to stay open. I curl up, wrapping my arms around myself, and say, "Please keep talking." I just want to hear his voice. It doesn't matter what he says.

I feel his eyes on me for a time, then he says, "The town is called Los Cazadores. The Hunters. As the name implies, it's a dangerous place . . ." And his voice is a formless wagon that carries me into sleep.

We walk down Los Cazadores' High Street as the sun rises. Nobody's out this early, save for the stable hands seeing to a few withered, bent-back horses in a barn with so many missing slats I can see straight on through to the other side. They fill the horses' feed buckets with sand. I've seen it before, in the worst of times, people filling their bellies and children's bellies and their animals with sand, just to keep away the pangs of starvation. Of course, they all die anyway.

"Why do they call the town Los Cazadores?" I ask the Bullet Catcher.

"Why do they call your town Sand?"

"It's our number one tourist attraction."

He half smiles and says, "Los Cazadores is an old gunslinger town. Years ago, it was bustling. Most have moved or passed on. Nevertheless, best we tread carefully."

Early on in the fighting between the gunslingers and bullet catchers, most towns picked sides. Everyone was swept up in the fighting, whether they had loyalties or not. I think Sand was an old gunslinger town too. The walls at Dmitri's were lined with framed, yellowed photographs of gunslingers, whose names no one remembers. Most of those allegiances are forgotten now. With the bullet catchers all but gone it matters little. But my bullet catcher reads from an old map, and he hasn't forgotten.

At the end of the High Street stands the small law house—more of a shack, truth be told—connected to an equally small brick jailhouse that might be able to fit two outlaws, if they weren't too particular about their personal space. Inside the law house, the sheriff dozes with his boots up on his desk. The room is cool and smells of bad tobacco. The sheriff's desk is scarred with a thousand notches, as though he picks at it with a knife in the slow hours. A half-empty bottle of snakebite lies on its side on the desk. The sheriff's snoring is loud, almost obscene, like animals rutting.

The Bullet Catcher takes one look at the lawman and pushes his feet off the desk. The sheriff wakes with a start and his hand moves automatically for his gun, but the Bullet Catcher pins the sheriff's arms at his sides like you'd hold the tail of scorpion to stop him stinging.

The sheriff shakes his head side to side, chasing away drunken dreams. He looks into the Bullet Catcher's eyes. Recognition crosses his face and his eyes go large.

"You know me," the Bullet Catcher says. "What work you need doing?"

The Bullet Catcher and the sheriff talk business. I stand by the door, still toting our furs. The general store, where we can sell them, won't open for a little while still. People begin stirring from their apartments, heel-toeing across the boardwalk and through the soft dirt of the High Street. Some head for work, many more to the watering hole for their first shot of snakebite. In the coolness of the lawman's house, the sun feels good on my back, and the warmth, coupled with the soft voices of the two men talking business, bring a half-remembered moment of my childhood to mind: my parents talking in the other room on some warm, lazy morning, and me, snug under my quilts, bathing in the sun coming through the open window. I let my eyes close and listen to the voices that are more like birds singing than words.

The Bullet Catcher wakes me with a hand on my shoulder.

"Everything okay?" I ask, sleepily.

"We have a job," he says. "But we have time. Let us sell the furs." He tips his wide hat to the sheriff, and leads the way to the general store.

The furs don't sell for much, and the Bullet Catcher seems on edge as we walk into the saloon around midday. The place is already full. The pianist plays something slow and clumsy to go along with the midday heat. His bent sweat-stained hat sits upside down on top of the baby grand, empty save for a few coins that doubtless the musician put there himself. The sawdust sprinkled around the boards does nothing to stop the rising smell of vomit.

There are a few professional girls here, resting their heads in the crooks of their arms along the railing running around the second floor, where the rooms you can rent by the hour are. Smoke curls from the ends of their long cigarettes. I'd rather be down here, in the danger of all these outlaws and guns, than up there. I'd rather wash dishes. I'd rather be dead. The drunks whistle at me, but I flash them a look I've learned from the Bullet Catcher, when he seems able to stare to the core of a person, and they stop whistling, turn back to their cards and drinks.

"Snakebite," the Bullet Catcher says and puts a coin on the bar.

"Two," I say, lowering my voice.

"Soda for the Cub," he says, dropping a few more coins. The heat rises to my face. It puts the hellfire in me, making me feel like a kid. Then I remember where I am, this squalid town, many years past its heyday. Living in the mountains all these months with abundant fresh water has spoiled me. Water is a luxury. Water with bubbles? Downright high class. Soda costs many times more than snakebite. I take small sips to draw out the drink and cherish the feeling of the bubbles going up my nose, making me feel, for a few moments, as young as the Bullet Catcher treats me.

"So what's the job? When do we start?"

"It has already started. We are doing our job." Then he looks at me and clarifies: "Your job is to stay out of the way, to be ready to run if you get in a bind."

"And what's your job in all this, exactly?" The novelty of the bubbles wears off, replaced with annoyance. He doesn't trust me to just say what the job is. He speaks guardedly, almost begrudgingly.

"It's not your concern. Focus on your task, fulfill it well, and leave me to mine," he says.

I sigh and go back to my soda. I convince myself I'm not interested, that it's too hot to worry.

"On your feet, Bullet Catcher," comes a voice from behind us. "I'm calling you out."

The Bullet Catcher half turns and looks over his shoulder. The man stands in the middle of the saloon, by himself. Everyone else has moved to the sides to give him room, to get out of the way in case bullets start flying. He's tall, thin, dressed in denim, with side-whiskers and a curled, waxed mustache. He rests his hands on his hips, but not on the butts of his guns, a show of confidence. The placement of his hands says, 'I'm faster than you, old man.'

"You have me confused with someone else," the Bullet Catcher says, sounding almost bored, and turns back to his drink.

The man wedges himself between the Bullet Catcher and me. There's a tattoo on the back of the man's hand: VI encircled inside a black band. Six: the number of bullets in the chamber of a revolver. Six: the mark of the gunslingers. But it's not the tattoo that grabs my attention. I've seen it before, inked into the skin of countless people back in Sand. Gunslingers flash their tattoos like sheriffs flash their badge. It's the gunslinger's hand itself that takes my breath away. His trigger finger's been amputated. In place of his finger a metal one has been implanted. The surgery is crude and grotesque. The metal digs into his hand, curling up the skin in bulbous pink and white scars where the bone and tendon have been removed. But the artificial finger seems to work like his others. When he balls his fist, flexing the muscles of his arm, the finger curls obediently.

I've only heard of such things, of people willing to do anything to become a faster gunslinger. I had never heard of anything successful though. Most of the stories that made their way back to Sand were of poor folks driven to obsession, volunteering their hands and arms for experimental procedures. Those who didn't die from the surgery or infection needed their limbs completely amputated.

The gunslinger rolls up his sleeve, and one side of the dark curl of his mustache upturns in a smirk. Tattooed on the inside of the man's forearm are a series of black handprints. Seven in all. One for each bullet catcher he's killed.

What could the Bullet Catcher be thinking? Is he wondering if any of those handprints represent someone he knew? I wouldn't fault him if he were to reach for the gunslinger's throat. But he's calm as ever. He studies the line of handprints for a long time, and maybe he's reading names or faces in the tattoos: friends, family, partners in crime.

"Plan on adding my hand to your résumé, are you?" the Bullet Catcher says, not taking his eyes from the gunslinger's tattoos.

"Right at the end of the line." The gunslinger smirks, pointing to the bare patch of skin after the last tattoo.

The Bullet Catcher slugs his shot of snakebite, stands, and says, "I'm your huckleberry."

Everyone funnels out of the saloon, trailing the two duelists. I'm caught up in the throng of surging bloodthirsty locals. I try to find the Bullet Catcher's eyes, but can only intuit my instructions from his back. I hear his voice in my head saying, 'Do what I told you. Stay out of this, Cub.'

The crowd lines the street, like the spectators of a macabre parade, and the two duelists begin the long walk to fifty paces. I find my place again, beside the Bullet Catcher.

"Let me help!" He pushes me away, gently but firmly.

"Out of the street," he says. "Watch what I do. Take notes." At fifty paces he stops and scowls down at me. The look dashes away whatever anger I feel, whatever thought of being forgotten and left out, and chases me to the sidelines. I do what he says; I watch.

"Inker!" the gunslinger calls to the anonymous faces lining the street. "Ready your needle, I'm going to need another tattoo today!"

The Bullet Catcher says nothing. His body is relaxed: his left foot just ahead of his right, legs slightly parted, fingers spread, arms at his side. A stiff wind blows sand down the street in puffs, like machine exhaust.

The gunslinger whips his revolver from its holster. I've only seen such quickness in one other person: my teacher. His hand is an arc of burnished gunmetal, a blur that releases six bullets as quickly as pumping machine pistons. He shoots and moves, flicks open the chamber and loads six new bullets in a single move. He hits the dirt and rolls to his right, the force of his movements flicking closed the chamber, readying his gun for another round of fire.

I'm transfixed by the gunslinger. By now, the moves of the Bullet Catcher feel common to me. I haven't mastered them by any stretch, but I've practiced them. Practiced them over and over. And so much practicing has destroyed the mystery of catching bullets. I've come to realize it's a dogged, workman-like discipline. A skill, not a trick. By comparison, the gunslinger seems an awesome sight: flourishing gunmetal, amber muzzle flashes. He breathes fire. His volleys are relentless. Most everyone in the Southland, young and old, call themselves gunslingers, simply for owning a gun. They get the tattoos and make up stories.

This is a real gunslinger.

I've never seen a duel last longer than two or three exchanges. But this fight stretches the minutes. The bullets ricochet off the Bullet Catcher's whirling hands into the dirt. A few bend back in the direction of the gunslinger, but they hit the ground at his feet or fly into the backdrop of the desert.

The Bullet Catcher has refused to show me the positions for bending bullets, only for catching them. "Not until you're ready," he says. So I take this moment to study the way he redirects the gunslinger's bullets. I narrow my eyes and try to identify the positions of his hands and feet through the whirling blur. At first I can hardly see him, but the longer I watch the more I understand. All this time, I've thought of what the Bullet Catcher does as strength, a force of will that's so strong it overpowers the bullet. But when I watch him, he doesn't swing or swat at the bullets, he meets the bullet with his hands and guides them in a new direction. It's not about muscle or strength at all. It's something else. That something else settles in my mind like a shape in fog. It darkens and coalesces, gains weight and shape, and just as quickly, before I can make out what it is, it dissipates and is gone. I want to be patient, but it hurts to feel so close and so far all at once. Frustration is a physical pain, a pain I've been nursing for nearly a year under the Bullet Catcher's tutelage.

The gunslinger smiles, enjoying the duel. It could be that it's been years since he's had to work this hard, but in the light of the high sun he doesn't sweat. The Bullet Catcher whirls and a bullet goes through the brim of his hat, flipping it off his head. The Bullet Catcher's wispy hair is stuck with sweat to his forehead. It beads down his face and off the triangle of his nose. The gunslinger laughs and fires round after round.

The sound of the guns is constant, mesmerizing, interrupted now and again by a ricochet glancing off something metal, the dull sounds of wood splintering apart by stray fire. An onlooker grabs his chest and slumps to the ground, struck by an errant bullet. The crowd swallows him up.

The Bullet Catcher pulls a bullet from the air, cups it in his hands, and turns it around. It tears through the gunslinger's leg. The sound of rending flesh sends electricity through the crowd. The gunslinger yelps and falls to the dirt. The bronze earth gulps at the blood pouring from the wound. Just like that, it's over.

The Bullet Catcher, chest heaving but calm, approaches the gunslinger in his long slow gait. The gunslinger fires the last three shots left in the chamber, but he does it just to finish the round. He's beaten and knows it. His smile is implacable. I run up to the Bullet Catcher's side and make the slow walk with him.

In seeing the hideousness of the gunslinger's wound, I come to understand the care with which the Bullet Catcher tested me, how the wounds he's given me have been instructional. Not meant to harm, but to teach. The slug from the gunslinger's gun has torn through his femur. The leg lies in the dirt at an unnatural angle. The white, living bone is cracked and exposed. His skin isn't punctured. It's torn. His body gives up his blood like it's happy to be rid of it.

His chest rises in urgent breaths, but he just keeps on smiling. "Well fought, Bullet Catcher," he says and spits in the sand.

The Bullet Catcher picks up the man's gun, plucks a bullet from the shooter's gun belt, and loads it into the chamber. There is a gleam in the Bullet Catcher's eye, not unlike that of his counterpart, something that says, 'I've missed this.'

The blood is pouring from the wound, slower now. The gunslinger's eyes have turned glassy, animal-like. He looks at me then, and something like recognition flashes behind his eyes. He points a bloody finger at me. He opens his mouth to speak, but before he can get out the first word the Bullet Catcher points the gun at the dying man's chest and squeezes the trigger.

Chapter Eight

Blood gurgles in the gunslinger's throat, an awful wellspring that makes my own blood run dry. The sheriff drops a swollen money purse into the Bullet Catcher's hand.

The undertakers in their dark suits and tall top hats fight through the scrum of townsfolk clambering to rob the dead man of his good boots, his guns, his hat. They load the body into a wheelbarrow and cart it away. The Bullet Catcher counts his money. I drift to the boardwalk and sit. My mind turns to the gunslinger. Who knows what a man sees in his death throes? But he had pointed right at me. Maybe it was a mercy, but damn the Bullet Catcher for ending him before he could finish what he needed to say. They had fought by the rules of the duel, and it had been as honorable as any blood sport can be. But the gunslinger was beaten and the Bullet Catcher killed him in cold blood. There comes a point when all your heroes disappoint you. And this is the first time I look at the Bullet Catcher and think that I might not want to be like him after all.

The sheriff is bright-eyed and sober now. He points out to the desert, and I know he's pointing to another town beyond the horizon, where more gunslingers might be wearing out their welcome with the fickle townsfolk who used to revere them.

The Bullet Catcher nods, looking grim. He looks off at the horizon toward where the sun is beginning to lull in the sky and shuts his eyes as though he doesn't want to see whatever lies out there, beyond that line of the desert.

"It's three days from here," the Bullet Catcher says, filling my pack with supplies: dried meat, and fruit, and coffee, and sacks of rice and beans. He takes his pack and begins filling it as well. "A town called The Bruise."

"Why don't we just go home? We have enough supplies and food for two winters."

"I agree. You will be heading home. Only I will go to The Bruise."

He says this and I turn away, looking north, toward our mountain. Only now that I've been away does it feel like home. I had thought that when I returned to civilization I might feel some sort of longing for living back in a town, surrounded by people. I even thought I might run away, like I'd thought of doing so many nights after failing another of the Bullet Catcher's tests. But I don't. The mountain is my home. We've been away for only a week and I miss it like it's been years. I want to go back, and after what the Bullet Catcher did to that gunslinger, some time apart might even be good. But there's another part of me that's hurt that he wants to get rid of me. Is it because I've been so slow to learn? If I weren't such a burden he'd want to take me with him, anywhere.

"How am I supposed to learn from you if you send me home?"

88

"It is for your own good, Cub. Today you learn that sometimes it is better to retreat than to press on. This is not a matter for discussion."

"You can't send me home. I won't go."

"I will buy a mule to help with the supplies. Even so, the load will be heavy so I don't want you to try to make the journey too fast. The sun kills more than any man with a gun." When he tries to hand me my pack, I cross my arms and refuse to take it. He drops it by my feet and stares me down. In this moment he looks more like a father, fed up with his daughter, than a teacher. "Please," he says. The word seems strange coming from him. Something in me melts, tells me not to disappoint him. "Please, Cub. Take the packs. Go home."

"Give me one good reason why I can't come."

The Bullet Catcher fixes me with a sharp look. "It is not your place to second-guess me," he says. He doesn't raise his voice, nothing about his tone changes, but I know him well enough to know when his calm is broken. He doesn't call me 'Cub'. His eyes darken. What is it about The Bruise that has him so on edge? The more he tries to drive me away, the more I need to follow him.

"One reason," I say, trying to make myself taller in front of him.

He looks at me a long time. Finally, he says, "I don't want you to get hurt."

I want to hug him for that, but the Bullet Catcher isn't the hugging kind. "I don't believe anything could hurt me as long as you're with me. Wouldn't it be more dangerous traveling back home by myself?"

He looks north as though judging the distance. Then he gives out a long sigh and begins repacking the bags, emptying most of it out and leaving it on the boardwalk in front of the general store. The shopkeeper reluctantly returns the Bullet Catcher's money and begins bringing the supplies back in to the store.

The Bullet Catcher hands me my pack. I sling it over my shoulder and look up at him, ready to go. He grumbles, takes off his hat and wipes his brow. "The young always want to grow up too fast," he says to himself.

"What's wrong with wanting to grow up?"

He just shakes his head and we set off.

He doesn't talk to me for a long time after that. He won't even meet my eyes. But he's wrong about me wanting to grow up too fast. It's that I don't want to be left behind. I've been left behind all my life. When they died my parents left me behind. Nikko forgot me at the orphanage. My whole life threatened to pass me by while I washed dishes.

I'll never be left behind again.

The desert that separates us from The Bruise rolls in high, shifting dunes, blown by a hot, relentless wind. At the end of the second day, we bed down and my muscles melt into the softness of the bedroll that never seemed so soft before. The heat coming off the Bullet Catcher pales the sun at midday. He's hardly said anything since Los Cazadores. I actually miss him calling me 'Cub'.

"How many men have you killed?" I don't know why I ask it. But I want to know. I close my eyes and imagine the Bullet Catcher's past as a bloodbath. He sits near the fire, staring, unblinking, into it.

"Many," he says.

90

I think back to the gunslinger in Los Cazadores, the line of handprints tattooed on his arm, how the Bullet Catcher had studied them so calmly. I have to remind myself that this man is not a monk or priest. He's a fighter, a killer. His surface is placid, but who knows what lies beneath? Is it possible to truly know such a person? Would he accept someone knowing him? Is that why he tries pushing me away?

"How many women and children?" I can't help badgering him. I want to know everything about him. That's a good thing, isn't it? Wanting to know everything about someone you care for. The spell of the fire seems to give a little and he looks at me. His eyes betray nothing. They hide his secrets, like a bandage covering a festering wound.

"What is your sudden fascination?"

I get up and sit next to him by the fire. I put my hand on his and say, "Whatever you've done in your past, I want you to know I have your back. No matter what. You don't have to send me away."

He squints at me, perhaps not taking my meaning.

"That's why you didn't want me to follow you to The Bruise, right? There's something from your past there. You can trust me."

He turns back to the fire and pokes it with a stick, making the embers glow bright orange in the burned charcoal. "Not so many," he says in a whisper.

"What?"

"Women and children. Not so many."

"But some."

"More than some."

"Will you tell me your name? You can trust me."

His eyes look suddenly heavy and tired.

"Why did you kill the gunslinger in Los Cazadores? You had him beaten."

"It's what I was paid to do."

"So if they paid you to dig a well, or till soil, or dole out snakebite you'd be happy to do that as well?"

"I might do some digging." He lies back and closes his eyes. "Get some sleep, Cub. Tomorrow will come whether we're ready or not."

I lie down and look up at the night sky. At this moment, the Bullet Catcher feels as distant to me as the stars. He doesn't trust me. Over our time together, I've come to think of him as something more than just my teacher. I've come to think of him as family. But maybe it's an illusion, like any other desert mirage: so real one moment and the next nothing more than bands of heat rising from the desert, a trick of the eye. The fire dims and goes out. It's winter up on our mountain. I close my eyes and imagine the lake, the unbroken plane of ice water and the snow falling in curtains over the mountaintops.

All the morning of the third day I've thought about what the Bullet Catcher said back in Los Cazadores. Maybe it would be best for me to turn around. I'd wait for him back on the mountain, like waiting out a dust storm in Dmitri's, hunkered down, windows boarded. But then I think about that lonely walk back under this sun, over those dunes. Walking in the shadow of the Bullet Catcher, which seems somehow deeper and darker than before, possesses a coolness, an aspect of shade. I've become so fond of his company, even after the incident with the gunslinger, even when he's giving me the silent treatment. If I left, I would miss the soundlessness of his breathing at night, his soft steps and long stride, his eyes, and scars, and his smell of fresh water even when we are three days into the desert without so much as a splash on our faces.

Toward evening, The Bruise rises over the crest of dunes. Surrounding the town in a halo is a field of deep violet flowers that seem to pulse in the heat, like living blood rising to the surface to make a bruise. The Bruise is bigger than Sand and Los Cazadores. It has more than one street and a water tower.

We stop and catch our breath. We pass the water back and forth and take in the town. "What waits for us in there?" I ask, standing beside him atop the dune overlooking The Bruise.

"Just a man," he says. "A man we've come to kill."

We circle The Bruise, stalking it. "The Bruise is a loyal gunslinger town," the Bullet Catcher says. "We cannot simply charge in and take our mark, nor can we post up in the saloon and wait for him. He is not like the man in Los Cazadores."

"The man in Los Cazadores seemed to know what he was doing."

"Yes," he says. "He was able with a gun. The stories his tattoos told were not fairy tales. But he was dull and made for a large target."

"And this man is smarter?"

"His is an angry intelligence. He is very dangerous. But this is the closest I've been to him in many years. He hardly ever ventures so far from Las Pistolas."

"Las Pistolas?"

"Las Pistolas is *the* gunslinger town. Almost a city. It's where they train new recruits. A thousand gunslingers call it home. It used to have a different name, but no one remembers it anymore."

"So who is this man?"

The Bullet Catcher shuts his eyes and says, "After tonight, he won't be anyone at all."

A few hours later, the lingering sunlight melts into darkness. The green mercury lamps flicker on and brighten, casting their light across the halo of flowers. The flowers sway in the swirling wind and throw ghastly shapes across the backs of the buildings. From town come the sounds of people closing up shop, making their ways home or to the saloons.

We wait deep into the night. Then the Bullet Catcher stands, dusts the sand from his clothes and takes off toward the town without a word.

At the edge of the field of flowers the Bullet Catcher stops. He looks at the flowers for a time. They are much larger than they seemed at a distance, the size of sunflowers. He leans down, brings one of the dark blooms close to his nose and breathes deep. He looks just like he does on those cold mountain mornings when, running full bore along the path, he stops to linger over a newly blossomed flower. But these aren't anything like the flowers from home. There's something frightening about them, frightening in as much as they exist at all, with no water and only the blazing sun overhead. The Bullet Catcher stands and puts his hand on my shoulder. The look in his eyes is soft and pleading.

"You've had your way," he says. "You've come to The Bruise. Now do as I say and wait here. Crouch down in the flowers, Cub, and wait for me to return."

Anger, disappointment, rises to my cheeks. "You're not serious," I say. "I didn't come all this way not to help. I'm not your mule. I don't just carry the bags."

He raises his hand to quiet me. "I do not think that of you. It is my responsibility to train you, but also to protect you."

I peer around him at the town. All of a sudden, in the grim shadows of flowers dancing on the walls, the green mercury light, the distant sounds of drunkards, the sound of the Bullet Catcher's voice that could be mistaken for fatherly concern, I get the feeling that he's right, that something terrible will happen tonight.

"Let's both go, then," I say, looking back up at him. "Like you said: sometimes it's better to retreat than press on."

The Bullet Catcher turns to look at the town, like he's truly considering it. I hope he sees what I see, these things like warning signs.

"No, Cub," he says without looking at me. "This is something I must do. It is a fight long put off." He takes a deep breath and turns to me. "Of course, you must do what you feel you must as well. But if you follow me, I will not be able to protect you."

I look down at my boots, the flowers growing up past my waist. When I saw them from a distance they were so beautiful. I could think of nothing better than rolling in them, smelling each and every one of them. I wanted to make wreaths, crowns, chains. How a few hours changes everything.

These deep purple flowers are a promise of bloodletting.

"I'm going with you. I can protect myself."

He does nothing for a long time, perhaps hoping I'll change my mind. But finally he turns and walks off toward The Bruise, moving through the dense field of flowers silently, without breaking a single stem. I follow him, exploding the petals like so much confetti.

Chapter Nine

Weaving through unlit alleys and the shadows at the edge of streets, we arrive at the water tower. From down the street drifts the sound of a honky-tonk piano and the wilted falsetto of a drunken chorus. Two broad-shouldered, strong-chinned men, crisscrossed with bandoliers, stand guard at the access ladder to the water tower.

We stalk them from the alley across the street, crouching in the shadows, breathing through our noses, eavesdropping on their conversation. The Bullet Catcher's eyes shine out, excited, focused. A controlled energy radiates from his body. I hold my breath and stare at the two men, as if it will make their conversation clearer.

"He's as smart and affectionate as any person I've ever met," boasts the one on the left with the angry-looking scar across his forehead.

"My little girl wants a dog, but I think she's too young. Don't think she could look after one proper," the other one says. He's squat and square and in the moonlight looks like a chunk of uncut stone.

"Josephine, the blacksmith's daughter. Her dog just had a

litter. Sheepdogs. Big and hardy. Those dogs don't need much looking after. They'll look after your girl, if anything!" The first man laughs, rolls and lights a cigarette, and hands it to the other.

Are these men gunslingers or fathers? I'd never considered that a person could be both.

"I want you to count to thirty," the Bullet Catcher says, "then you will walk across the street and create a distraction for the guards."

"Then what?"

"You'll see me before they do. When you do, hit the ground. Make yourself flat." The Bullet Catcher retreats into the alley, his words trailing after him, the tail of his coat flapping like a tattered cape.

I start counting.

Thirty bullets on belt. Twenty-nine bullets on a belt. Twenty-eight bullets on a belt. The Bullet Catcher's going to kill these men. Twenty-five bullets on a belt. The man on the left has a dog. Nineteen bullets on a belt. Is not saving the man with the dog the same as killing him? Eleven bullets on a belt. If they die, the dog will go hungry. The other one has a kid, probably a wife. What happens tonight will affect more lives than those of these two men. Their families. Their friends. Four bullets on a belt. Hard to believe, but I've never thought about actually killing a person. My imagination always skips to the end: the man dead in the dirt and me standing over him. It seemed such a heroic pose. One bullet on a belt.

Pushing down my thoughts, I screw my face into what I hope is one of worry and skitter into the street.

"Help!" I yell. Back at the orphanage I shouted for help so often I was afraid of wearing it out. And Nikko always came running, until he was gone. "Help me, please!" I run over to the two men and collapse onto the old splintered wooden fence surrounding the water tower.

"What's the matter, darlin'?" the man with the dog asks, his voice filled with concern. His eyes are big and kind and already watering at the sight of a frightened girl.

"It's my brother. I was supposed to be watching him. I just turned my back for a moment, I swear!"

"That's all right, sweetheart. You're working yourself up into a skinny little dust storm. This town ain't so big that your brother could'a gone far."

The other man, the one with a little girl, steps up to take a closer look at me. "Come to think of it," he says, "this one does look awful familiar. You and your family just passing through?" He turns to his partner and says, "We see any other kids run by here today?"

The man with a dog, with the long, angry scar running across his forehead, and eyes that are big and kind, doesn't have time to answer. The Bullet Catcher's arms rise from the shadows like Death's scythe. I hit the ground, just like I was told. The Bullet Catcher grabs the man by the chin and shoulder, and yanks in opposite directions. The man's eyes go wide, his neck pops, his body goes limp. The Bullet Catcher launches himself at the other man. I can only watch as he pins the man to the ground, his knees on his arms, and presses a hand over his mouth. The man screams into the Bullet Catcher's palm. With the elbow of his other arm, the Bullet Catcher presses down on the man's windpipe until the man goes still.

The Bullet Catcher stands over the body and looks at me.

"Are you okay, Cub?" he asks.

This is the largest role I've ever had in someone's death. A part of me wants to run away and vomit in the purple flowers, but I make my eyes leaden. I stand, not bothering to dust myself off. "What's next?"

"The water tower. That will get us the attention we need."

I climb the water tower behind the Bullet Catcher, placing my hands where he last gripped the cold metal. The memory of his handprints is cold and warm at once. After this, even if I wanted to, could I ever again wash dishes without thinking about the men lying dead below? How I helped kill them? Who are we if we kill people who love their children and dogs? Who is good and who is bad, when they are the ones eager to help find lost children and we are the ones stalking in the shadows?

We're only a few rungs from the top, where a catwalk circles the swell of the tower. I can hear the water breathing inside, slapping the sides of the tank like the deep bellow of something wounded.

The Bullet Catcher is not good at going unnoticed. That's my area. As soon as he shows his face in town, people perk up and pay attention. So it seems somehow unnecessary when he pulls from his coat the brown stick that at first I mistake for a candle and shoos me along the catwalk, to the other side of the water tank, unspooling wire behind him. When he produces a trigger and twists the wire to the end of it, it hits me: he's going to blow a hole in the water tank.

"Cover your ears, Cub," he says, and presses the button.

Squeezing my eyes shut, I hug the sides of my head, and curl away from the sound of the blast. The catwalk shakes and groans like it's about to break away, but in the end it holds fast to the far side of the tank. I open my eyes. The water pours out of the blasted side of the water tank, falling, getting sucked up by the parched dirt below. The dry, exposed sides of the tank catch fire: a signal torch to set the whole town running.

The townsfolk gather around the water tower. Parents with babies in their arms emerge from their apartments and hold buckets under the falling water, or kneel and scoop at the soft bronze mud. It reminds me of how my father would line dozens of buckets in front of the house whenever rain clouds began boiling in the distance. He'd sit out on the porch and stare at the horizon until the clouds moved on or gathered around.

Snakebit men tumble out the bat-winged doors of the saloons and make their way toward the burning water tower, drawn by the heat and light. Some fire their guns in the air, thinking the burning water tower a bonfire, something to celebrate. Others wear deadly expressions like undertakers wear black.

The Bullet Catcher perches on the catwalk, watching the people gather below. The water slows to a trickle. Bits of the water tower splinter in the heat and fleck off the sides like dry paint, tumbling down into the crowd that parts for the falling missiles.

"Who are you, stranger?" a voice hollers up from the crowd. They haven't seen me. I press myself against the far side of the tank. The flame is starting to die, and the shadows are returning. I'm the unnoticeable girl.

"I am looking for the man who calls himself Bullet," the Bullet Catcher calls down.

A murmur rolls through the crowd. Gathering up their children, who had wandered into the street with sleepy, bemused looks, the parents haul their full buckets back to their homes. Some of the drunkards lose interest and crawl back to the saloon. Those who stick around are the serious type, with their dusters hanging loose on their shoulders and their hands on their hips an inch away from their shooters. I reach into my coat and grasp my gun. The feel of it quiets my heart.

"If you wanted Bullet, you didn't have to go burning down the water! Ever hear of asking, polite-like?"

"Produce Bullet or I'll burn down more than just your water."

He means it. The Bullet Catcher has never taught me to bluff.

From the crowd there's a flash of gunmetal, a yellow burst of light from the mouth of a gun. The shot rings out. The Bullet Catcher barely seems to flinch. The mob around the tower huddles together, looking in the darkness like a single living mass. Then a sliver of the black mass, the shooter, falls away and crumples to the ground without a sound, killed by his own bullet.

Another murmured conversation rolls through the crowd before the man speaks again. "Come on down then, stranger. We'll take you to Bullet." There's a new element to the voice: fear. Now they know whom they're dealing with. This isn't some drunkard with an arsonist's bent. This is a man who catches bullets.

The Bullet Catcher raises his chin, perhaps to look for the moon, but even that has taken to hiding behind the clouds tonight. The only light comes from the fire, reduced to charcoal and embers now, the green mercury lamps, flickering down the streets, the yellow light, shining through windows. "Half hour," the Bullet Catcher calls down. "Your man will meet me in the flowers."

"He'll be there. Try not to burn down anything else on your way out of town." And with that, the crowd disperses, knowing the Bullet Catcher won't make his move until they're a safe distance away.

The Bullet Catcher crouches in the flowers, balancing on the balls of his feet, his eyes level with the tops of the full blooms.

I lie on my back in the field, unneeded, like a fifth leg on a horse. I'm safe, not because of the Bullet Catcher, but because I'm unnoticeable again. And I'm not even sure I mind. I can't shake the feeling of helping to kill the guards. It lingers and hurts more than I suspected it would. How will I feel if *I* have to kill someone, someday?

"Did you know they had pets and children?" I ask.

"Who?"

"The guards we killed."

He comes over and crouches next to me. I close my eyes to keep from crying.

"It hurts terribly, Cub. It always does. But push it down. It won't help you."

"So you knew, or you at least suspect it of everybody?"

"That someone I kill could have a family? Friends? A full life of kindness and good deeds? Even the worst people are capable of great kindnesses." He looks up at The Bruise and says, "Just as good people are capable of terrible misdeeds."

Can I kill knowing that anyone could have a double life? A life where they're sober and loving, where they take their big, scarred hands and carefully cradle the bodies of their children, and another where they strap themselves with belts of bullets and kill people for looking at them wrong?

I sit up and bring one of the purple flowers to my nose and breathe deep, like the Bullet Catcher did earlier. My breath catches in my throat and whatever I last ate threatens to come back up.

"They smell rotten," I say, getting to my feet so I can breathe the fresh air above the flowers. "Like dead bodies left out in the sun."

The Bullet Catcher pulls me back down low so I won't be seen. "The flowers of The Bruise are special," he says, risking taking his eyes off the town to look back at me. "They flower year round, rain or drought. Their purple color has been known to make the weak of heart pass out from their beauty. Yet they smell of the dead. They're beautiful and terrible all at once."

I examine the flowers and think of the Bullet Catcher, his skin a network of scars, beautiful and terrible. Is that because his teacher was so much harder on him than he is on me? Running my hands over my tiger-striped arms, I'm reminded how much he tries to protect me.

"I've never seen anything like them in the Southland."

"They are of the North. The old warriors there used to paint their bodies with the dye derived from the petals. They'd trick their enemies into thinking they were fighting the dead risen back to life."

"I think you were right, when you told me to go home. Maybe I wasn't ready for this."

"No one with a heart is ever ready." He takes a deep breath and lets it out slow through his nose. "Cub, know that it was not easy for me to tell you to go home."

I've seen people cry from happiness now and again. Orphans when they were adopted. One or two of the girls back in Sand when their beaus proposed. Even a gambler, once, who took everyone else at the table for everything they had. But I never understood it, how happiness could make you cry. Until now, because it takes everything I have to force the tears down. It's as if he'd flat out told me he loved me.

The deaths of the guards still hurt, but I push the feeling down like the Bullet Catcher told me to. I crouch on the balls of my feet beside the Bullet Catcher, shadowing his posture, making my eyes narrow slits. "What can I do?"

"You're doing it," he says. "Stay low. Stay out of the way." Then the Bullet Catcher puts his hand on my shoulder and says, "If I go down, I don't want you fighting. If things look bad I want you to run. You will keep your mind from revenge. You will not look back."

"I don't know if I like you enough to avenge you."

"I know you, Cub. You're sentimental."

He's right. I would try to kill the man who killed him, no matter that I've never killed a man before. No matter that even my small part in killing the guards left me feeling nauseous and guilty. For the Bullet Catcher, it's worth it. I'd pour my life out like snakebite if it meant avenging him. When I first ran after him, he was just a means of escaping my old life, the small, uninteresting thing I called living. And, maybe, my way of keeping Nikko alive in my heart. Though now I feel silly that I ever thought that way. The Bullet Catcher did not choose me. I chose him. He did not spirit me away like a fairy godmother. I was a stowaway. And because I chose him and because he accepted me, I love him.

I am sentimental like that, exactly. And I'm about to tell him as much, but I don't have the time.

A voice comes startling out of the dark: "When I saw the fire I knew it was you." It could only be Bullet's, though it's different than I imagined, almost boyish.

The Bullet Catcher puts his hand on my shoulder and pushes me lower into the flowers, out of sight. I search, but can't see the gunslinger. Despite the boyishness of Bullet's voice, I still expect a giant of a man, all muscles and shoulders. I imagine a side of the mountain breaking off and standing up into the shape of a man. I picture the moon coming down from wherever it's hiding and sprouting legs and arms to go along with its face.

From the other side of the field comes the soft swishing sound of legs slowly pushing aside the dense flowers. A slim figure, silhouetted by the green light of town, comes into view, maybe fifty yards away, and stops. He looks directly at us.

"It's good to see you again, old friend."

The Bullet Catcher doesn't breathe. I don't breathe either.

"How I wish you wouldn't insist on playing these games." Bullet's voice is amiable and annoyed, like a schoolboy scolding one of his schoolyard friends for breaking the rules of some frivolous game.

There's a soft sound, the breeze passing over the field, and when I turn to where the Bullet Catcher was crouched a moment ago, he's gone, with just the indents of the toes of his boots left in the earth.

Then I hear the fighting, the soft, wet sound of fists being thrown, spilling blood across knuckles and flowers, breath knocked from lungs, bodies tumbling across the ground. When I look all I can see are flowers, shaking with excitement. The Bullet Catcher and Bullet fight in the dirt, throwing punches, scratching, clawing, kicking, biting. Every now and then I see a head, or the broadness of a back, rising above the purple horizon. They pull apart and scramble to their feet, only a few yards apart. Bullet's back is to me as he draws his revolvers and fires. He empties both chambers, twelve shots in a second flat, then disappears into the flowers, emerging a second later with reloaded guns. They are so close to one another the Bullet Catcher has no time to catch or bend the bullets, but he manages to dodge, moving preemptively away from the shots, reading the tornado of the gunslinger's moves. This is nothing like the duel in Los Cazadores. They fight with everything they have. There is no honor nor rules; each man thinks only of killing the other.

The shots come so close together they sound like cannon fire, each sound reinforcing the one before it into a cacophony of noise. I move closer, weaving around the tall green stalks, trying to not so much as bend them, lest I draw Bullet's attention. Maybe I can sneak up behind him.

Then it happens. The most unexpected of all things: the Bullet Catcher grunts, spins half around, and falls into the flowers.

Bullet hit him.

The Bullet Catcher told me that if he went down to turn tail and run. To not look back. But until now I thought it impossible that anyone could shoot the Bullet Catcher. So I hadn't considered it. Not seriously.

Bullet rises from his half crouch, holsters one of his guns and reloads the other slowly as he approaches the flattened bed of flowers where the Bullet Catcher went down. His back is still to me as he stops and looks down at the Bullet Catcher. He's saying something, but my ears are ringing from the gunfire. He spins the chamber of his revolver, flicks it closed, and points it at the Bullet Catcher lying on the ground.

I'm running. Caution abandoned, I bolt full tilt through the flowers, not away, but toward the fight. I draw my shooter. Bullet doesn't make any sign that he hears me. His ears must be ringing, like mine. Just a few yards away I stop and level my gun at the back of his head. I don't think about my guilt over the guards in town, I don't think about how I'll feel after killing this man. My ears burn, my eyes sting with salt, my nose is full of smoke. I chose him. He let me stay. I was his stowaway. And when it comes down to it aren't all children stowaways? Just because I came to him nearly grown did that make me any less his? He any less mine? In my mind, I hear the Bullet Catcher saying, 'Run. Keep your mind from revenge.'

But this isn't revenge. This is an intervention.

Just then, Bullet turns a fraction toward me. There's something in the shape of his nose, and ear, the arc of his eyebrow, that I recognize. But there's no time to think. The gun goes off in my hand. It doesn't make a sound, but my hand tingles from the explosion. Bullet's head pitches forward and he

108

grabs his cheek. The blood pours between his clenched fingers, but I've missed. It was just a glancing shot. My fingers fumble clumsily with my gun, opening the chamber and trying to find a bullet to reload. The gunslinger half turns and focuses a dark almond eye on me. His face is squeezed into an expression of pain and anger, but when he sees me, his eye goes wide and his jaw slack.

"Imma?" he says.

I look up. The gun drops from my hand. "Nikko?"

Chapter Ten

It only lasts a moment, our reunion. Then Nikko's head cocks forward violently. He staggers, collapses. The flowers fold beneath him. The Bullet Catcher rises behind him, his arm wrapped around his midsection, a rock in his hand. I'm too stunned to move. Nikko's alive. And not only alive but here, right here, in the flowers on the outskirts of this far-flung Southland town. And he's a gunslinger. This all feels like the sudden conclusion to a long-drawn-out family feud, my brother fighting with our father. And then I remember that the Bullet Catcher isn't our father.

The moon comes out from behind the clouds, casting everything in silver light. The Bullet Catcher picks up my brother's gun. He stands over Nikko, his eyes gleaming in the moonlight, looking murderous. He pulls back the hammer with a terrible click.

"Don't!" I yell.

The Bullet Catcher turns and looks me up and down, like he's trying to remember my name. "It must be done," he says, but he resets the hammer just the same. His expression is empty. All the murder has left him. He looks lost. He looks

110

old. At this moment, he seems nothing more than an old man who's walked into a room only to forget why he'd done so.

I approach him slowly. "Is this why you brought me?" My mind is spinning. There is a history between the Bullet Catcher and my brother, a different one than the Bullet Catcher told me, and that history couldn't have been as angry and violent as it is now without them having once been close. "You brought me to meet my brother, didn't you? You knew that if I were here you wouldn't be able to go through with this, with killing him. You want to save him. That's it, isn't it?"

"Save him? From what?" His voice is dreamy and faraway.

"From being a gunslinger."

He looks softly at me, like I'm some naive child, and shakes his head. "The life of a gunslinger is not something to be saved from. It is a choice, the same as being a bullet catcher." His expression hardens and he looks back down at Nikko. "And you forget that I did not want you here at all."

There's nothing to say to that. It hurts. And he's right. He hadn't wanted me here. All this time he had had only one thought, and that was to kill Nikko. But now that he has the chance, he doesn't pull the trigger. And maybe that's for my sake.

The wind whistles through the flowers. Music rattles from town. I look at Nikko in the moonlight. He is just how I remembered him, but with a new hardness to his features, stubble on his cheeks. He's taller than before, and has that same desperate skinniness, those same dark eyes as when I last saw him. His shoulders are narrow, like mine. His face, with his high, prominent cheeks and large, almond eyes, is pretty rather than handsome. His hair shines black in the moonlight.

He wears the dark clothes of a gunslinger and a black glove on his right hand. I crouch on a knee and run my thumb over the roughness of his cheek. He's not a mirage. He's flesh and blood. He's alive. He's right here.

Shouting comes from The Bruise. Orange torch flames add themselves to the green lamps. The Bullet Catcher's eyes sharpen. He shrugs off his old age and a brilliance comes back into his demeanor.

"Grab the packs," he says.

"What about Nikko?"

"He's too dangerous to leave here. He comes with us." He strips Nikko of his guns and bandoliers and throws them into the flowers. He lifts my brother as though he weighs nothing. "No time to argue. Follow me." He turns and runs off around the perimeter of town, holding his side, keeping low in the flowers.

We circle around and enter on the far side of town. As we weave through darkened alleys, the only person we run into is a drunk, passed out, leaning against the side of an apartment building. From the outskirts of town comes the sound of the gunslingers combing through the flowers.

"Why don't we run into the dunes?" I ask when we stop to catch our breaths.

The Bullet Catcher cocks his head at the stables, a little ways down the street. "We'd never make it without horses," he says.

We enter the barn through the back. It's abandoned save for the soft whinnying and clatter of hooves. Most likely the night watchman is out in the flowers with the gunslingers and townsfolk.

The Bullet Catcher chooses an evil-looking black stallion with a diamond on his forehead, flared nostrils that look like smoke flues, teeth like the scorched metal of a furnace grate. The horse I choose is small and brown, with big intelligent eyes. Her tail flicks back and forth. When I come close, she steps forward and presses her forehead against my hand. I feel as though she's been waiting for me. By the way the Bullet Catcher frowns at my choice, I can tell there are faster horses in the stable, but there's no time for discussion. He says nothing.

The Bullet Catcher saddles his horse. He lifts Nikko and rests him over the horse's back, before swinging himself over the saddle. I follow his lead, pulling the saddle straps tight around the horse's belly. He hands me his pack and I tie them on like saddlebags. I swing up on the saddle clumsily. The horse looks back at me as though double-checking my work.

"First time?" the Bullet Catcher asks.

I nod.

"Ride in rhythm with your horse or you'll hurt her back." Before I can ask him what he means, he flicks the reins and takes off, galloping through the open doors of the stable. I do the same and my horse trots after the Bullet Catcher as fast as she can.

We turn out of the barn and gallop down the street. For someone who has only ever gone as fast as a slow wagon train the speed is terrifying. The horse bounces me up and down and I can feel my pelvis and spine fracturing with every painful bump. I shut my eyes and grab onto the horse's mane for dear life. The horse grunts with every bump; I'm hurting her as much as she's hurting me.

"Open your eyes!" the Bullet Catcher yells. I force my eyes open. The Bullet Catcher's pulled alongside me, screaming commands. "You're hurting your horse! Keep your eyes open! Sit up in the saddle!"

I do as he says. I learn quickly to rise when my horse does, to fall with her. Soon we are like the same thing. She stops grunting so painfully. The Bullet Catcher speeds off in the lead. Nikko hangs over his horse's back, still unconscious, hair flapping in the wind. And my horse, now that I've stopped hurting her, gallops after them.

The lights of The Bruise fade into the distance and disappear behind the tall dunes, but we don't slow down. Nor are we heading back to our mountain.

We've been galloping at full speed for maybe an hour. The moon has retreated again, and the night is black and starless. The Bullet Catcher slows and motions for me to move alongside him.

"Do you hear it?" he yells over the sound of our horses.

"Hear what?"

"Prick your ears, Cub!"

I tune out the sound of our horses, their hooves, their dry, tired breathing, the pulse of my horse's heart through the saddle, and then I hear it, a distant sound growing louder: more horses.

"Gunslingers make good riders," says the Bullet Catcher. "They are gaining on us."

"What will we do?"

"Go to ground. There is a place half an hour's full gallop from here. It's risky."

"Is there nowhere else?"

114

"Only one road lies before us. We will see what happens."
He whips his reins and takes off like a bullet.

Our horses gallop tirelessly, weaving through the dunes. Ahead,
a tall plateau rises up from the desert. The ground levels out and
turns hard-packed. It looks impassable, but the Bullet Catcher
doesn't slow; he whips the reins, driving his horse harder. The
sound of the gunslingers' horses is loud in my ears, and when
I look back over my shoulder, a line of specks, a deeper shade
of black than the night, bob along the horizon.

When we're nearly at the base of the plateau, a black wall
rising out of a black night, the Bullet Catcher pulls his horse
sharply and rides alongside the towering rock. We ride along
the wall and now I can hear the gunslingers' voices, yelling
after us. The Bullet Catcher's eyes are fixed on the wall, like
he's expecting it to magically open up to us at any moment.
Suddenly, he pulls the reins and dives his horse into a thin
fissure that I don't see until I've galloped past it.

"Hell!" I scream and pull my horse around to double back.
The sound of the Bullet Catcher's horse, galloping on the
stone floor, echoes off the narrow walls. I am not so far behind.
There are sharp turns in the passage, and though I pull hard
on my horse's reins, I can't get her to turn quick enough. I
turn late and my legs scrape against the walls of the canyon
that are made of soft shale that breaks away easily. Still, it
hurts like hellfire. I take another turn late and the walls rip the
saddlebags from the horse. The food and gear clatter to the
canyon floor, lost. Holding closer to the horse, I lean forward
over her neck, so that I can hear her breathing, short and quick

and exhausted. Behind me, the sound of hooves is closer than ever. The gunslingers must know about the passage too.

The passage widens. Rounding a corner, the Bullet Catcher has stopped in the middle of the path, his horse maneuvered sidelong across the width of the passage.

"Stop!"

I pull so hard on the horse's reins I fear I'll break her neck. She digs in her hooves and nearly throws me off. Behind us, the sound of horses is deafening.

The Bullet Catcher jumps down from his horse and leads it by the reins into a cave set into the rock, the ceiling so low that he and the horse have to duck to enter. I jump down and follow, leading my own horse into the hiding place. The horses settle down on their haunches and the Bullet Catcher takes Nikko from his horse's back and lays him down on the cave floor.

The sound of hooves grows even louder, filling the air with dust, vibrating the loose pebbles at our feet. The gunslingers appear, riding single file at breakneck speed. They ride through the narrow canyon like bullets through a barrel. Then they're gone, the sound receding down the tight canyon pass. When the only sound is the low ringing in my ears and the only sign of the gunslingers are the imprints of hooves in the dust of the canyon floor, I finally let out my breath.

The Bullet Catcher's face is ashen. The scars and lines of his face have a kindness, like the smile lines of a man who grins with his whole face, but his eyes are injured. Then I remember the field of flowers, the shock of seeing the Bullet Catcher reel back, shot by Nikko. His arm is wrapped around his midsection. The blood on his fingers—his blood—is thick and brown and drying.

"Let me look at that," I say, reaching out a hand. He recoils, his eyes gleaming like an animal's. Then he relaxes.

"Thank you, Cub," he says, "but I can tend to myself." He strips his coat, unbuttons his shirt, and pulls off his undershirt, drenched in blood. When he sees my eyes go wide, he says, "It is not as bad as it looks. The body has a lot of blood. We do not need every drop."

The Bullet Catcher tears his undershirt into long strips to use as a field dressing. He produces the curved surgical needle and a flask. He unscrews the cap and pours medicinal alcohol over a needle to sterilize it.

Nikko lies on the cool cave floor, breathing soundly as though in an easy sleep. A large bump has developed on the back of his head, ruining his perfectly kempt black hair. I dampen a cloth and wipe the dirt from his face. That face that is so much like mine. That face that I haven't seen in so many years. Training to be a bullet catcher, you learn to keep bandages and a needle and thread handy. I have my own med kit, small enough to keep in my pocket. I clean the cut on Nikko's cheek, made by my bullet graze, and sew the shallow wound closed. Ever since the fight in the flowers, things seem to have progressed at double speed, in the space of a breath. But now, in the cold and darkness of the cave, everything has slowed down, returned to normal. Anger wells up suddenly within me.

"You knew that Bullet was my brother."

"I did," the Bullet Catcher says through gritted teeth as he threads the curved needle through his flesh.

"And if I hadn't been there you would have killed him."

"More likely, he would have killed me."

"You know what I mean."

The Bullet Catcher stops, the needle trembling ever so slightly in his fingers, his wound bleeding fresh. "Yes. I went there to kill him."

I shut my eyes against the tears.

"There is a history between the two of us that you do not understand," he says, restarting his sewing. He sighs painfully and cuts the thread. He pours clean water over his bloodied side and wraps himself with the dressings made from his torn shirt.

He stands, bending at the waist for the low ceiling. Feeling along the wall, he makes his way to the mouth of the cave. He presses himself close to the wall and peeks around the corner. Then he slips around the edge into the canyon. His steps descend the pass. Then gunfire, shouting. I jump to my feet, bang my head on the ceiling. The Bullet Catcher reappears at the mouth of the cave, whirling and sweating, throwing bullets back at his pursuers. He dives back into the cave. A gunslinger follows close behind him. He aims his gun at the Bullet Catcher's back and fires. The Bullet Catcher spins around, his hands flashing, and the gunslinger hurtles backwards against the canyon wall. He got his own bullet in the chest. The Bullet Catcher stands ready, his hands dangling at his side, watching the cave entrance for more gunslingers. My gun is loaded in my hand. Boots scuffing the dirt, muffled voices, come from just around the bend, but no one follows after the first gunslinger. After a while the sounds recede and the Bullet Catcher relaxes. He lowers himself against the wall. He's pale from the gunshot, pouring sweat.

I pocket my gun and take a seat on the cold cave floor. "You told me my brother was dead."

"He is dead, in a sense. He's dead to me."

"But not to me!" I yell, half turning to the Bullet Catcher, not wanting to meet his eyes. "How could you lie to me?"

"If I lied, I did it for your own good. You do not know the things he's done."

"Could it be any worse than the things *you've* done?" When he doesn't answer I let out a slow breath and say, "So when you told me that pain waited for me in The Bruise, this is what you meant."

The Bullet Catcher just looks at me, his eyes watering from his own pain.

"So what? Are we stuck here?" I ask, wanting to change the subject.

The Bullet Catcher takes a stick, places his hat on the end and thrusts it out into the moonlight. A shot rings out and flicks the hat up. It dances in the air as bullet after bullet rings through it. Finally, it hits the ground. From high on the cliff edges, where the gunslingers must be perched, comes the sound of laughter. The Bullet Catcher tosses aside the stick, splintered by bullets and, with a new one, retrieves his hat from the lip of the cave.

"What are they doing, playing with us?"

"Seems that way."

"Great."

Nikko stirs. He sits up, blinking, holding his head, dazed. He touches his cheek and runs a finger along the railroad of stitches.

"Nikko . . ." I start, but I don't know what to say after all these years. There's too much. I want to ask him every question

119

under the sun. Where he's been. What's happened to him. How he became a gunslinger. But all of these things get knotted in my throat and all I get out is his name.

"Imma," he says, his face forming into a brilliant, uncontainable smile.

I can't help myself. I wrap my arms around him.

"I missed you every day," he says, kissing the top of my head.

If this is a dream, I don't want to wake up. All I want is to hold Nikko in my arms while he kisses my hair. But the Bullet Catcher clears his throat loudly, and says, "Remember yourself, Cub."

I had grown used to, even fond of, the Bullet Catcher's name for me, but in front of my brother it makes my cheeks burn. Reluctantly, I pull myself away from him. Nikko takes out a small pouch, pinches some tobacco and sprinkles it onto a strip of yellowed paper. He rolls it, licks it closed, and offers it to me.

"I don't smoke."

He smiles again. "I'm glad. It's a bad habit." He offers the cigarette to the Bullet Catcher, who takes it. Nikko pulls a box of matches from his pocket and lights the Bullet Catcher's cigarette. Then he rolls and lights one for himself.

They smoke together in silence. They do it calmly, peacefully, as though everything else can wait until the paper burns down to the end. I feel terribly young in front of them. Nikko draws a deep, confident lungful of smoke and exhales Os, just like the Bullet Catcher does when he smokes from his pipe.

There are a few sticks of dried brush and moss in the cave. The Bullet Catcher takes what there is and makes a small fire. The three of us sit around it. No one talks. Not because there's nothing to say, but because there's too much. Especially for someone as glib as the Bullet Catcher. And what about Nikko? Is he a big talker? Or is he quiet too? He's my brother and yet I know so little about him. I want it to be as easy as falling back into our old roles from when we were younger. When he would stomp around the yard of the orphanage with his chin up and I would follow right behind, holding his hand, his skinny little shadow. But that was so long ago and so much has happened since then. And then there's this gulf between Nikko and the Bullet Catcher, the only two people in the world I care anything about. And me in the middle: the bridge spanning the two sides. I might just break apart from the tension. Our shadows, cast onto the cave wall, dance in the flickering firelight, larger and more animated than us. In the cave, the shadows occupy a greater space than the light.

"Where have you been all this time?" I ask, breaking the silence.

"That's not really the question you want to ask. You want to know why I didn't come back for you."

I poke the fire. "I want to know why I wasn't important enough. I want to know if you ever intended to come back for me or if it was just something you said so I'd let you go."

"He is a liar, Cub," the Bullet Catcher intervenes. "It is his nature."

"That's the pot calling the kettle black, you old hypocrite," Nikko says. When he speaks to the Bullet Catcher his voice is full of anger. But then he turns to me and his anger empties. In that emptiness I can't help but imagine the events that transformed him from the boy I remember into the man sitting across from me, wearing the dark clothes of a gunslinger, a history of muzzle flashes and blood, spilled in sepia, as in a photograph.

"I was always coming back for you."

I want to believe him, but I don't, and it's as though all those years back at the orphanage, waiting for him to come back for me, were for nothing. I feel foolish. "Even if that were true," I say, "it's too late. It's years too late. So much has happened since the orphanage. I rescued myself. I'm a bullet catcher, like you wanted to be once. You didn't grow up telling me stories about the gunslingers. The gunslingers were the bad guys, remember?"

"And you don't think the bullet catchers were just as bad as the gunslingers? We were simply too young to know any better." He turns to the Bullet Catcher and says, "What do you have to say old man? Am I wrong? You wouldn't lie to your student, would you?"

"She knows the bullet catchers were no saints."

"So what's the difference?" Nikko asks, turning back to me. "Where you were living, before you met the Bullet Catcher, there were street gangs, right? Local thugs, many no older than children, that would flash a knife or some sand-choked old gun and take whatever trinkets or coins you've on you?"

"Every town has gangs."

"And could you tell me the difference between any of those gangs? Was what they wanted so different? Money. Territory. Power. That's all anyone ever fights for. Would you say one was better than the other?"

"They called themselves by different names. They wore different colors. You could tell the difference that way."

"Yes. Exactly my point. But other than their colors, their names? Because what's in a name?"

I don't say anything.

I look to the Bullet Catcher, but he's silent as well.

"Nothing. There is no difference. Do you think it's any different with the bullet catchers and gunslingers?"

"Nothing is ever so simple," the Bullet Catcher says.

"And yet, wasn't it you, old man, who once told me not to confuse complexity with profundity? So let's cut through it. Have you told her about your past? About what you've done?"

"I know he's done bad things," I say softly, closing my eyes to the shadows and light.

"I do not lie to my pupils."

"Saying nothing is the same as lying. Imma, you don't know half of who he is."

"You told me Nikko was dead," I whisper, my eyes still closed.

Silence. We both seem to be waiting for the Bullet Catcher to argue, but for a long while he says nothing. "You're right," he finally says. "But I do not lie for my sake, and you know it, Nikko."

"But you did lie," I say. "If you didn't do it for you, then why did you do it?"

"I did it to protect you," he says. "Nikko knows the truth of many things, but he doesn't know what to do with it. It tears him up from the inside. And it is my fault, in a way. I did not want to make the same mistake with you, Cub."

"And what about giving her a choice?"

Again, the Bullet Catcher grits his teeth, says nothing. And we all lapse into silence.

In the silence, I think about how good it is to hear Nikko's voice. It's been made rough by sand and smoke, but it's still the voice of my brother from my childhood. It almost wouldn't matter what he said. I thought him dead. Hearing his voice, being in his company, it's a kind of miracle. After a lifetime of losing, I feel like I've finally been given something back, something that I thought I had lost forever. Haven't I lost enough for one lifetime? Don't I deserve a little bit of good luck?

If only we could have reunited years ago, when we were younger. Then everything would be simpler. But like the Bullet Catcher said, 'Nothing is ever so simple.'

Chapter Eleven

Morning comes. Deep in the canyon, the daylight arrives late and lasts only an hour, nothing more than a camera flash. That hour is so bright and the cave so dark that, after the light passes, my vision is full of colored orbs that float on the surface of my eyes. In that blunt darkness that follows the light, I reach out for Nikko's hand and hold tight. I'm afraid when the light returns he'll be gone. A ghost.

Nikko and me pass the time exchanging old stories. His favorite subject is Mom and Dad. He tells me of the good days on the homestead and the orphanage. It's odd to think that there were some good days sprinkled into my past. Alone, I tend only to think of the bad times. But Nikko brings with him all the long forgotten goodness of our past.

"They loved us," he says. "Right up till the end."

"I feel like I used to know that. But it's been so long, I guess I'd forgotten. Or maybe I was too young to remember for sure."

"But I wasn't," he says. "They would pick you up out of your crib and spin you around in their arms and press their faces into the top of your head and whisper it, that they loved you, and sometimes they'd shout it. I think it would kill them all over again to see us like this. They would have hated us being apart."

"What are you saying?"

He smiles and drops his voice to a whisper. "I'm saying come with me. I'm saying it's the only way all three of us get out of here unharmed. I know how much the Bullet Catcher means to you. I won't let anything happen to him. I promise."

I swallow hard. I look at him a long time. I don't say yes, but I don't say no either. I don't say anything at all. For the first time it occurs to me that what Nikko and the Bullet Catcher both want is for me to pick a side. That's what all of last night's talk had been about: trying to win me over. My cheeks turn hot. The heat runs down my throat to my stomach. How could they do that to me? Make me choose between them?

"Cub," the Bullet Catcher says, and when I look at him I can tell he's been calling me for a while. I try to set aside my thoughts. I cross the cave to the Bullet Catcher and crouch down beside him. He lowers his voice and says, "This situation is untenable. There is only one path open before us. We will need to use Nikko as a hostage. We might be able to escape if we put him between the gunslingers and us. They won't shoot if they think they might hit him."

"You're wrong," Nikko says. "My men will be posted up on the cliff face. They'll have you surrounded on both sides of the cave. I'm useless to you as a shield."

The Bullet Catcher considers this for a while. "Then we'll bargain," he says. "You'll tell them to let us go, or we'll kill you."

"You wouldn't!" I grab the Bullet Catcher's shirt and look into his eyes. "You wouldn't hurt him."

126

The Bullet Catcher first looks at my hands where I hold onto him, then he scans up to my face. "Let me go," he says flatly.

And I do, suddenly frightened of him.

"Tell me you won't hurt him."

"I will do what I must to ensure that we live another day."

I stand and take a step away from him. "I won't let you hurt my brother."

He looks from me to Nikko, and then back to me. The only sound is the drip, drip, drip of the water coming through the cracks of the cave. The three of us hold our breaths. Then the Bullet Catcher leaps at me. His hand is in my coat, quick as a pickpocket. He grabs the gun and pushes me away. The Bullet Catcher points the gun at Nikko and for a few moments we stand there, the three points of a standoff. The Bullet Catcher advances slowly on Nikko. Nikko backtracks until he comes to the wall. He presses himself against it like he's trying to dissolve into the rock. His eyes are trained on the end of the pistol.

I run to Nikko and wrap my arms around him, putting myself between him and the Bullet Catcher.

"Move, Cub," the Bullet Catcher says.

"Don't call me that!" I turn to look at him, trying to make myself tall to protect Nikko. When we were small I was always the one hiding behind him and he always protected me. Now it's my turn to return the favor. I just never thought I would be protecting him from the Bullet Catcher. "I won't let you hurt him."

The Bullet Catcher lowers his gun ever so slightly. I can hear him swallow. "This is the only way," he says. "I know you wish it were different, but it isn't."

"What about giving her a choice, Bullet Catcher?"

The Bullet Catcher doesn't move. He watches us impassively.

I shouldn't have to choose. It isn't fair. But if experience has taught me anything it's that life isn't fair. Nikko is alive and it's a miracle. But to keep him I have to sacrifice the only other person I love. But what else can I do? And besides, what will happen to the Bullet Catcher if I side with him? Would he be better off or would he be gunned down as soon as we tried to escape? Maybe going with Nikko is what's best for everyone.

I turn to Nikko and rest my head against his chest. His heart is racing fast. He holds my head gently in his arms. "Promise me you won't hurt him."

His heart beats faster. "I promise," he says.

I turn back to the Bullet Catcher. "Please," I say. "Throw down the gun. I don't want anyone to get hurt." The Bullet Catcher just stares at me. He doesn't look betrayed or angry. His eyes shine, catching the fading light coming from the canyon. He drops the gun and kicks it across the ground.

Nikko picks up the gun and flicks it toward the mouth of the cave. "Move." We all walk single file to the cave opening and Nikko shouts out, "Stand down! We're coming out!" Nikko steps out first, waving the gun at the Bullet Catcher to follow. I stand at the lip of the cave, still in darkness. And when I step over into the light of the canyon it feels like crossing a threshold into a new place that I don't understand at all.

On both sides of us are Nikko's gunslingers, smiling, spinning their guns. Without looking at me, Nikko says, "Imma, this is your first lesson. As long as the end of your barrel touches the Bullet Catcher's flesh, he's helpless. But all he needs is an inch and a moment. Don't give it to him."

Before I can ask him what he's talking about, Nikko's gunslingers descend on the Bullet Catcher. They drag him to the ground and bind his hands behind his back. Nikko stands over him and puts the pistol to the back of his head. He cocks the hammer.

"Wait! Stop!" I run at them but a gunslinger grabs me and holds me back. I struggle in her arms but she has me tight.

For a moment it looks like Nikko might actually shoot the Bullet Catcher, but then he turns to me and says, "That's how you beat a Bullet Catcher." He resets the hammer. The gunslinger lets me go. Smiling, Nikko walks over to me and presses the gun into my hands. I look down at the gun. He pinches my chin between his thumb and forefinger and lifts my eyes to meet his. "Don't worry," he says, smiling down at me. "No harm will come to him. I know how much it would hurt you. And I never want to be the one who causes you pain." He squeezes my shoulder and goes to help the other gunslingers drag the Bullet Catcher to his feet. When they march him to the horses he goes without a fight.

I look back into the darkness of the cave, where my horse rests, looking at me with eyes that I project all my guilt into. I extend my hand to her and make a few clicking sounds. She comes to me and I press my head against hers and pet her.

"Tell me I've done the right thing," I whisper into her broad face.

Up ahead, Nikko swings his leg over the saddle of what had been the Bullet Catcher's horse. When he sees me hanging back, he trots over and says, "Are you okay? You look a little green."

I look up at him, at his black eyes and dark hair flecked with brown, at the cut on his cheek that's bleeding anew. Just a day ago I thought all those parts of him were dead and gone. His hair turned to dry straw, his eyes rotted out to reveal the caverns of his skull, his blood sucked up by the desert sand. And then I think of the Bullet Catcher, back in The Bruise. He would have killed my brother even though he knew what it would do to me. I think all this and I know I've made the right decision, no matter how much it hurts to see the Bullet Catcher led away with his wrists and ankles bound.

I try to smile up at Nikko but I can't manage it. "I'm fine," I say. "What were you saying before? Something about a lesson?"

His smile brightens. "Imma, if you're going to be a great gunslinger, you'll have to pay better attention."

"Who said anything about me becoming a gunslinger?"

After a day in the cramped cave, Nikko's horse wants to gallop. It wrestles with the bit in its mouth. It trots circles in the dirt. Nikko pulls the reins, calming him. "I did," he says. "It's in your blood, Imma. One day you'll be a great gunslinger. Like I am. Like Father was."

I don't know what to say. And I must look shocked, because Nikko smiles gently and laughs.

"Now let's ride. I'll tell you everything when we get home." He kicks his horse and they shoot off down the canyon. I watch him round the bend, then raise my eyes to squint at the sharp canyon edge and the brutish blue sky beyond, before mounting my horse and following Nikko.

PART II

Chapter Twelve

Once, many months ago, before we travelled to Los Cazadores, before Nikko came back into my life and everything changed, the Bullet Catcher told me that the burden of a gun can't be measured by its weight. He told me that the burden is too heavy to measure. But when I started training with Nikko he told me a gun was my right. He told me that gunslinging was in my blood. I think he might have been right about that. But he was wrong about one thing. Back in the cave, Nikko told me gunslinging and bullet catching weren't so different. They are. When I was training with the Bullet Catcher, he made me repeat the same lessons over and over. I learned, but my progress was slow, and my mind felt blasted, my thoughts polished away. I was a stone in a river and the Bullet Catcher was water, grinding me down, turning me to sand. But with Nikko as my teacher, gunslinging comes easy. My progress feels exponential. To hold a gun is to hold lightning. Nikko was wrong.

Bullet catching is water.

Gunslinging is electricity.

* * *

We rode into Las Pistolas after a day's ride from the cave. We dismounted our horses and stable hands took them away. I waited, standing in the middle of the street, not knowing what to do or where to go. I waited for Nikko, who was ordering a couple gunslingers to take the Bullet Catcher to the jail.

"Don't rough him up," he said. "Just take him there. Give him something to eat and drink."

I wanted to go too. I didn't know what I could say to the Bullet Catcher, but I wanted to make sure he was okay, that Nikko's men followed his orders and didn't hurt him. But then Nikko wrapped his arm around my shoulders and said, "I have a surprise for you."

Nikko led me to a large building. The entrance was made of marble blocks and I felt like I was entering a cave. A man opened the glass door for us and stood aside to let us in. He gave a half bow to Nikko and said, "Pleasure to see you again, sir." Nikko smiled at him and led me to the top floor—ten stories up. I had never been in a building so tall. He showed me into an apartment.

"This is all yours," he said.

"What do you mean—all mine?"

"I mean it's yours. Your new home. This was my apartment—well, one of my apartments—but I want you to have it."

I went from room to room, from the bedroom to the sitting room to the kitchen and bathroom. There was a feather bed and settees and couches. A writing desk. Shelves overflowing with books. Beautiful carpets with swirling weaves atop polished wood floors. There was a claw-footed tub that filled with cool

134

or warm water in moments from a tap in the wall. Nikko told me the water traveled through pipes buried in the ground. But there were no rivers or streams and often I wondered where the water came from. The water seemed like a miracle.

"This is all mine?" I asked, pressing my nose against the tall tenth-story window and gazing at the town below.

"It's all yours," Nikko said.

The night of our arrival, Nikko took me to eat at his club. Over dinner, I asked him about our father. He smiled and led me to a private room, where white-gloved waiters served us drinks and lit Nikko's cigar for him. It was there that he told me the story.

Emiliano Moreno, my father, was a mechanic, like his father before him. He grew up in Polvo, a town not so far from the border between the Northland and South. It was famous for its market where merchants from the North came to barter with Southerners. This was all before the gunslingers, a time when bullet catchers were common.

Most bullet catchers worked as private security for banks or wealthy families. But some were mercenaries and outlaws. In my father's time it was not unheard of for a single talented bullet catcher to ride into town and leave with whatever they wanted. Women, men, all the money in the town's bank vault, casks of snakebite. How do you stop someone who can't be shot? But Polvo was a large town, a city really, with huge tenement blocks, a market larger than most towns, and enough water that everyone could take a bath every day without worrying that there wouldn't be enough to drink. It was too big for

135

one person to cause problems, even if that one person was a bullet catcher.

When he was old enough, Emiliano went to work with his father in the repair shop that had been in the family for three generations. They fixed everything from guns to water recyclers to steam engines.

My father was somewhere around my age, fifteen or sixteen, still an apprentice to his father, when a bullet catcher named Andanza came to town. For three days Andanza caused no end of trouble in Polvo. She stole from merchants. She went to the bank and walked out with two bags of silver, one slung over each shoulder. She drank and caroused all night and when one tavern keeper tried to give her a bill she stuck a gun under his nose and dared him to insist. Lawmen came to arrest her and there was a shootout. By the end of those three days Polvo had lost so many lawmen that everyone agreed to let her have whatever she wanted and hope that she moved on sooner rather than later.

My father and his father kept their earnings from the shop in a small safe under a false bottom in the floor of the family house, so they didn't pay much attention to Andanza or the small chaos she was making. But Grandpa liked to play cards with his old war buddies after work, down at the saloon, a few blocks from the shop. One day, Andanza was there. She had been there most of the day. It was at this time, with Andanza dead drunk and my grandpa a few tables away, playing cards for pennies, that the tavern keeper tried to sneak the money Andanza owed him out of her wallet while she dozed at her table. He got the wallet out of her pocket and started counting out the money. Andanza woke, saw the tavern keeper, and broke his wrist. He dropped the wallet, wrestled his hand free and went running for cover. Andanza drew her pistol and peppered bullets at the retreating tavern keeper. Then all hell broke loose. There were a few drunks with guns who thought as long as Andanza was distracted they might be able to gun her down and collect the bounty on her head. There were three or four of them and they surrounded her on one side. But Andanza was too fine a bullet catcher, even when she was dead drunk. The townsfolk drew their guns and fired. Andanza swung out her arm in a long arc and bent the bullets back around. My grandfather was on the ground, his hat pulled over his head. He got one of the bullets right through his neck. Wrong place, wrong time. Andanza stumbled out of the bar and to Polvo's great relief, she had gone by sunrise, moved on to the next town.

Emiliano left Polvo too. He couldn't stay in the place where his father was murdered. He opened up his own shop in another town. By that time, more people were arming themselves against the bullet catchers. Most of his business was gun repair. He became somewhat famous for it. He could fix most any gun. Then he started making his own guns and people came from all over to buy them.

When the gunslingers formed, promising to put an end to the bullet catchers, Emiliano went to his local chapter and joined. He was a natural. Because he knew everything about guns, he knew how to get the most out of them.

Eventually, he closed the repair shop and struck out with a posse of gunslingers. They traveled across the Southland hunting down and killing bullet catchers. He had many handprints tattooed on his arms. But he was always looking for one bullet catcher in particular: Andanza. Sometimes he'd hear a rumor about her, that she was in this town, or that she was headed to that town. But he was always a step behind her.

Then, one day, Emiliano was drinking in a saloon. He had been on the road for years by that point, and had quit paying attention to the names of the one-horse towns he travelled through. It was early and the saloon was relatively empty. He ordered a snakebite. Another patron pulled up the stool next to him. He expected it to be one of the gunslingers from his posse, come to share a drink, but when he turned it was Andanza. He could hardly believe it. He slugged his drink, stood and said to the bullet catcher: "Your name is Andanza. You killed my father. I'm calling you out."

Andanza laughed and said, "I've killed a lot of people's fathers. What makes yours so special?"

Emiliano squeezed the handles of his guns so hard the wood creaked. "Because he was *my* father. And because I'm going to kill you."

Andanza had probably heard similar lines a hundred times or more in her life, and I don't suspect she had any cause to think that Emiliano would be the first to make good on his promise. She smiled and said, "We'll see, gunslinger. We'll see."

Out in the street, they counted out the paces and stared each other down. The whole town caught wind of the duel and turned out to line the street and watch.

"On three," Andanza called.

Emiliano nodded, his fingers an inch from his guns.

"One!" Andanza called.

Emiliano's heart beat dull and slow, like it was pumping mercury.

"Tw—!"

Before Andanza could finish, Emiliano drew his pistol and fired. Andanza raised her hand to catch the bullet. She swiped at the air and staggered forward with the momentum. She opened her hand and it was empty. She looked down. A red dot was developing around a smoking hole in her chest where Emiliano's bullet had pierced her. She looked up. Emiliano spun his gun and holstered it. Andanza took another step forward and fell down dead.

Emiliano approached her slowly, in case she was playing possum. He nudged her onto her back with the toe of his boot and her eyes were wide and empty.

"That was mighty unsporting," said a bystander.

"She didn't deserve any better," said Emiliano. That night, he rode out of town with his posse, his father avenged and his conscience clear.

When Nikko finished, the lights in the room seemed to have dimmed. When he had begun, the sounds of conversation and the clack of billiards could be heard from the other rooms in the club. But now everything was quiet. It was very late and when I looked out the window the night was dark and still. I didn't know what to make of our father's story, other than it was a piece of our history I hadn't thought possible until a couple days ago. And I wondered how much of my father was in me. How much of my brother. I said, "I never even saw Father hold a gun."

Nikko shrugged. "He gave it up once he met Mom. Anyway, how would you know? You were so young. Did you even know what a gun was?"

I said, "You're born knowing."

That was three months ago. And in all this time I have never visited the Bullet Catcher. I want to tell him I'm sorry. I want him to forgive me. I want to know about the bad blood between him and Nikko. But I put it off, not ready to face up to any of it. I have gone so far as to avoid the street that the jail is on entirely. Whether it's remorse or loyalty to Nikko that keeps me away, I don't know. But every day that I don't visit him makes the prospect more difficult.

Nikko and I practice gunslinging every morning. The practice field, where we meet, is surrounded on four sides by artificial dunes built up to absorb stray shots. During the day the field is full of recruits practicing their aim, but it's early and we have the whole place to ourselves. Nikko always teaches me in private. It's one of the only times of day we get to spend together, just him and me. Everyone wants a piece of his time.

The sun hasn't yet broken over the dunes, but the light beyond the field vibrates, hinting at the heat of the coming day. The air is cool and milky blue. Across the field, Nikko strides toward me, carrying a valise, wearing a smile ear to ear. He's always like this first thing in the morning, and his smile never fails to alight one in me as well. Every night, when I lay my head on my pillow, before falling asleep, I look forward to his smile the next morning.

I have waking nightmares alone in my rooms, when it's so dark I can't make out the shapes of the furniture, when I begin to believe I've dreamed the whole thing, that, in the morning, I'll wake in the Bullet Catcher's camp, under the canopy of my tent, or worse, back in Dmitri's, on my cot, the fat tavern keeper yelling at me to start my morning shift. And in these dreams, Nikko is dead. Odd as it sounds, I miss the cave, where I could be close enough to hold on to him.

"What's that?" I ask, pointing to the valise.

"Show and tell!" His voice is a loud, joyous laugh. He puts the valise on the ground and unlatches the locks. For a few seconds he fiddles with something behind the lid. I feel like we're young again. He eyes me mischievously over the top of the open valise, then, theatrically closing the lid, he reveals a mechanical glove, worn over his right hand. It looks like the bullet-catching glove he built when we were children, only all grown up, just like him. A brass exoskeleton stretches along the glove, the sharp metal arching over his fingers and the back of his hand, like the gothic buttresses of the northern cathedrals I remember from my books. It hums with energy, making my teeth chatter.

He beams with pride. "I've been working on it ever since we were kids. I perfected it only a few months ago."

"It catches bullets," I say, awed.

"Exactly," he says. "The bullet catchers might be all but gone, but they're still a nuisance. They're an idea. Killing a man? No problem. But killing an idea. That's tricky."

"And the glove kills ideas?" This is why my favorite moments are before we start talking. Nikko's voice is joyous. He laughs

141

easily. But his words put me on edge. Times like this remind me that he's not the brother I grew up with. He's grown up. A young man with a history I only half know.

"The bullet catchers aren't people anymore. They're legends. And with each passing year the legend grows." As he talks he flexes the fingers of the glove. Holding it up to the light, he goes through the bullet-catching positions the Bullet Catcher taught me. How far did Nikko get with his training? He only goes through the basic steps. "The legend grows because no one can catch bullets anymore. People are beginning to think bullet catching was magic. Parents tell their children how great the bullet catchers were. Kids play bullet catchers and gunslingers in the street."

"What's so bad about that? We wanted to be bullet catchers when we were kids. We played those same games. We thought they were magic."

He looks at me a moment, snapped from his reverie. Then he smiles and says, "Sometimes I forget how young you still are." He takes out one of his guns and spins it on his trigger finger, thinking. "No. You're right. It's not bad, exactly. It just makes people—" he scans the sky, looking for the right word—"more difficult. But the glove will show people that bullet catching isn't magic. It'll show people that bullet catching isn't even special.

"Today, though," he says, "the glove is a tool for your next lesson. We're going to play gunslingers and bullet catchers, just like the kids. Only we're going to use real guns and live ammo."

I draw one of my guns. It's heavy in my hand. But when it comes to shooting, it'll be like a feather. I look from the gun to Nikko. "I'm going to shoot at you?"

142

He smiles. "Don't worry. You won't hit me. If you make me break a sweat, I'll be impressed."

He turns and marches across the practice field. With his back to me, walking with the ease and surety of a teacher, the ends of his long coat picked up by the wind, I could easily mistake him for the Bullet Catcher. It's amazing how time changes people. None of us are who we were yesterday. Would any of us even recognize our younger selves? And what would our younger selves think of the people we've become? Nikko smiles more than he used to. But it's that something behind his smile, that splinter just below the skin. Life's always this way: the joy mixed with unease.

"Remember!" he calls to me. "Shoot at where I'm going to be, not where I am! When you're ready!"

My guns flash. One shot right at him to get his feet moving. Then I empty both barrels, scattering my shots around the area I anticipate him to be. It's easy to forecast the way a target will move once you know what to look for. Every second hints at the second that follows. It's in the way the air changes. The way Nikko's breath shortens. The way he grunts when he changes direction. A twitch in his face. The direction of his eyes.

To be a bullet catcher is to react, to be an echo of your opponent. But Nikko has taught me to act before my opponent.

"Don't react!" he says. "Act!"

At first, I'm too slow and my aim isn't sharp enough to make him work. He doesn't bother catching or bending the bullets. He dodges lazily, gleefully, a child playing a game. Sweat pours down my face. I blink it away. Reload. I tap the triggers faster. My accuracy tightens with every round. The gulf between

Nikko's movements and my own converge, moving closer until the difference is so minute anyone watching would have difficulty judging which one of us moves first. We synchronize. We could almost be dancing.

I keep going, not feeling the weight of the guns. My hands and feet and fingers work automatically. I find the spot I know he'll be in a moment's time and fire. His eyes go wide. He grunts, trying to change direction. Every muscle in his face clenches in concentration. At the last moment he reaches out his gloved hand and swats away the bullet. Just in time. The bullet passes around him, through the tail of his coat. Neither of us stops to admire the close call. Nikko rolls to his feet and plants himself, square to me, in parting the clouds, a bullet-catching pose. I keep shooting. Nikko's gloved hand is a blur. There is no time to dodge anymore. I am too fast, too accurate. He bends the bullets into the ground at his feet.

I sense it in the air first. It almost has a smell, like ozone and sweat. He doesn't redirect my last shot into the ground. He spins and swings his arm out. I hit the ground in a puff of dust and the bullet sings past my ear.

I keep my face buried in the ground, suddenly exhausted, huffing the golden dirt. I stay there until Nikko comes over and offers his hand. He's all smiles again. Sweat dapples his forehead.

"Well done, little sister," he says, pointing to the sweat on his forehead. "And you've made more work for the tailor." He puts his finger through the bullet holes in his duster. Looking skyward, he follows the rising sun for a moment with his eyes and takes a big breath. "Enough for now?"

I smile and nod, not knowing exactly why—for the sheer physical elation that comes from hard work, for the sake of sharing a smile with my brother.

"Breakfast, then," he says, beaming. Helping me up, he rests his hand on my shoulder and steers me toward town. I look up at him and trace the scar on his cheek that I gave him that night in The Bruise. My old habit of tracing scars. He catches my hand, gives it a gentle squeeze, and lets it down. I lean into him and close my eyes, trusting him to guide me. It's enough that we're here together. That is reason enough to smile. My guns dangle from my fingers, suddenly heavy again, still hot from shooting. I finally holster them.

"Proud of you," he says, giving my shoulders a squeeze. And we laugh, for no reason at all.

Chapter Thirteen

We climb the dune and look out over Las Pistolas, my brother's home. My home. Las Pistolas was once a booming silver town, but when the mines ran dry the people left—everyone except those too old or young or sick to make the trek across the Southland to somewhere new. Nikko says when he took control of the gunslingers the first thing he did was move everything to Las Pistolas. Without silver, the one thing the town had going for it was that it lay at the heart of the desert. The hub of the wheel, some call it.

Nikko and I walk down the gentle slope into town. When Nikko moved the gunslingers here most everything was abandoned, falling apart. Instead of tearing everything down and building it back up, he ordered the old buildings to be patched and reinforced. As the town grew, to keep everything tight and centralized, Nikko ordered the planners and carpenters to build up, not out. It hadn't grown into a city so much, but several towns stacked on top of one another. Most of the buildings are at least three to four stories, with one story sitting atop the other like a child's poorly aligned stack of blocks. Metal stairs wind up from one level to the next, and across each story stretches a floating metal boardwalk affixed to the sides of the buildings. They creak and groan with foot traffic and let down sheets of trapped sand on the people below. The sound of machines is everywhere: humming electricity, whirring engines, firing pistons. White steam. Black smoke. The air is bilious and reeking. An airless, monochrome sky hangs above the town. Besides training new gunslingers, Las Pistolas is an industrial town. The factories turn out guns and bullets that ship to all corners of the Southland.

Everyone calls Nikko 'sir' or 'Bullet'. Sometimes I forget that my brother and Bullet are the same person. Bullet strikes fear in others by the mention of his name. Bullet doesn't match my image of Nikko, whose voice is always soft and unguarded with me, who hugs me and kisses my cheeks and the top of my head. The only one who speaks to my brother like an equal is his lieutenant, a man called Cloak.

"In the Northland," Nikko says, stretching his arm out to an imaginary vista, "there are giant buildings of metal and concrete, so tall they scrape the sky. They make Las Pistolas look like the boondocks." The North is one of Nikko's favorite subjects. He says that he lived there for a time, before he was sent back down to the Southland. He talks endlessly about the cities, the paved roads, the flying machines, the motor buggies, the beautiful, fashionable people. "Once you see it, Imma—once I take you there—nowhere else will ever be good enough." There's a far-off look in his eyes and I know he's seeing the cities of the North projected over the crooked, sooty buildings of Las Pistolas. Nudging him with my shoulder, he snaps out of it and smiles down to me. "One day," he says.

Cloak meets us at the edge of town. He whispers something into Nikko's ear, holding onto his arm to draw him close. Cloak dresses almost all in black: black coat, black shirt, black waistcoat, black trousers, black boots. He wears a black leather glove over his shooting hand, like Nikko. Even the chain of his fob watch is lacquered black. He's the only person I've ever met, besides a few traveling salesmen, who wears a tie. It's always perfectly straight and bleached white, a target he dares anyone to aim for. He hides his nose and mouth behind a bandanna, like he's robbing a bank. Nikko says the industrial air bothers him, but I imagine that behind his bandanna lies a crooked row of yellow fangs. But his eyes are beautiful: big, and pale gray. He keeps those big eyes on me as he whispers into my brother's ear.

Nikko turns to me and says, "Sorry, Imma, business. Rain check on breakfast," and heads off with Cloak down the wide, even road bustling with people and coaches and horses and the occasional motorized buggy, toward the industrial end of town. I can't imagine what the cities of the Northland must look like. Las Pistolas is the biggest place I've ever seen. Las Pistolas has water towers like other towns have gravestones.

I head home. The doorman opens the door for me and tips his hat with a smile. "Morning, Miss Moreno," he says. I return his smile and drag my feet up the ten stories to my apartment. After only a few months, I'm almost embarrassed by how ordinary living in Las Pistolas feels. Mornings, first thing, the water is full of small ice crystals that catch the light like any precious stone. But I no longer excite at the feeling of the water on my skin, of scented soaps, of the medicated salts relaxing my tight muscles after training. I bathe, and dry, and dress without any of the ritual or care I used to practice.

When I first came to town, we struggled to find me something to do. I was a novice gunslinger, and it wouldn't have looked good if Nikko gave me any real responsibility. So Nikko came up with the title of Overseer, and told me to tour the Academy and the factories and report back any faults or deficiencies I might find. But it was all just to keep me busy. How would I know what was normal and what was deficient in a gunslinger operation?

Still, in the beginning, I made a habit of spending a little time every day at the Academy. I sat in on some demonstrations, took part in a few drills, but all those children with guns—in the beginner courses, many weren't even teenagers—made me nervous. And the students in the advanced classes treated me with mild disdain when I sat in on their lectures. I stopped going after a few weeks.

I leave the apartment and head for the saloon. I head there most mornings after training with Nikko. After all those years living and working in Dmitri's, any saloon feels like home. I'm comfortable amongst the old men and women who fill up the bar before midday, whose hands don't stop shaking for nothing, the people who couldn't grip a gun if their lives depended on it. In Nikko's kingdom, these people are outsiders, tolerated because of who they used to be. They're old tigers. They have the stripes, but their teeth have all fallen out. The old gunslingers and me have become fast friends, naturally. They look at my arms and legs and recognize my stripes as their own. They know another outsider when they meet one.

The old gunslingers hail me as soon as I come through the batwings. I sit beside Hartright. Besides Nikko, she's my best friend in Las Pistolas. A knife scar runs diagonally down her left cheek. She has a mouthful of gold teeth, seven fingers, and two deep brown eyes. Her shooter, a rusted antique, sits by her drink on the table. In her old age, Hartright is nothing but tall tales and twinkling eyes. As soon as I sit down and order breakfast she launches into the story she didn't have a chance to finish telling when last I saw her, when Cloak had come to fetch me for Nikko and Hartright shut her mouth mid-sentence.

"And then I said," Hartright says, chuckling, "Old Wakefield, that's not your horse, that's your wife! You should have seen the look on his face, young'un." She wipes tears from her eyes, her whole body shaking with the laughter she'd pent-up over night. "Blind as a bat, he was, without his glasses," Hartright croaks out between laughing fits. Then, as though she was only reminded about her own glasses by her story, she pats her pockets and shirt until she locates them sitting across the bridge of her nose. "I ever tell you about when Wakefield and me found the oasis filled with mermaids?"

"No," I say, smiling ear to ear. "Can't wait." I've heard this story at least three times. I don't care. I don't smile easy. Never have. So anyone who makes me smile is worth sticking close to. Maybe that's why I'm here. Maybe that's why I chose Nikko.

By midday Hartright is all but passed out, resting her cheek in the crook of her arm, her hand wrapped around a bottle of snakebite. But she still manages to tell stories out of one side of her mouth. Some mornings I might order lunch, read a book from Nikko's library, and wait for Hartright to wake up so she can tell me more stories. But today I'm restless and when Hartright lays her head on the table I say my goodbyes to the rest of the old gunslingers and go looking for Nikko.

Not everyone in Las Pistolas is a gunslinger. Gunslingers don't stoke the fires in the factories, or work the assembly lines. Gunslingers don't work the markets or saloons. Many of the families who moved to Las Pistolas did so to be close to their sons or daughters training at the Academy, or in the hope that if they ever had children they might be looked on favorably when it came to admission into the Academy. In the street, I flag down a man in a dirty red flannel shirt. He wears a pair of goggles, pulled up on top of his head. Two black rings of coal dust encircle his eyes.

When I ask if he's seen Nikko, he doesn't know whom I'm referring to. "Bullet," I say, "Have you seen him today?"

"Aye," he says. "I passed him on my way out of the ordnance factory." He points the way to the far side of town. I tip my cap and push on.

Though I was supposed to, I've never visited any of the factories. The smog hangs heavier over the belching smokestacks. I can see them from the west-facing windows of my apartment, and even from that distance they look bleak. Up close, the factories seem almost animated, breathing out the sooty air. I enter by the service entrance where motorized buggies and horse-drawn carts bustle away shipments of bullets.

Inside, the machines groan. Workers with arms as thick as my legs heave bars of lead to machines that heat and pound them into malleable wire. Operators stand over giant presses that shape the metal into bullets. There's a small army of children sitting on stools between rows of crates. In one crate are the unpolished bullet jackets. They take them one at a time, dab polish on the end of their finger and rub up the copper until it shines. Then they deposit the polished jacket in the crate on the other side. I'm reminded of the factory owners who frequented the orphanage, looking for cheap labor and small hands. Did Nikko acquire his workforce the same way? And what happens to the children once their hands get too big for polishing bullets?

A worker points me up to the foreman's office, up a steel staircase, black with coal dust. Nikko, Cloak and the foreman sit around the foreman's desk. When I knock and enter they stop talking and look at me.

Nikko smiles. "I didn't expect you here," he says. "How was your morning?"

"Hartright kept me company."

"That's about all she's good for," Cloak says.

Nikko laughs and says, "You wouldn't know it to look at her, but Hartright was once a great gunslinger. She used to ride with Dad. She has two arms full." In this town, where so many famous gunslingers make their home, I've learned that 'two arms full' means they have tattoos of bullet catchers' handprints running the length of both their arms. "Hartright and Wakefield," Nikko says. "Mean bastards. Wakefield's dead now and Hartright's retired, of course."

I think of Hartright, passed out back at the saloon, slumbering snot bubbles into the crook of her arm. She's so skinny her clothes outweigh her. Her wrinkles overlap one another. To look into her eyes you'd never think her capable of hurting a fly, and in her stories she never talks about killing anybody, she never talks about Dad. In her stories, she and her friend, Old Wakefield, were nothing but troublemakers, getting into harmless scrapes, knocking over booze wagons at worst, but mostly encountering all manner of mythical creatures—mermaids, gargoyles, angels, demons. But if Nikko is telling the truth, her gun wasn't always just a paperweight.

I shake away the thought of a younger and more violent Hartright. "I saw children working down on the factory floor," I say.

Nikko shifts in his seat.

Cloak says, "It's the best way to make bullets."

"I don't care. Nikko, if your childhood self could see those children, what would he say? Don't you remember how the Brothers and Sisters lined us up for the factory owners? How it felt when they went down the line examining our fingers like the hides of cattle?"

Cloak is about to say something, but Nikko raises his hand and Cloak shuts his mouth. "Those children aren't orphans, Imma. Do you think me so heartless?"

"Then who are they?"

"The children of the machine workers and coal shovelers. They all make a fair wage. We aren't slave drivers."

"It's still not right."

Nikko stares at me, considering. "Maybe you're right," he finally says. "You are the Overseer, after all. I promise I'll look

153

into it." He smiles and stands, stretching his back. He turns to the foreman and says, "We can finish our conversation another time."

The foreman bows his head.

Nikko turns back to me. "Let's go to my office. I have a surprise for you."

In his office on the top floor of the tallest building in town, Nikko slumps into his large, red cushioned chair, kicks his boots up on his desk, and lets his head hang back to stare at the ceiling with closed eyes. For a few moments he lets Cloak and me see how tired he must be. Then he opens his eyes, smiles, and languidly waves his hand at Cloak. Cloak goes over to the little table that contains a bottle of snakebite, seltzer, and glasses. He pours three shots and hands them around. Nikko opens a drawer in his desk and pulls out a wood box, about the size of a shoebox, and puts it on the desk in front of me.

"What's this?"

"Open it," he says jovially. I unlatch and open the lid. Inside is a pair of shiny new revolvers. The steel is polished to a mirror. The bone grips are engraved and when I pick up one of the guns I see that it reads: Immaculada Moreno.

"What are these for?"

Nikko shrugs. "Because every great gunslinger needs a couple trusty shooters."

He raises his snakebite and knocks it back. Cloak pulls his bandanna from his face and sips reservedly from his glass. This is the first I've ever seen him without his bandanna. His face is the opposite of what I expected. He's closely shaven, with a soft jaw, and a dimple in his chin. His attractive mouth is downturned on both sides. He's much younger than I thought. Wearing his bandanna, when I could only see his eyes, I'd mistaken him for an older man. The desert sun can do that, tan the skin and bleach the eyes, make them look ancient. But he can't be much older than Nikko, if at all.

Nikko smiles up at Cloak when he drinks and reaches around to pat him on the back. Nikko splashes a bit more into his glass and says, "Don't look so serious, my friend. We can be ourselves in front of Imma. If you can't rely on family, on whom can you rely?"

Cloak sips again and lets his shoulders relax.

"We've been talking," Nikko says, his hand resting on the small of Cloak's back. "You're going to ride with us tomorrow when we head out on gunslinger business."

"Tomorrow we'll ride to Bad Pines," Cloak says. "It's a nothing town. Maybe a dozen or so people. But they have water. A lot of water. More than they need."

"And what are we to do?" I ask.

"Make them share," he says.

Nikko laughs. "The Southland is a big place," he says, gesticulating its size with his hands. "We're all in this together. Everyone has to share."

"You can consider this a test," Cloak says.

"A test of what?"

"Loyalty." Cloak rests one of his hands on the butt of his gun.

"I'm loyal to my brother," I say, putting my hand on my gun. This is how gunslingers growl.

"That's enough," Nikko says.

155

"I told you she wasn't ready," Cloak says. "She's lazy. She still thinks of herself as a bullet catcher, not a gunslinger."

"I said that's enough." All the humor has drained from Nikko's face. He's pale, his eyes hard and serious and staring through Cloak.

"Best thing to do would be to kill the old man."

"Cloak!" Nikko yells. He rises to stand toe to toe with his lieutenant. "You've said quite enough. Outside. We'll speak later."

Cloak backs off, looking diminutive stacked against Nikko. He knocks back the last of his drink, grabs his hat, and leaves.

Nikko's hand sits on the butt of his gun until Cloak closes the door behind him. Then Nikko relaxes. He sits on the edge of his desk. His face is serious but kind.

"Are you happy here, Imma?" There's concern in his voice.

"You wouldn't kill the Bullet Catcher, would you? You promised." How could I possibly stop him if he made up his mind to kill him? What if Cloak and the rest of the gunslingers pressured him into doing it? Whose loyalty means more to Nikko—mine or the gunslingers'?

"Cloak's just talking. He likes to growl."

"You're not answering my question."

"Do I have to?"

I slump into the back of the chair. "Why are you making this so difficult? Just tell me everything will be okay." I tap my still full glass with my fingernail and refuse to look at him.

"Cloak's right about one thing," he says. "You haven't been giving gunslinging your all. You get away with it because you're a natural, but you spend too much time with Hartright and the others. You spend too much time reading up in your apartment.

You should be auditing at the Academy. You should be touring the factories. Just think, if you had done what I asked you to months ago we could have already been fixing the problem of children working at the factories."

"There never should have been a problem like that in the first place."

He nods and says, "You're right." We fall into silence.

"Tell me you're happy," he says again. When I don't say anything he says, "You're not a prisoner. If you leave, no one will chase you."

"You wouldn't chase me?"

Nikko's face turns grim.

I sigh and say, "If I leave, what would happen to the Bullet Catcher?"

Nikko rubs his eyes. "I'd have to kill him. I'd make it quick."

My mouth drops. "Is that a threat? Is the Bullet Catcher ransom?"

"I'd have no choice," he says, crouching in front of me. He puts his hands on my shoulders, holding me. "My men will demand his blood. It's already difficult enough to explain to them why I haven't killed him. They relent to honor our promise. But the promise is between both of us. Without you the promise is broken." He wipes away the tears running down my cheeks. "Please," he says. "Look at me."

I do what he says.

"There we go." He smiles and wipes away the last of my tears. "There's nothing to worry about. A promise is a promise. Everything will be okay."

"And you," I squeeze out. "What will happen to you if I leave?"

"What will happen to me?" he repeats. "I'll hate myself for failing you twice in the same lifetime." Nikko pulls me close and holds me.

I close my eyes and let go of everything, and sink into his shoulder.

Chapter Fourteen

"Imma, wake up! You're missing the day!" Nikko calls from the doorway.

"Ten more minutes."

"Now!" he says. "And be quick about it!" He comes into my room and throws open the curtains. "It's a special day."

I bury my head in my pillow, blocking out the late-morning light.

"It's your first ride!" he says, coming over and putting a knee on the bed. "It's the first time we get to ride together." He shakes me by the shoulders.

"All right, I'm up, I'm up!" I can't help laughing, like when we were young and he would tickle me until my stomach and face ached from laughter. With Nikko close, my muscles feel stronger, my bones less creaky. Despite my wanting to be gloomy after yesterday's argument, I can't help but feel light and happy.

"Five minutes," he calls back as he leaves. His footsteps skip down the stairs. I'm left alone in the room. The light coming through the windows is white and punishing. The ride will be blistering.

"Exciting day," Cloak says, deadpanning. My horse, No-Name, is waiting for me, already saddled. I run my hand along her neck. She purrs, cat-like, and I swing up onto the saddle.

"It *is* exciting," Nikko says, riding up, all smiles and energy. "Today you learn what it really means to be a gunslinger. We're peacekeepers, the people who keep things fair and orderly in the Southland."

"Like lawmen," I say.

"That's part of it, sure," Nikko says. "But lawmen are loved, thanked, well paid. Don't expect any thanks. The things we have to do are often unpopular, but they're for the greater good."

"Beneath every pretty clock face lie the springs and gears," Cloak says absently.

"Resident philosopher," Nikko says, grinning.

Cloak grumbles to himself, kicks his horse, and rides on ahead.

"What did he mean?"

Nikko watches Cloak as he rides on ahead. He says, "You'll understand when we get there." Then he clicks his tongue and his horse gallops away.

I lean over No-Name's neck, pet her mane, and whisper, "Let's go." And she does. That night in The Bruise, when the Bullet Catcher and I stole her to make our escape, seems so far away. In the months that we've lived in Las Pistolas, No-Name's gotten bigger, faster. I could never settle on a name for her. Besides, I've never felt that she really belonged to me. She tolerates me in the way friends tolerate one another's lesser points. It's not my place to name her, so No-Name it is.

160

I fall into pace alongside my brother. He turns and smiles at me before hunkering low on his saddle, urging his horse on faster. His laugh carries after him on the wind. I speak into No-Name's ear, "Faster, girl!" She whinnies and chases Nikko's dust trail. I let my eyes close, enjoying the wind on my face, no longer afraid of going fast.

We pass a week beneath the desert sun, but it's one of the easiest journeys of my life. No-Name is young and happy to gallop unendingly. There's plenty of water, and Cloak can cook wonders with just the barest ingredients. All I have to do is ride. But out here there is little in the long listless hours to distract me from thinking about the Bullet Catcher rotting away in jail. So far, I've made it a point to avoid the jailhouse. Now I make a promise to visit him as soon as I get back to town.

Bad Pines really is a nothing town: one potholed street, lined by a row of ramshackle buildings. At the end of the street sits a bent church, the steeple fallen through the roof. If there were ever pine trees they died long ago. The people of Bad Pines, old men and women, empty into the street when we approach. Their faces and hair are sand colored and ashen, as though they live their lives in a windstorm.

It seems miraculous given everything else about Bad Pines, but the town sits on the banks of a gushing river that emerges from a natural spring, pumping endless water from beneath barren rock. The water roars for no more than fifty yards before disappearing again beneath the earth. The river is like a blue stitch, disappearing beneath the cloth. I imagine the water plunging into the earth, an endless, lightless, waterfall. The sound is beautiful and deafening.

Still on his horse, Nikko leans toward me and says, "We've been trying to set up some sort of peaceable trade agreement with these old goats for months now. But so far, nothing."

"If they don't want to trade, they don't want to trade."

Cloak looks at me like he's never heard anything so naive.

"They have more than they need," Nikko says. "In the desert, everyone has to pull the rope equally. They don't use the water to farm. They don't irrigate. Without it the earth is barren and the soil is too acrid to till. They use the water for nothing."

"They certainly don't use it for bathing," Cloak says. Nikko laughs like he always seems to when Cloak says something cruel.

"So if they won't negotiate what are we doing here?"

"Good question, little sister."

"We call it aggressive diplomacy," Cloak says.

"We make them agree to trade," Nikko says. "But we still give them fair terms. We aren't monsters. Look at how they live. This is for their own good. You'll see."

Nikko and Cloak trot to meet the congregation. I hear the Bullet Catcher's voice in my head: 'Only monsters must convince themselves they're human.'

Nikko leans over one side of his horse, his elbow in his lap, smiling with his teeth. "Good morning!" he hails.

A wrinkled old man steps forward and says, "We've already told you, gunslinger, we won't make no deal." He's tall and spindly. His skin and bones don't fill out his clothes. He wears a coat with missing buttons and threadbare lapels that might have one day been fashionable. He looks like a salesman, lost for years in the desert. The rest of Bad Pines gather behind him, their withered faces making their eyes big and pathetic.

"Mayor Jezek," Nikko says impatiently, "our offer is more than fair. We have people who can help make the soil fit for farming. Think of all the good you could do with the money. And it never hurts to have us on your side."

"We have no need for your fancy farming or money," Jezek says, gathering a bit of steam. "We have no need for fancy clothes or machines. We have water and food enough."

"We can offer protection."

"Protection? You the only people come out this far. There's a lot of desert between us and everyone else."

Nikko dismounts. He walks slowly up to Jezek, looking at his feet the whole time. He stops when his boots nearly touch the old man's, then he looks up and stares him in the eye, not saying anything for a time. Jezek is a good foot taller than my brother, but he shrinks under his gaze.

"Fine, Jezek," Nikko says in a slow drawl that only amplifies his annoyance. "We offer you protection from ourselves. Consider it a promise. A promise that no harm will come to you or your people." He spits in the dirt. He peers around the side of Jezek's willowy frame and says, "Your women are old, but my men aren't picky."

This is the final straw for the old man. He makes himself as tall as he can, sticks his finger in Nikko's chest, and says, "You best get on your horse and ride back to whatever damned place you came from. My people *are* old, but we can still defend ourselves, need be."

The people of Bad Pines produce weapons from beneath their rags of clothing. Those without guns shoulder pitchforks or shovels or scythes. Nikko and Cloak burst out laughing. Nikko puts his hands on his knees and doubles over, like the sight of this small rabble of old men and women, wanting nothing but to be left alone, is the funniest thing he'd ever seen.

"I like you, Jezek," Nikko says, recovering from his laughing fit. "Damn me, but I do. I can't help it. That's why I'm going to extend my offer one more time. But mark my words: this *is* your last chance." Nikko draws his gun and taps it against his thigh, a metronome keeping time. "There's no reason we have to come to violence, friend."

"No deal," Jezek says, his voice trembling.

The townsfolk don't even have time to raise their weapons. Nikko and Cloak's guns chatter back and forth, then fall silent. White smoke from their guns rises into the air. The people of Bad Pines lie dead on the ground. Everyone except for Jezek, that poor old man. He's frozen with fear. Finally, his shaking hand goes for his gun. Nikko grabs Jezek by the wrist and squeezes, forcing his gun back into its holster. Nikko stares up at him, a smirk cast over his face. Slowly, Jezek turns. When he sees his people, dead in the dust, he lets out a strangled sound from deep in his throat and his knees buckle.

Nikko slowly reloads his gun, pushing each bullet into the chamber with his thumb. He bends down on a knee, so he's face to face with Jezek. Nikko makes a show of scanning the street, and says slowly, "And to think, you could have saved them." Then he puts his gun to the old man's heart and pulls the trigger.

I want to call out for him to stop, like I did to the Bullet Catcher when he was going to kill Nikko, but it all happens so quickly. Nikko waves for Cloak, who dismounts and comes up to him, crouching beside Jezek's body. They speak for a few minutes, but from where I am, still astride No-Name, my skin frozen and goose-pimpled, I can't hear them.

Nikko gives me a quick glance and must sense my shock, because he doesn't bother coming over or trying to talk to me. He and Cloak begin gathering up the bodies, dragging their heels through the dirt, piling them together like dry tinder for a fire. Nikko finally comes over to me, still sitting frozen on No-Name.

"Better get out of the sun," he says. "The back of your neck must be getting awful red." He smiles that same smile I've grown used to, but I'm suddenly afraid of him. When he reaches for me, I jerk away, twisting so I almost tumble off No-Name, but Nikko catches me. I turn to wood in his arms, not daring to move.

Nikko bites his lip. "Are you all right?" he says with concern.

"I'm fine," I croak. For the first time in my life, I want to get away from him. He doesn't let go of me right away, maybe trying to figure out what's come over me, but finally he lowers me to the ground.

"Why don't you go down to the river and splash some water on your face? It looks like you've had enough today. You don't want to see what Cloak and I still have left to do."

He walks back to Cloak, who's prying loose boards from the buildings, turning them to skeletons. They add the dry wood to the pile of bodies. I head down to the river. No-Name follows

165

at my side, bowing her head and nudging at my shoulder until I reach over and scratch her muzzle.

The cold water reminds me of the Bullet Catcher's lake, and for the first time I think that back in the cave I made the wrong choice. The children working in the factory, the veiled threat about killing the Bullet Catcher, and now this. I have only ever loved two people in my life, and up until this point, despite the bad things they might have done in their lives, I had thought they were both good people. By the river, I lie on my back under the eaves of a wilted, sun-blasted willow and No-Name lies beside me. There's precious little shade and No-Name takes up most of it, but the roaring water helps wash away any thoughts of the Bullet Catcher and Nikko and the poor townsfolk of Bad Pines.

"Imma . . ." Nikko calls from up the bank.

"What?" I answer without opening my eyes. The air is suddenly thick with smoke.

"The smoke is drifting down to the water," Nikko says. "Might want to move off. Bad for the soul to breathe human ash."

Nikko shakes me by the shoulders until I open my eyes. I let him take my hand and pull me to my feet. He wraps his arm around my shoulder and leads me away from the smoke, drifting down over the water. The smell is thick and oily.

"This water," he says, leading me farther down the bank, "is more valuable than a handful of lives. When people are counting on you for their food and water, their livelihood, sometimes you have to make hard decisions. I have to weigh the lives of this town against the thousands of people all around the Southland who are counting on me."

His voice is warm, soothing. His words make a certain amount of sense, but I can't scrub away what I saw in his face when he killed those people. That ruthlessness. I stare at the water and imagine throwing myself in. When it dives back into the earth would it take me with it? Would it take me all the way to the rotten core of this world, all broken bones and pale, waterlogged flesh?

"I know it sounds cold, little sister. But you'll understand one day. Our people need the water."

"Our people?" I shout over the roar of water. "And what about the people who aren't *ours*?"

Nikko smiles and runs his fingers through my hair. Ash falls over my face and shoulders. "Eventually, Imma, there will be no such thing. One way or another."

Out of the corner of my eye, I see the slightest rustle in the thick bushes that manage to grow through the dirt, along the banks of the river. Anyone else would think it a bird or lizard, but I know better just by the sound of the rustling. Through the dense brush comes the glint of the sun off a drawn pistol. I don't think. I draw and half turn toward the sound. My finger taps the trigger. My palm slaps the hammer as it strikes again and again. Six shots in a second, filling the bush. Another second passes, followed by the sound of a body going limp and collapsing.

Nikko only turns once it's over. Cloak comes running down the slope to the river, guns drawn. Following our line of sight, he holsters his guns and steps through the brush. He drags the body out onto the bank. The would-be-assassin is bare-chested, his face and body cut by bush thorns. He has

167

a baby face and a feathery moustache. If he's any older than me, he doesn't look it. The youngest boy in this village of old men. I shot six times. He has six holes in the skinny target of his chest and gut.

Nikko looks from the body, to me, his face glowing with joy. "Good shooting," he says, clapping me on the back, pulling me toward him in a suffocating hug. "I'm so proud of you."

I holster my gun before I drop it. I bury my hands in my pockets so Nikko and Cloak won't see them shaking.

"Look at you," he says sympathetically, "You're as white as a sheet. It's been a long day and a longer ride to get here. Why don't you get some rest in one of the houses?"

"That's fine," I manage to say. Darkness creeps in at the corner of my vision. I feel lightheaded. My only thought is to get to a bed, out of sight of Nikko and Cloak, before I pass out. I'm afraid of showing them any weakness.

As Nikko leads me away, I turn and watch Cloak shoulder the dead weight of the body and carry it up the bank, after us. Like in training, I feel with a gun in my hand I can't miss. But it's not the shooting that makes killing hard.

It's everything that comes after.

Nikko leads me into one of the houses, nothing more than a shanty, and sits me down on a bed in a bare room. For all I know it could be the bed of the boy I just killed. Nikko kisses me on the forehead and brushes the hair from my face.

"Just rest," he says. "You saved my life today."

Then he leaves and I'm alone in the mostly empty room. I draw one of my pistols and hold it in my palms. Already, the polish has scuffed. My reflection in the metal is that of a funhouse mirror. I run my thumb over my name carved in the bone handle. The gun drops to the floor and lands with a dull thud. And I fall backwards onto the bed. I close my eyes and I'm swallowed up into a depthless, black whirlpool, falling into the center of the earth.

Chapter Fifteen

I hardly remember the days following my killing the boy at Bad Pines. The first person I ever killed. At some point, minutes or hours later, Nikko came to the small, bare room where I lay, somewhere between waking and dreaming, and told me it was time to leave. I remember closing the door behind me, then Cloak setting fire to the building. Around me, Bad Pines burned. A mound of stinking, burning flesh lay in the center of the wide, blackened road. I doubled over and vomited. Then I was astride No-Name, holding tight to the reins, riding away as the flames and smoke and ash rose into the brazen sky. For miles, the ground was blanketed with soot.

Somewhere along the way, we crossed paths with a gunslinger caravan traveling in the opposite direction, back toward the ruins of Bad Pines. They drove huge wagons with miles of bronze tubing stacked and tied to them. Their horses groaned under so much weight. On the ride back, Nikko sat with me most nights, around the fire. He spoke to me about this and that, nothing I can remember, but his warm voice did me good all those cold empty nights when I could manage no thoughts of my own.

"Incredible, isn't it?" he said on one of those nights. "We'll be able to pump water whenever, wherever we need it. In a desert, he who controls the water, controls the people." Nikko spoke on and on excitedly, but all I could think of was Bad Pines.

When we get back to Las Pistolas, I instruct the doorman not to let anyone up, and lock myself away in my rooms. It is only then, all alone, out of the blinding desert light, free from the company of my brother and Cloak, that I turn over what Nikko meant when he said 'control.' I think of what life was like back at the orphanage or in Sand, how water was always at the forefront of everyone's thoughts but how there was never enough on our lips. It is like that all over the Southland. Promise a person enough water to drink for a day, a week, a lifetime, and then ask him for anything in return, and I doubt there is less than a handful of men and women alive who'd refuse. I pull closed the curtains and get into bed. But what about power in the hands of a good person? After all, Nikko was good to me. But then I think of Bad Pines, and all my rationalizing turns to so much hot air. Finally, after going back and forth like this for hours, I sleep.

I stay locked up in my room for three days, refusing every summons or note from Nikko. I need to be alone with my thoughts. Then, on the morning of the fourth day, I wake to find Nikko, sitting in the big chair in the corner, reading a book.

"Morning," he says. "I've come to find out when you're coming back to us."

I turn over on my side so I'm facing the wall, away from him. The wallpaper is a pattern of sun-bleached flowers. I don't know their names. When I think of flowers, I think of the ones at The Bruise that smelled of death and decay. I don't care for flowers.

Nikko comes around the bed and crouches in front of me. Brushing a strand of hair from my face, he says, "The first time is always hard. We all deal with it in different ways. After my first kill, I didn't speak for a long time. All I did was drink."

I don't want to talk to him, but still, inexplicably, it's good to hear his voice. After days of self-confinement, with my loneliness returning like a bad friend, that same loneliness I felt every day after Nikko left me in the orphanage, I'm glad to have him close to me.

"Tell me the story," I say, my throat sandpaper. Nikko hands me a glass of water that I drink out of the side of my mouth, not wanting to sit up.

"It was a gunslinger," Nikko says. "I was still apprenticing under the Bullet Catcher at the time. The gunslinger was old and snakebit. Still he recognized the Bullet Catcher and me as his student easily enough. The gunslinger shot only at me, perhaps thinking I was an easier target. He shot me in the gut. I thought I was going to die. But I managed to send the last bullet back his way. I hit him square in the chest. More luck than anything. I wasn't even trying to hit him. Just instinct. Pure desperation. The Bullet Catcher just stood by, with his arms crossed.

"I must have passed out, because the next thing I knew, I was in bed, bandaged up. On the nightstand there was a plate with a rusty-looking bullet on it. Turns out, it was another gunslinger who took me in, fixed me up. He and his wife took pity on me when the Bullet Catcher left me for dead in the street. When I was well enough, I went right to the bar. I was so overcome with guilt that I planned on drinking myself to death.

"That's when the gunslingers took me in, sobered me up. One of the old gunslingers recognized me as our father's son. Said I was the spitting image of him. He told me all the memories he had of Dad. He told me about our gunslinger blood."

I sit up against the headboard, looking at the glass of clean, cool water in my hand, wondering what town it was siphoned from, not wanting to think about it. The water doesn't seem like such a miracle anymore. It tastes thick and metallic in my mouth.

Nikko smiles at me, straightening up. He pats my hand and begins to stand.

"Tell me a story about our parents," I say, looking for an excuse to keep him near, for anything that will keep me from thinking of Bad Pines, if only for a few minutes.

Nikko sits back down on the bed and says, "What would you like to know?"

"I don't know." And then, because I can't think of anything else, I say, "I don't remember the day they died, Mom and Dad."

"You're better for it."

"Don't spare me. You haven't anything else." My voice is colder than I mean it to be.

Nikko sighs. "You're angry. I understand that. You must feel toward me just how I felt toward the Bullet Catcher. You think I've robbed you of something, putting you in a position to take someone's life. In a sense I have. I'm sorry for it. But sometimes you have to give something up to gain something greater."

"And what do you think I gained from killing that boy?"

Nikko takes my hand, looks me in the eye, and says, "Now you know what you're made of. Now you know who you are."

"A murderer?"

"A gunslinger. Your father's daughter."

We sit in silence, both of us letting the meaning of Nikko's words sink in. Then I put my hand on his and say, "Please, tell me how they died. I deserve to know."

"The bullet catchers killed them. Dad was a well-known gunslinger by the time he retired. He had two arms full. That's why he picked that sorry plot of land for our homestead. Dad was no fool to think farming desert sand would be easy. He needed somewhere remote to keep us safe. But the bullet catchers found him anyway. One night, they surrounded the house, burned Mom and Dad out, and shot them down. Do you remember anything of that night?"

"Nothing."

"Years before the attack, Dad dug out a tunnel through the basement that led far enough away to escape unnoticed. That's how we got out. I carried you. When I was old enough, Dad told me what to do in case anyone came for him, which direction to walk. To the west, he said. Away from the sun in the morning, toward it in the evening. You really don't remember that?"

"Maybe. Or maybe I'm just imagining I do. I wish I remembered more about them." So it had been Nikko who saved me. I had known that once, if not explicitly, then instinctually. But somewhere along the way I'd forgotten. A thought crystallizes within me—something that started so many months ago in The Bruise—that no one is ever good or bad. That there is no such thing as true evil or righteousness. Because when I'm with Nikko, there is no doubt in my mind that he loves me. There are people who are incapable of love, but my brother is not one of them. And those who love cannot be rotten, not all the way through. But I have no doubt that Nikko is also, in many ways, a monster.

We sit together on the bed, not talking, not looking at one another. Maybe Nikko's thinking of Dad, or maybe nothing at all. Holding the glass of water, all I can think of is how it came to be in my hand, and who might have died for it.

After a while, Nikko gets up, smiling. "There's a celebration tonight. We broke ground for the aqueduct at Bad Pines yesterday."

"I'd just as soon skip it." Murder is bad enough, but the ghoulishness of celebrating it makes my stomach churn.

"It'll be good for your spirits. You could use some cheering up. And besides, I've been telling everybody how you saved my life. I'm sure there will be a lot of people who'll want to buy you a drink, myself amongst them." He gets up to leave and says, "Promise me you'll come." His eyes are big. He clasps his hands together, pretending to beg.

"Maybe," I say, trying to smile, though the shape of it feels wrong.

"Good enough," Nikko says. He kisses my cheek and leaves.

Night falls and the sounds of the celebration drift through the windows. The streets are lit up bright with lamps and torches. I get out of bed for the first time in days and head for the jail.

On the street, I pull my hat low over my face, flip up the collar of my coat and walk with my head down, my hands in my pockets. But I'm no longer the unnoticeable girl. Everyone recognizes me. It's not so late but many of the gunslingers are already drunk. I'm accosted by the mass of people in the street who pat me on the back and shake my hand for saving Nikko. I've never experienced this kind of attention before and I'm flustered and strangely happy to have so many people smiling my way, so many people wishing me well, so many people noticing me. Gunslingers, three times my age, who bear their tattooed arms with sleeveless shirts and waistcoats, tip their caps to me as I pass them in the street.

The jailer and his deputy sit at the big desk they share, playing cards. They look up at me with sun-blasted slowness. All the doors and windows in the jail are batted down to keep out the cold of the desert night. Inside, amongst the flickering oil lamps, the air is warm and thick-smelling with sweat and smoke. The two men don't say anything, don't tip their hats. The jailer spits tobacco into a spittoon, and the brown juice dribbles down his chin. The deputy works his cheekful of tobacco as slow as a mule chewing cud. They sit and stare at me, waiting for me to speak.

"I'm here to see the Bullet Catcher," I say, probably a little too loud. The two jailers share a wordless look.

"Ain't nobody s'posed to see him less Bullet give the say-so," says the deputy. These two look and sound like hicks from the sticks, but the jailer's fingers fast-twitch just above the butt of his holstered shooter. Nikko's too smart, too demanding, to let just anybody guard what might be the last bullet catcher in the world. These two know what they're doing.

"I'm Bullet's sister, if you didn't already know."

"We do, ma'am," says the jailer, his hand still hovering. "But with all due respect, Bullet's sister ain't Bullet."

Peering through the open door that connects the jailer's office to the cells, I can see the Bullet Catcher's heels, propped up through the bars of his cell. If our positions were switched, would he have left me to rot in a jail cell? Wouldn't he at least have visited me? Could what Nikko have told me be true, that the Bullet Catcher just left him to die after being shot by a gunslinger? It doesn't fit with the man I've come to know and love.

"The old man give you any trouble?" I ask, because I'm not ready to leave. My brain stretches for a way to see the Bullet Catcher without having to ask my brother for permission, but nothing comes to mind.

The jailer and his deputy share another wordless look.

"Best customer we've had in quite some time," the deputy says.

"Quiet as a church mouse," the jailer adds solemnly.

"I'll be back with word from Bullet," I say.

"Yes, ma'am. Gotta be a written order, too. Notarized. Can't take chances with this one, you understand."

Tipping my hat, I turn and walk back into the cold. It's getting late, but Nikko will be at the celebration. He never seems to sleep much anyway. And when he does, it's with one eye open. He doesn't trust anyone, except for Cloak. And me, maybe. At least, I hope so, because I'm about to test just how far that trust goes.

A gunslinger party is easy to mistake for a riot. I walk back toward Nikko's offices, along Main Street, amongst the guns igniting in the cold night air, orange like fire. There are no fireworks, just the constant popping of guns. The street is filled with people. Lowering my head, I make myself small and dart through the raucous crowd.

I push my way to the entrance to Nikko's club. But the guard tells me that during celebrations Nikko likes to spend time with his gunslingers. I find him at the Screeching Owl. The Owl isn't just some dusty old drinking hole. The high, vaulted ceiling is more akin to a church than a saloon. A gilded chandelier hangs in the middle of the room, giving off warm electric light. Usually, the room is filled with square tables with white tablecloths. The bartenders, done up in black suits, come right up to your table to take your order. They serve tea in beautifully painted teapots and little finger foods that are so good you wonder why they don't make them bigger. Nikko's taken me here a handful of times. He says that all the best restaurants in the Northland are like the Owl.

Tonight, the gilded bar-room has turned into a free-for-all. The gunslingers have climbed behind the bar and are serving themselves. They shoot holes in the ceiling and take potshots at the light bulbs of the chandelier. The tables have all been pushed to the sides or upended to make room for dancing and fighting.

Nikko, done up to the nines in a bow tie and dress jacket, sits at a table with Cloak and a few of his other lieutenants. They lean across the table to better hear one another over the noise, and every now and then they sit back and watch the celebration as though they are far removed from the action, like they are watching animals in a menagerie.

I don't go up to Nikko right away. I spot Hartright and her gang of old-timers cowering around a table in the far corner, clutching their bottles. I zigzag across the mayhem over to them and Hartright finds an unbroken chair on its side and sets it right for me. She hands me a glass and I just hold it, taking the time to scan the bar. Shave away the bravado and recklessness and the scene isn't much different than Dmitri's, or any other drinking hole in the Southland. Maybe the gunslingers are a bit better fed, but they still have that hungry look of any Southlander. Their eyes are red and yellow and clouded over. Their skin is ashen. Dirt shakes from their hair and clothes. Their breath is acrid from snakebite.

"You're the talk of the town," Hartright says.

"Thanks, I guess." When I look at Hartright she grimaces, trying to smile. "This doesn't change anything, you know."

Hartright grumbles and says, "You're wrong there, young'un. Sure, it doesn't change anything for us, our gang of ol' good-for-nothings, but for you . . ." She trails off. Her eyes become sober and piercing. "But for you, everything will be different. Your whole life just went upside down."

"How do you mean?"

Hartright takes a swig from the bottle and clears her throat. "Let me put it this way," she says, "once you know something, you can never un-know it. Once you do something, you can never undo it. You carry it with you forever."

"Like the first time you kill someone," I say, replaying the moment in my mind.

179

"You never forget," she says. She looks at the bottle like she's angry at it, before taking another drink.

"Quite a celebration," I say, for lack of anything else.

"*This* is how the old celebrate," she says. Though I haven't taken a drink yet, she tips more snakebite into my glass until it's full up to the brim. Hartright points her bottle at Nikko, sitting against the wall, humoring some young drunk spitting into his ear.

"Look at this poor bastard," Hartright says. The boy in question can't be much older than me. The hair on his chin looks like the shorn thread from an old quilt, long and patchy. His cheeks are clean and ruddy from snakebite. At first, Nikko tries to nudge him away gently, nodding his head. But with each passing second, Nikko's face grows darker. The boy leans on Nikko's shoulder and doesn't stop talking. Hartright shakes her head and watches.

When Nikko finally manages to push the boy away the look he trails after him freezes me in my boots. It's the same look he had in Bad Pines. That ruthless look. He tries to keep that side of him a secret from me, but he can't help but let it out in fits and flurries. Most everyone has a side they try not to show others: a jealous side, an insecure side, an angry side. But Nikko's isn't a normal darkness. His is the dark side of the moon: scarred and cold. That's what I learned at Bad Pines. All these trained killers are afraid of him. Unless they're so snakebit they forget. Nikko watches the boy weave through the crowd back to the bar. Nikko beckons Cloak, who leans in close and listens as Nikko whispers something in his ear. Cloak nods solemnly. He pushes his way through the crowd and hauls the boy out of the bar.

180

The bottom falls out of my stomach. Whatever Nikko has planned for the boy, it won't be good. I start to get up to chase after them, but Hartright puts her hand on my shoulder and pushes me back onto my seat.

"You don't want to see none of that, young'un. Plenty of opportunities in your future."

I watch the door for a time, listening to the gunshots, trying to pick out the one meant for the boy. But all the gunshots sound the same. Nikko watches the door too. Then he stands, and starts to leave, shaking hands, smiling, patting everyone on the back. He finds me in my corner, flanked by Hartright and my entourage of old gunslingers, and his smile melts away. He knows that I've seen everything. He nods at me, like an admission, and I can think of nothing else but to nod back. Hartright pretends to be looking at something else. Nikko waves for me to follow him.

I knock back my drink. It lights a fire in my stomach.

"Have any stories you want to tell, Hartright? I could stand to smile."

"Ain't no more time for that. Godspeed," she says, and pours me another drink. I knock back that one too and follow Nikko into the street.

Nikko waits for me outside the bar. Cloak is back at his side, but there's no sign of the boy anywhere. There's a splatter of red on Cloak's white tie that he wipes at distractedly with a handkerchief. Nikko's all smiles when he greets me, but it's a painted-on expression.

"Enjoying the celebration?" he says.

"Not really."

Cloak wets a corner of his handkerchief with his mouth and dabs at the stain. Nikko clears his throat until Cloak stops and tucks the handkerchief into his coat sleeve.

Nikko smiles out of one side of his mouth and says, "No, not really your thing, I suppose." He loosens the knot in his bow tie and undoes the top button of his shirt. "Listen, Imma. Whatever you saw in there, it's not what it looks like."

"It looked like you dragged a boy into the street and shot him for annoying you."

Nikko and Cloak erupt in laughter, laughter so large and surprised-sounding that it's almost convincing.

It's Cloak who explains. "Imma, we've been shadowing that boy for weeks now. We suspected he was the ringleader of a group funneling guns and ammo out of town to sell on the black market."

Nikko picks up the story. "We figured the best way to deal with him would be at the party, when he'd be nice and drunk and off his guard."

I want to believe Nikko, but the story sounds too clean, too rehearsed. And besides, I've already seen what he's capable of. I look away from him, down the street. Perhaps I'm looking for where they may have dragged the body, heel marks in the sand, but there's only thousands of spent shell casings, boot prints running in every direction, drunken gunslingers stumbling in Ss or passed out on the boardwalks.

"I want to visit the Bullet Catcher," I say, still not looking at Nikko.

Nikko doesn't respond. He begins rolling a cigarette.

"Now why would you want to go and do something like that?" Cloak asks, speaking for Nikko.

"That's none of your business."

Nikko licks the cigarette closed, lights it, and takes a long drag. "I don't think that will be possible, Imma. What would people think? It wouldn't look good."

"I don't care what people think."

"No, of course not. That's not your job. It's mine. I'm sorry. The answer is no."

The night grows colder. I wrap my arms around myself, and dig at the ground with the toe of my boot, thinking. I swallow and work up my courage. "I know what I saw here tonight."

"All you saw was the removal of a dangerous sectarian," Cloak says.

"Then you wouldn't mind if I told anyone about it. It's not like anyone would be missing someone like that?"

Cloak steps closer to me. "Is that a threat?"

I look straight into his eyes, refusing to so much as blink. "How could it be a threat if you haven't done anything wrong?"

The look in Cloak's eyes says he wants to strangle me. But Nikko puts his hand on his shoulder and says, "Okay. That's enough. Your imagination is running wild tonight, Imma, but if visiting the Bullet Catcher is that important to you, then of course you can see him."

Nikko hands Cloak the cigarette, which he takes and puts between his lips. Nikko digs through his pockets for a slip of paper and pencil. Cloak turns his back so Nikko can use it as a writing surface. Cloak takes long drags and watches me as Nikko writes the note on his back.

Nikko signs the letter. Cloak initials it. Then Nikko gives me the note, and says, "If it makes you happy, then I'm happy."

I pocket the note. "If I did what that boy did—if I looked at you wrong, would you do to me what you did to him?"

Nikko's expression turns serious, his eyes suddenly big and wounded. "I would never hurt you," he says. "I would never let anybody else hurt you."

"I hope so," I whisper, before turning and walking away.

I return to the jail, but the place is shut up tight, the lights out. So I head back to the Owl and help Hartright finish her snakebite. We sit and don't talk for a long time, but finally, perhaps recognizing my pensiveness, Hartright retells the story of the sirens of the Southland that sing poor lovesick travellers deep into the desert, and how she and old Wakefield resisted them, at least for a little while. She socks my shoulder at every punch line and I can't help but smile.

Chapter Sixteen

The next morning, the light coming through the curtains is so bright I swear the sun is sitting right outside my window. The yellow heat vibrates in my skull. By midday, when I still haven't risen, Nikko sends a runner to check on me. When I tell him I'm dying, he just chuckles and tells me it's a hangover—the first and, hopefully, last of my life. He dissolves a couple tablets in a glass of water and makes me drink. The concoction tastes vile, but it does the trick. After half an hour, still foggy, but finally free of the headache, I rise and dress.

Though I know it's useless, I search the street outside the Owl and in the neighboring alleys for signs of the boy, but I don't find anything. The boy has vanished. Disappearances, I'm told, are not an odd occurrence during a gunslinger party. That's why the gunslingers either get blind drunk and try not to worry or sit in the corner with their guns drawn beneath the table, sipping water until the party's over.

Cloak shadows me all morning. I see him out of the corner of my eye as I search down alleys or interview people who I think might know something about the boy. As afternoon approaches, Cloak reveals himself to inform me that Nikko wants to meet at the practice field, anxious to make up for the practice I missed that morning. Then he departs, and I'm left to stare out at the desert, beyond the edge of town, that endless plane of sand and sun.

So much empty space to hide a body.

When I meet Nikko at the practice field, he doesn't say anything other than to tell me he cleared out the cadets so we could have privacy. He doesn't mention last night, not even to ask if I went back to see the Bullet Catcher.

I sleepwalk through the lesson. When it's over, Nikko comes trotting up to me from the other side of the field, his hair stuck to his forehead with sweat, that familiar smile on his face.

"I don't know if there's anything else I can teach you," he says, clapping me on the shoulder. "What can I say? You're perfect." I want to keep my distrust in my heart. After last night, I'm walking on thinner ice. My mistrust will keep me safe. But how can I help but smile when he speaks to me like this? When he smiles? And regardless of what it means to be a gunslinger, it feels nice to be good at something.

"You think?" I say, heat rising to my cheeks. We lie on the slope of the dune and watch the sun go down. Nikko rolls a cigarette but doesn't light it.

"I'm so proud of you, Imma," he says.

"Shut up."

"I am. And I'm not just talking about how much progress you've made as a gunslinger. I'm talking about everything that's gone on. I know you don't like the conditions at the factory, to say nothing about what went on at Bad Pines. I've been

186

thinking about it. Maybe you're right. Maybe I've grown too used to not having to compromise." He props himself up on an elbow and looks at me. In the fading light, he looks impossibly tired, so much older than he is. The light catches the wrinkles in the corners of his eyes and shines through his hair where it's just starting to thin.

"I'm so glad you're here," he says, his eyes shining. "You're going to make me a better person. I've already given the order that the children should be taken out of the factories. Kids their age should be in school."

I don't say anything because I know if I do my voice will shake. I try to look cool and unaffected, but Nikko sees through me and beams his huge smile. And I think that it was wrong to condemn Nikko as a monster. Monsters don't change. Monsters don't try to better themselves. I push down all my suspicions and fears and make myself believe Nikko is telling the truth. Because I need to. Because no matter what, he's my brother and I love him. And maybe it doesn't matter what he's done. Maybe it doesn't matter what any of us have ever done, all the large and small crimes that mount up and weigh us down over a lifetime. Maybe all that matters is how we conduct our lives once we know better.

We lie in the dunes until the moon rises, full and crisp white. "There's a final test that everyone has to take before they become a bona fide gunslinger. I think you're ready."

"What's the test?"

"I don't know. It's supposed to be different for everybody. Usually one of the teachers at the Academy decides what the test will be. On special occasions I come up with something.

But the charter states that since you're my sister, I'm supposed to keep my nose out of it. For impartiality's sake. Cloak's come up with the test."

I bite my lip at the sound of Cloak's name.

"I know you two haven't gotten along so well, but you don't have to look so worried. The test is just a formality, something to mark the occasion. It's not a *real* test."

After Nikko and I part, I go to the jail to see the Bullet Catcher. I don't know what I'll say to him. I don't know if he'll even want to see me. But I have to go. I owe him an apology and so much more. I flash Nikko's note to the jailer and his deputy and walk right into the cells without saying a word.

The Bullet Catcher stands by the far wall in his cell, leaning his shoulder against the cool brick and gazing up at the barred window. I stand in front of his cell, my hands on the bars, looking at the sawdust on the floor. It's been months and I've forgotten how to talk to him.

The Bullet Catcher is the first to speak. Without taking his eyes off the small window he says, "Your final test is approaching."

"How do you know about that?"

"I've been informed. A sage sparrow comes to my window and sings the news to me."

I open my mouth to speak, but he holds up a finger.

"Hear that?" he says, pricking an ear. From beyond the window comes the sound of birdsong, like small bells chiming. A gray and white bird hops onto the sill, cocking its head left and right in that nervous way birds do, twittering to itself. The Bullet Catcher gazes up at it, like he's listening intently to the bird. Then the bird stops, hops once or twice along the sill, and jumps off, back into the moonlight. My heart sinks. Could being cooped up here so long have shaken something loose? Is it my fault?

"Are you—do they talk to you, the birds?"

The Bullet Catcher smiles from across his cell. "When you converse with an animal you are only speaking to yourself. It is good practice. It is good for reflection."

"Then how did you know about the final test?"

"The jailer and his deputy talk. Their voices carry."

I breathe out, relieved. The Bullet Catcher comes over to the other side of the cage. I grip the bars so tightly my hands turn white. I thought about visiting him every day, just to check to see if he was okay and maybe to try to explain myself. But with each passing day, it became harder to visit him. I imagined his face, full of anger and betrayal. But when he comes over to me, he puts his hands over mine, and when he speaks, he does so softly.

"It's good to see you," he says.

"Back before The Bruise, I told you I had your back—" My voice falters. I don't know how to go on from there. Standing before him, it seems impossible that I could have gone all these months without visiting. I miss him more, being with him, than at any point since I betrayed him—because that's what it was, a betrayal.

He just pats my hands, like I don't have to go on. And I don't, because I still don't have the words—I may never have them.

His gnarled old hands feel somehow soft when he holds my hands in them. "Nikko's done terrible things," I say. "He shot down a whole town. I think he killed a boy for no reason. And who knows how many others he's killed."

The Bullet Catcher doesn't say anything. He just keeps on holding my hands in his.

"But he told me that he thinks I'm going to make him a better person. He says he wants to change. I don't know what I'm supposed to do."

The Bullet Catcher lets go of my hands and sits on his bedroll. "Nor do I," he says, "but to become a better person is a worthy goal for anyone."

The cell beside the Bullet Catcher's is empty. The door is unlocked and open wide. I go in and sit on the cot. We sit with our backs to one another's, the bars between us. "Did you know my father was a gunslinger?"

"Yes, I knew."

"Did you know him?"

"In a way. By reputation." He clears his throat and says, "I was in a town called Santa Marías, near the Salt Ocean. I had been tracking a gunslinger for weeks and had finally caught up to him hiding out in a relative's house near the edge of town. We had dueled most of the night and when morning came I was dog-tired and he was dead. I was drinking and eating eggs in the saloon when a couple bullet catchers I'd never seen before came in looking to round up a posse to track down another gunslinger they said lived a day's ride east from Marías. I was so tired my eyes ached. My bones felt brittle like sawdust. But that kind of tired, the tired that comes from fighting, it makes you want to keep going. It's a bloodlust. I volunteered. Ten of us rode out that evening. Three bullet catchers and seven

190

townsfolk, armed to the hilt. Along the way, they told me many tales of the man we were off to kill. They told me he was evil, that he was a monster, the stuff of nightmares. And that was enough for me. I believed in such words back then.

"I was surprised when we arrived at the gunslinger's homestead. I had expected a fortress, but it was just a squat little house, like any other on the frontier of the Southland, though it was well tended. I remember the freshly painted porch and the vegetable garden out back. It would take a lot of work to make anything grow in dirt like that, but sure enough the vegetable garden was sprouted with all manner of things."

"Stop. Don't say more." I know that place. I remember that house.

"We did not give any warning. We surrounded the house and opened fire. I was full of so much hate. I hated this man I had never met. Someone lit a torch and set fire to the house. The townsfolk never stopped shooting.

"The winds were too strong and kept blowing out the fire. It did not burn completely. After a while, we worked up the nerve to approach the house. Inside, picking through the rubble, we found the gunslinger. He was not even wearing his guns. He was holding a woman in his arms. To think, from the stories I'd been told, I was shocked he was just a man."

I close my eyes and don't even bother trying to stop the tears. Let them come, I tell myself.

"But it wasn't the sight of the gunslinger and his wife that made me realize my folly. It was what I saw next. All around the house, in every room, there were toys and children's clothes. There was a highchair in the kitchen. A small, wrought-iron bed with bright sheets thrown hastily off. I searched everywhere for the bodies of the children. My blood had run cold, my mind was blank. When I found the trap door, I pulled a rug over it. I did not tell anyone. And the others did not care about the children. They were as good as dead, way out there, all on their own. We had done what we came to do.

"I doubled back that night and followed the passage to where it emerged in the hills just a few hundred yards from the house. I found the children a few hours later, taking shelter under a shallow ledge, jutting out of the side of a rock face. The boy, no older than nine or ten, was clutching his small sister in his arms to protect her from the stinging wind. I did the only thing I could think of. I put them on my horse and rode off, brought them to an orphanage, the closest place I thought they'd be safe."

We're silent for a long time. I don't know what I'm feeling. I think I'm supposed to feel something, but it's too much. I only feel tired. From the other room come the voices of the jailer and deputy arguing over their card game.

"Why are you telling me this?" I finally manage to say.

"Because Nikko was right. It was not fair to keep the truth from you. If I were a better man, I would have told you right away. I would have told you that it is because of who you are, because of my regret over what I did, that I was so quick to want to chase you out of my camp, that I was so hesitant to train you.

"When Nikko first sought me out, I recognized him straight away, like I recognized you. You two look alike. But he looks more like that gunslinger, your father. And you look just like that woman I found in his arms. In the eyes and nose. When

I told your brother this story he ran from me. He joined up with the gunslingers and led them to me. It broke my heart. I had destroyed his life a second time."

"He told me you left him for dead after he was shot."

The Bullet Catcher thinks about this for a time, and then he says, "Perhaps it is easier for him than the truth. What I did was worse."

I rest the back of my head against the cool metal bars and close my eyes. I imagine that day with the Bullet Catcher outside my house, my mother and father rushing Nikko and me through the trap door. Our father giving Nikko some last instructions, kissing him, knowing it would be the last he'd ever see his son and daughter, and closing the passage behind us.

"I think you've said more to me today than all our other days combined," I say, pulling myself out of my thoughts.

"I told you. I've been practicing."

"I should go," I say, not opening my eyes. I want to get up and leave. I think that I don't ever want to see him again.

"Imma, back then, I thought I could not make mistakes. I thought I knew everything. I was already an old man, but I suppose a lot of young people feel that way. I have done terrible things in my life. The lesson I learned that day, outside your homestead, I've had to relearn again and again. Like me, your brother has done terrible things, but he is still your brother."

"And what about my father? Was whatever he did bad enough to kill him?"

"I convinced myself it was. But it had little to do with him. I didn't know him personally, but I suspect he was neither good nor bad. He was just a man."

193

"No," I say. "He wasn't just a man. He was my father." A silence falls between us. "So what am I supposed to do now?" My voice is a whisper. "What am I supposed to do when there is no right side or right answer? When on one side there's a man who killed my father and on the other is a man who kills innocent people?"

"I do not know. Don't go looking for answers from someone feeling truthful."

I stand to leave. The Bullet Catcher doesn't move. When I'm at the door, I turn back and say, "I don't think I'll be back."

The Bullet Catcher stands and goes over to the bars, hangs his arms outside the cell, and says, "Remember how you felt after every test up on the mountain. These are hard lessons, Imma. And learning them is painful. But do not confuse pain with failure."

Chapter Seventeen

Last night, when I returned home from visiting the Bullet Catcher, there was a messenger waiting for me. He gave me two notes. The first was from Cloak, informing me that the test was set for the following night. The second was from Nikko. It read: *Good luck.*

The next day passes quickly and night falls like a black curtain. In my apartment I sit on the edge of my bed as the light fades. Then I gather up my belt and guns and strap them on and leave.

Torches line Main Street, lighting up the facades and elevated boardwalks like the corridor of a nightmare. As in a dream, I walk farther down the passage, fearful of what may lie at the end, but unable to turn and run away. The entire town has turned up to see Bullet's sister take her final test. They push and jockey for position along the street. Younglings flash toy shooters at their friends and yell, "Bang! You're dead. I shot you!" Their friends calling back, "No you didn't!" I can't help but think who these younglings will be one day, when they carry real guns, fire real bullets, kill real people.

When I approach, everyone stops and looks at me. Nikko stands in the street, and when I walk up to meet him the crowd closes in around us. My gun belt hangs loosely around my waist. My guns, cleaned and polished, wait in my holsters, the straps unbuttoned. The chambers are full. My reloaders are prepped. The night air is as cold as the day was hot. There are no stars in the sky. In my mind, I've prepared for anything. I want nothing but to get this over with.

The crowd stirs; cattle readying to stampede. But when Nikko raises his hand, everyone falls silent. "Today," he calls to the crowd, "Imma becomes a gunslinger!" The crowd erupts, goes crazy; they hoot and holler and stamp their feet, making the ground rumble. Nikko raises his hand again, commanding silence. He waits a beat. The crowd holds their breath. Tomato-red faces looking ready to explode. Nikko lowers his hand and shouts, "Let the test begin!" The crowd explodes again, even louder than before. Guns shoot wildly into the air. Barmen emerge from saloons with glasses of snakebite on trays.

Nikko whispers in my ear, "I'm so happy for you." As though my success is a given, as though the test is already over. I breathe a little easier. Nikko stands aside, his arms crossed.

The crowd parts to let Cloak through. His gun is drawn in his left hand and with the other he pulls along a figure, hands bound behind his back, face hooded in a canvas bag. A few feet away from me, Cloak stops and kicks the back of the hooded man's legs, forcing him to his knees. He pulls off the hood.

The Bullet Catcher's face is pale. His eyes and cheeks are swollen and bruised. He wheezes when he breathes, probably from cracked ribs. Since parting from the Bullet Catcher yesterday, I have done nothing but think about what he'd done. He killed my father, and regardless of how he'd helped me, regardless if it was he who found Nikko and me and delivered us to the orphanage, I had made up my mind never to forgive him. But when Cloak pulls off the hood and I see the Bullet Catcher's face, bloodied and bruised, his bright eyes filled with blood, I forget all that. I rush to him, kneeling down to hold up his slumping figure. I cup his cheek in my hand, and he looks up into my eyes. His face is calm, giving away nothing.

"What's the meaning of this, Cloak?" Nikko yells.

"This is her test," he says, pulling down the handkerchief from over his mouth, smiling thinly.

"This is completely improper," Nikko says, struggling to control his voice. He grabs Cloak by the arm and says in a low growl, "This is not what we talked about. Dammit, you're making a liar out of me."

"This is precisely why her test was up to me," Cloak says, his smile disappeared. "You're too close to her to see that *this* is the best test of her loyalty."

They stare at each other like two dogs in a pit, sizing one another up. Nikko grimaces in a way that pulls the skin of his face tight, making him terrifying and sad in the flickering torchlight.

"Listen to me this once," Cloak says softly so the crowd can't hear. He rests his palm intimately on Nikko's chest. "You've said to me you want us to be a family." Then Cloak looks at me and raises his voice loud enough so everyone can hear. "It's no secret, Imma, that I don't trust you. Not fully. Your history is entwined with the Bullet Catcher's. That is why this *is* the only proper test. You must choose. You must show me—you must show your brother—where your loyalty lies. You do this and there will be no more distrust. No more suspicion. You will be a gunslinger. And your brother and I will be behind you, come what may."

Nikko's face slackens. He looks at Cloak's hand on his chest and then at me. He turns to me and grimaces. "I'm sorry," he says.

"The test is simple," Cloak says, turning to me. "All you have to do is prove your loyalty to your brother. Take out your gun and put a bullet in the Bullet Catcher. He won't be untied. He won't resist."

I search for help in Nikko, but he won't meet my eyes. The Bullet Catcher is still in my arms. I don't want to let him go. To do so would mean that I'd have to make a decision.

Cloak crouches in front of me, staring straight into my eyes. What I expect to find in his depthless gray eyes is arrogance, deceit. But his look is earnest and mad. "One day," Cloak says, "when this is all over, barely even a memory, we'll all be sitting together, you and me and Nikko, and you'll understand that I did this for the both of you, to bring you closer together. One day, you'll see that I'm right and you'll thank me." He rises and moves to stand beside Nikko. He whispers something in his ear and Nikko closes his eyes and nods.

I look into the Bullet Catcher's scarred, battered face. If only I hated him as I thought I did, this would all be so easy. Think. Hellfire, just think. I could shoot the Bullet Catcher. Become a gunslinger. Take my place by my brother's side. What then? Would I be the next Cloak? I love Nikko, and I know he loves me, but I don't want to be like him. I will never be like him. I could shoot Cloak. What then? I get gunned down by the mob of gunslingers. Turn the gun on myself? That would seem to solve a lot of problems. Is it selfish that I don't want to die? But killing myself wouldn't solve anything. They'd send the Bullet Catcher into the darkness right after me.

Time stands still. Everyone waits on me. Slowly, I let go of the Bullet Catcher and rise to my feet. He doesn't take his eyes off me. His face is the calm center of a storm. My hand moves on its own, sliding my gun from its holster. I hold it in both hands, feeling its weight, reading my name etched into the bone. Cloak stares down at me, radiating self-righteousness. The crowd begins to stir impatiently. But Cloak spelled out the rules simply enough: there's no time limit to this test. And then I think back to that first test of the Bullet Catcher's. There had been a hint hidden in his words. He'd told me where he was going to aim. Was there something hidden in Cloak's instructions? Something I could use to save the Bullet Catcher?

The answer comes to me like a flash of light.

I crouch in front of the Bullet Catcher. He furrows his brow, his face a question mark. When I click open the chamber of my gun he seems to understand. He smiles. I take a bullet from the chamber, click it closed, and holster the gun.

"Open your mouth." The Bullet Catcher does. I put the bullet on his tongue and he closes his mouth. I stand, wiping my hands. Cloak glowers at me, bemused. "Done," I say.

"What do you mean? You've done nothing." He nearly yells it.

"Like you said: the rules of the test are simple. You told me to take out my gun. I did. You told me to put a bullet in him. I did. His hands remained tied. He didn't resist. I met all the conditions of your test."

Nikko listens to my explanation, and despite the history between him and the Bullet Catcher, he can't help but smile too.

The Bullet Catcher looks up at Cloak and sticks his tongue out, showing Cloak the bullet. When he speaks, his voice is tired and scratchy. "Would you rather I swallow it? That way you could say she put a bullet in my gut." That's what sends Cloak over the edge. He cocks the trigger of his shooter and presses the barrel into the Bullet Catcher's forehead. The Bullet Catcher leans into the barrel, unafraid.

Cloak screams at me: "You know damn well what I meant! You've failed the test! You've chosen this old goat over your own brother!"

The shot rings out. Some in the crowd hit the ground; others crane their necks to get a better view. The sound of the bullet hitting its target is sharp and metallic. Blood sprays across my face. When I wipe the blood from my eyes, the Bullet Catcher is still kneeling in the dirt. Cloak sprawls on the ground gripping his shooting hand, screaming. His gun lies in the dirt, covered in blood.

Nikko, by my side, spins his gun on his finger and holsters it. "That's enough, Cloak," he says. "Don't be sore over losing."

Cloak writhes in the dirt, gripping his hand.

"Oh, get up," Nikko says. "You act like you've never been shot before." Cloak gets to his feet, and when he looks at Nikko, he doesn't look angry, he looks hurt. He tucks his bloodied hand into his coat and pushes his way through the crowd, leaving his dented shooter in the dirt.

Nikko looks after Cloak, the smile melting from his face. He starts to follow him, but thinks better of it. He runs his hand through his hair and watches Cloak until he's gone. Then he turns to me and ruffles my hair. "I'm proud of you, sis. You used your wits today. It's a powerful tool, a person's intelligence." Then he says, low and serious, "But I worry about the day when you'll discover it's not always possible to think your way out of danger." Nikko raises my chin with his hand until our eyes meet, and says, "But don't worry. On that day, whenever that is, I'll be there with you. You can count on me."

Nikko signals to the crowd. Two large gunslingers come up and, taking the Bullet Catcher under the arms, drag him to his feet. "Take him back to his cell," he says. As they haul him away, the Bullet Catcher spits the bullet into the dirt.

Nikko takes me by the wrist and thrusts my hand in the air. The crowd goes crazy. There's a mad rush as everyone makes for the saloons, ready for the party to begin.

Noticing my eyes, still fixed on the street where they hauled away the Bullet Catcher, Nikko nudges my shoulder, and says, "Smile! You're a gunslinger!"

Chapter Eighteen

Cloak isn't seen for two weeks. I hold my breath, hoping he's gone for good. But then he does return and Nikko does everything he can to keep him close. Now it's impossible to meet with my brother without Cloak hovering somewhere nearby. Under Cloak's shadow, I feel Nikko slipping farther away from me. And nothing has changed. Despite what Nikko said, children still work in the factories, their faces blackened with coal dust, their eyes hollowed by sleeplessness, their fingers bearing the callouses of middle-aged men and women. I spend my days in the factory, arguing with the foreman, writing entreaties to Nikko. But I'm not even sure Nikko sees those reports. It would be easy for Cloak to intercept them.

Over the weeks following the test, I don't visit the Bullet Catcher. After the test, I know I still love him. I know that, like with Nikko, nothing could keep me from loving him. But I haven't forgiven him. I might never forgive him. Maybe forgiveness isn't important. Or maybe it's just unnecessary. So I keep my anger close and spend most of my nights in the saloon with Hartright. I drink more. Sleep less. My feather bed makes me miss my thin sleeping roll high up in the mountains, where the air is cool and thin. In sleep, I sweat out the alcohol and when I wake in the morning my bed smells like a saloon, like my small room in the back of Dmitri's used to smell. I keep a bottle in the drawer in the nightstand, and I dull the headaches with a few sips in the morning. But Nikko doesn't seem to notice. The drinking doesn't affect my aim.

Thinking of the Bullet Catcher locked away in his cell doesn't help my drinking. When I agreed to go with Nikko, he told me he would lock him up to keep him safe. At the time I thought that made a certain kind of sense. There were a lot of people who wanted the Bullet Catcher dead. And it's a hard life up on the mountain. The scarcity of food in winter. The cold and loneliness. When Nikko promised to keep the Bullet Catcher safe, I'd thought of those traveling circus acts that tour the Southland. The larger troupes always had some sort of menagerie, and while the animals were usually fake—odd taxidermy creations mashed and sewed together: a cow with the head of a horse, rabbits with the tails of foxes—some of the shows really had rare animals, great golden eagles with feathers the color of the desert, sulking timber wolves pining for the mountains, gazelles with striped hides and twisting, devilish horns. I imagined the Bullet Catcher's twilight years spent in the same manner as those caged animals. He would be a curiosity, something that astonished simply because he existed. How did I not see how terrible a fate that was until now? How had I blocked out how defeated those animals in the menageries looked, penned up, dragged around, ogled at by unwashed children and snakebit men and women? Maybe because I traded the Bullet Catcher for the promise of his safety, and now, after the test, I know his safety isn't guaranteed. Or maybe because Nikko and I continue to drift apart and there seems to be nothing I can do about it. Maybe because now it feels like I bargained the Bullet Catcher away for nothing. Fools gold and glass diamonds.

Late last night, the bottle nearly empty between us, and most of her drinking companions already retired for the night, Hartright gave me a long, concerned look and said, "I think you ought'a take it easy, kid. This stuff makes more problems than it solves."

I was slumped forward in my chair, my chin buried in my arms crossed on the table. I was pondering the last few inches of snakebite at the bottom of the bottle, but when she spoke I cocked an eye at her. "What do you know?" I said, and drunk as I was, I could tell I was slurring badly.

"Not much," she said. "But more than you." Then she poured the rest of the snakebite into her glass. I think she did it just to keep it from me.

Morning breaks. I produce my bottle of snakebite from the bedside drawer and take a pull. Then I stumble through my morning routine, from my apartment to the factories. I observe the same dead-eyed children performing the same tasks I see every day. Then I write another report and make the long walk across town from the factories to Nikko's office to deliver them. He's hardly ever in these days, and usually I leave them on his desk. But this time I find Cloak sitting in Nikko's chair, his boots kicked up on the desk.

When he sees me, he waves me in, and smiles, and says, "Bullet's out."

"I'll come back."

"Nonsense. You're dropping off your daily report, right? I'll make sure it gets to him."

"I'll just wait till I see him next."

Cloak stands and crosses the room. His spurs jangle sharply with every step. I stand my ground, refusing to look fearful in front of him. He closes the door and stands in front of me. "It could be a while until you see him, Imma. You better just give it to me." He holds out a black-gloved hand like a claw.

"Screw you." I turn to leave and he grabs me by the shoulders and spins me back around. He throws me against the wall and pins me there. He lets me go and grabs the papers in my hand. I refuse to let go and they tear in half. He balls up what he got in his fist and drops it to the ground.

"You're wrong about me, you know. You think you're the only one with Bullet's best interest at heart. But you're the one that's hurting him. He was happy before you and the Bullet Catcher showed up." He points to the crumpled paper on the floor and says, "And that's the last one of those I want to see. He has more important things to worry about than children. Do you think it's easy to be the leader of so many gunslingers? Gunslingers are like wolves and when the alpha looks weak others start to get ideas that they might make a better leader. You make him weak." He steps back and straightens his tie. His bandanna guards his mouth, but his eyes smile. He opens the door and steps aside. "I'll tell Bullet you said hi." I run out of the room, ashamed of my fear. My arms where Cloak grabbed me ache, and I know that under my coat purple handprints are developing on my skin.

It's growing late. I don't go home. I go straight to the saloon. Hartright sits at her table like she's been waiting for me. I sit down next to her and knock back glass after glass of snakebite until I can't remember why I was upset in the first place. All that's left is a tightness in my chest, like a snake coiled around my heart. And the more I drink, the tighter the snake constricts.

I wake on the thin cot of a jail cell. It's sometime between midnight and dawn, and the cell is deathly cold. A chill runs through my bones. I'm covered in sweat.

"Sit up, Cub." The Bullet Catcher's voice drifts from the adjacent cell and fills the entire space. "Sit up," he says again. I pull myself up. My stomach lurches. I lean back against the bars and the coldness of the metal sends an electric shock through me. I'm crying, though I don't remember why. The Bullet Catcher reaches through the bars and holds me up, steadying me. The chill evaporates in his arms. I'm suddenly warm, as though someone has thrown a blanket over me. "Breathe slow," he says. "Take deep breaths."

"I'm dying," I croak.

"No, you've only had too much to drink."

I do what he says. I breathe. Then I bend over the cot and throw up green snakebite and whatever it was I ate at the saloon. The Bullet Catcher holds me so I won't fall off the cot. I heave for a while after that, though there is nothing left in my stomach. Then I lean back against the bars and close my eyes. The Bullet Catcher lets me go and wipes my mouth with his sleeve.

"I'm sorry, Cub."

In my stupor, I have no idea what he's talking about. "For what?"

"For this," he says. "For everything."

I swallow. "Just don't let me go."

I wake, remembering little of the previous night. I'm covered in bruises from a fight that comes back to me in snatches, like music carried on the wind. I remember shouting at someone at the bar, standing quickly and my chair toppling over. Then the street, alight with the lamps burning behind windows. A lot of yelling. Hartright trying to put herself between me and whoever the other person was. The last thing I remember was Hartright getting thrown to the ground. I kicked whoever it was between the legs. But the bruises tell me that after that I must have lost the fight.

The Bullet Catcher watches me from the other cell, like he's trying to coax me back to life with his gaze. And then I remember waking up in the cell in the middle of the night, and how he held me and spoke to me. And I realize, with surprise, that I'm not angry with him anymore. It turns out, when it comes down to it, forgiveness is easy. At least when you love someone. I forgive the Bullet Catcher everything, and it feels like shedding a tremendous weight.

After that, I visit the Bullet Catcher every day, and I realize how lonely I was when I had neither him nor Nikko to talk to. It was the same loneliness that defined my days from when Nikko left me behind to when I chased after the Bullet Catcher. Loneliness is a kind of desert. It's wide open and desolate, and if you're not careful it will kill you.

On a warm afternoon, a week later, I lie on the cot, staring at the low brick ceiling and the bars of the top of the cage. The door to my cell is wide open. The Bullet Catcher leans against the wall looking up at his window. His face and ribs have mended from the test. Scars on top of scars.

"What should I do?" I ask, as much to myself as to him. "How do I make everything right?" But that's not exactly what I want to ask. Sometimes, alone in my rooms, I say what I really want out loud and it sounds too ridiculous to voice to anyone else, even the Bullet Catcher. I want to know how I can set the Bullet Catcher free. I want to know how to make sure he's safe. And I want my brother to love me. I want him to choose me over Cloak.

"The way forward is dark and complicated," he says dreamily. "If I told you what to do, you would always second-guess yourself. It is better that you do what you believe to be right."

"The last time I did that you ended up in jail."

"You are wiser than the person you were yesterday. But I will say this much: you should drink less. It clouds your mind, makes you slow." Then the sparrow's birdsong like the sound of bells rings lightly from outside the window. It flits up to the windowsill, twittering all the while, before hopping down onto the Bullet Catcher's hand. The Bullet Catcher stares into the bird's black marble eyes and the

208

bird stares back. After a few minutes, he lifts it back to the window and the sparrow hops off and flies away. Then he looks at me and says, "Cub, I cannot tell you what you should or should not do."

"I know why Nikko hates you, but why do you hate him so much? I mean, anymore than any other gunslinger." The thought has been niggling at me over the last few weeks, ever since the Bullet Catcher told me about him and my father. In the quiet between us, the question bubbles to the surface, and as soon as it comes out, I wish I could take it back. I don't want to know.

The Bullet Catcher massages the bridge of his nose, takes a deep breath, and says, "Before, I told you that Nikko quit me after I told him about your parents. I told you that when I saw him next he led a posse of gunslingers to kill me. I only narrowly escaped. What I didn't tell you—" the Bullet Catcher's voice catches in his throat, his emotions, for once, getting the better of him. He clears his throat and finishes—"What I didn't tell you was that I was only the last of the bullet catchers he hunted down. In those days, word spread slowly between the few of us that remained. We were scattered, hidden. But Nikko knew all our secrets. I had shown him. He struck us where we least expected it: in our homes, amongst the company of friends. He saw it as recompense for what I did to the two of you. That is how he rose so quickly through the ranks of the gunslingers. For that brutality, he was deemed, at his young age, a capable leader.

"When I heard of his visiting The Bruise, I was overcome with thoughts of revenge, and I let it get the better of me."

The more the Bullet Catcher reveals to me of Nikko, the more I realize how little I know my brother. The sorrier I feel for him. The more horrified I am by what he's done.

Thinking all this, I sit up on the cot and rest my hand on the Bullet Catcher's shoulder, like he had done so many times when I was scared or unsure. He puts his hand on mine and lets his head hang. We stay like that for several long minutes, until he raises his head, looks back out the window and says, "The hour grows late, Cub."

He's referring to my dinner with Nikko. He promised me this dinner weeks ago and assured me Cloak would not be there.

"I'll come back tomorrow." As I'm leaving, I turn back, meet the Bullet Catcher's eyes, and smiling best I can, repeat my promise, "I'll come back tomorrow."

I wait in the hallway, outside Nikko's office. The electric lights flicker in that way that's still foreign to me, yellow and over-bright. Give me a gas lamp any day. Somewhere in the building someone flushes a toilet. The boiler gurgles down in the basement, the sound seeping through the floorboards. Footsteps clank across the elevated boardwalk a story below Nikko's window. All sights and sounds I've never managed to grow used to in this town.

Nikko's door is opened a crack, letting a blade of yellow light and the sound of hushed voices into the dim hallway. I move closer to the door, careful where I step across the creaky floorboards, and putting my ear close, listen in on Nikko and Cloak's conversation.

"You're wrong. I know her. She will never accept it," Nikko says, sounding exhausted.

"In time she will see it as a gift. She'll thank you." Cloak's voice is firm.

"How can I risk it? She goes to see the old man every day now. She's slipping away."

"And this will bring her back."

Daring to ease the door open just a few more inches, I peer into the bright room. Nikko sits in his chair, elbows on his desk, his head in his hands. Cloak stands over him with his hand on his back. Then Cloak swivels Nikko's chair toward him and crouches down to look him in the eye, resting his palms on Nikko's thighs.

"It will be a blood pact between the two of you. She passed her test, but only by avoiding the point: that she has to choose. She has to choose between you and the Bullet Catcher. And besides, we have no choice in the matter. You know that. It's tradition. What would all those gunslingers who look up to you, who fear you, think if you were to give your sister special consideration?"

Nikko rakes his fingers over his face. His eyes are bright and shining. He doesn't say anything.

"They would turn on you," Cloak says. "It would ruin everything. In time your sister will understand and respect you for it. She will love you for your strength."

Cloak gets to his feet and holds out his hand to Nikko. "Tell me you trust me." In private, speaking with Nikko, his voice is soft and warm. Nikko takes his hand and lets Cloak lift him up. Cloak pulls him close and embraces him.

211

"I trust you," Nikko whispers into Cloak's shoulder. Cloak moves his hand to the back of Nikko's neck. He touches his lips to his cheek before moving them to Nikko's lips. They inhale deeply, their arms around one another, and kiss.

When they draw away from one another they smile at the other's smile. I don't know what it is exactly, but with Cloak running his fingers through Nikko's hair, their noses so close they're nearly touching, Nikko glows. He looks more himself in this moment than ever before. In this stolen moment Cloak inspires love in my brother. But it was never Nikko's capacity for love that I doubted. It was everything else: his anger, his hate, his judgment.

Can I forgive Nikko for the things he's done? How can I begrudge my own brother when I've forgiven the Bullet Catcher? Maybe the difference is that I hated the Bullet Catcher for killing two people. And in the end, it's only coincidence that those two people were my parents. But who knows how many hundreds of people Nikko has slaughtered? What's the difference: two versus hundreds? The death of my parents is personal. The death of the bullet catchers is trivia. But that is only my feelings clouding the facts. The truth is that the crime multiplies with every death.

But maybe I don't have to forgive Nikko. Maybe it's enough to understand why he did what he did. How can I know for sure that I would have acted any different if I had been as hurt, as angry, as strong as he is? Yes, I can love him without forgiveness. As for Cloak, his relationship with my brother is the same as any other bad relationship. Sometimes you just fall in love with the wrong person. Cloak wants me to choose between Nikko and the Bullet Catcher, but if I'm going to help Nikko I need him to choose me over Cloak.

Nikko fixes his hair and straightens his shirt that has become crooked in their embrace. "My sister will be here any moment."

"I'll leave you to it then," Cloak says, stealing another kiss from Nikko as he heads for the door. I retreat to the bench along the opposite wall, and when Cloak appears I try not to betray anything of what I've seen.

Nikko takes me to his club, where they take our coats, though not our guns, and set us up to dine in a private room. The table is long and could easily sit twenty people. Nikko and I share only a corner of the table. The electric lights along the wall are dim and amber. The rest of the large room is cast in shadow. It's as though Nikko and I exist in a bubble of light. Outside that bubble is darkness, and somewhere beyond that, the quiet clacking of billiards and muted voices.

Nikko's in a fine mood. We talk all through the first two courses about nothing at all and I can't keep the smile from my face. It happens like this sometimes, that when I'm around my brother and we're talking and laughing, I forget everything else. It's not until there's a lull, as the waiters collect our empty plates and refill our water glasses, that I remember that no matter how much I want things to be simple between Nikko and me, we still need to have that hard conversation. I need to tell him that I think Cloak is bad for him. I need to tell him that he has to choose me over Cloak. And I need to make him choose before Cloak makes him. But then I think of that look on Nikko's face when they kissed, and I can't bring myself to say anything, not tonight. What's the difference if we have that conversation tonight or tomorrow? Tonight has been so perfect, and Nikko seems so happy, I don't want to ruin it. So instead I say, "Why didn't you tell me about the Bullet Catcher? That he was part of the posse that killed Mom and Dad?"

Nikko's smile disappears. And I think: there I go, ruining it anyway. But he doesn't look angry. He clears his throat. "So you know. I suppose he told you, then." He takes a deep breath and lets it out slowly. "I didn't tell you because I know what the Bullet Catcher means to you and I knew it would hurt you. I guess I wanted to protect you."

I think about that for a while. Then I reach across the table and take his hand in mine. We share a smile.

"I should have told you," he says. "You're old enough to know everything and to make your own decisions. It's only that sometimes when I look at you I still see my baby sister from when we were at the orphanage. Remember when you used to hide behind me when anyone bigger came close?"

I look down at the tablecloth, a little shy of the past. And when I look back at him I say, "You don't have to worry about hurting me. I think I could handle anything at this point." I roll up the sleeves of my shirt. The electric light catches the pattern of the scars running up my arms, making them look bright white and angry.

Nikko looks at the scars and swallows and rubs his own arms and I wonder if he has matching scars beneath his shirt. But if he does, he doesn't show me. "I reckon you're right," he says. "I do believe you could handle anything."

I roll my sleeves back down, suddenly self-conscious, like my bullet-catching scars are somehow sacrilegious in this gunslinger town. "Was it the Bullet Catcher who told you about his role in Mom and Dad's—in their deaths?"

He leans back in his chair. "It was."

"What did you do when he told you?"

He takes a deep swallow of his water, sets it down. But he doesn't say anything.

"Do you ever regret what happened between you and the Bullet Catcher?

"There are lots of things I regret."

Then the dessert comes, sweet chocolate cake like I'd only read about in stories. Nikko changes the subject, and I think we are both grateful. We talk and laugh all through dessert and coffee and I would have been happy if it went on through daybreak.

Outside the club, readying to part ways, he hugs me and says, "Why don't we do this more often?"

"I don't know," I say, pulling back and smiling up at him.

"Well, we must make it a regular thing," he says. "Once a week, if not more."

"I'd like that." This is my real brother, the one who smiles easily, the one who glows like a lightning bug, who doesn't look like he has a malicious bone in his body. I can't help but think of all the dinners to come, and how they will lead to even more time spent together. I imagine all those early promises Nikko made me when I first came away with him, of journeying together to the Northland and seeing those great cities with skyscrapers and flying machines and millions of

215

people. I think of soft snow falling on paved streets. I think of Nikko and me side by side and neither of us wears a shooter and there's not another gunslinger for a thousand miles. And then I remember Cloak, and the conversation that I still need to have with Nikko. And all those thoughts and hopes vanish like smoke.

"There's something I wanted to speak with you about," Nikko says, holding my hands in his. "It's something Cloak and I have been discussing. What you said at dinner, about being old enough that you can handle anything—" But when I hear Cloak's name, my expression must drop, because Nikko cuts himself off, squeezes my hands tighter and says quickly, "I know you don't care for him, but he's not as bad as you think. He's smart, and he wants what's best for us."

"What is it, the thing you wanted to tell me?" I ask, unable to hide the suspicion from my face. Behind Nikko's voice, I hear Cloak's words.

Nikko looks through me. His forehead is furrowed in thought. He starts and stops several times, but finally all he does is smile and say, "Forget it. It can wait."

But I know what the something is. I'm sure it's whatever Nikko and Cloak were discussing when I overheard them in his office. It's been on my mind all evening. But I can't bring it up without letting him know I was spying on him.

"Are you sure?" I say. "You know you can tell me anything."

He smiles again. "I know," he says. "It's nothing, believe me." He puts his arms around me and I put my arms around him. We lean into one another, holding tightly. "I love you," he says.

"Me too."

216

And then we part. Nikko heads back to his apartment and I start off toward the jailhouse to discuss the evening with the Bullet Catcher. But when I turn onto the street with the jailhouse, I stop. The barred windows of the jailhouse burn yellow in the night at the end of the darkened street. I remember what the Bullet Catcher told me earlier, that I would have to make my own decisions, that I would have to rely on myself to know what's best. I kick distractedly at the small rocks in the street before turning around and heading home.

Chapter Nineteen

Everything had seemed so simple over dinner. But later that night, alone in my room, my head is swimming. What was it that Nikko and Cloak were discussing in his office? What does it have to do with me? How can I free the Bullet Catcher and do what's best for Nikko? By the time the sun rises, I have no idea what I am going to do.

The next morning, I sit in the bath until the warmth thaws the sleeplessness from my bones. I do my usual rounds at the factories. Have my usual fights with the foremen. I avoid the jail. I avoid the saloon. Evening settles into the landscape as I return home. A note waits for me on the nightstand. I open it and it's written in Nikko's hand:

MEET ME AT MY CLUB. 10 TONIGHT.

The note gives me a chill. I think of that half-overheard conversation between Nikko and Cloak and I am sure the note has something to do with it. Again, I want to ask the Bullet Catcher for advice, but I won't go to him. Besides, what can I do but meet Nikko? Last night, I had put off what we needed to talk about. I had put off forcing him to make all the hard decisions that needed making. Our meeting tonight might be my best chance to try again. And besides, I *need* to know what Nikko and Cloak had been talking about when I eavesdropped on them. It's the same feeling you get sitting on the lip of a deep well dropping in stones, putting your ear close to the darkness, listening for the bottom. That little something inside you that makes you lean closer to the edge. In the Southland, some of those wells go down for what seems like miles, deep, deep into the earth in the hope of digging out even the muddiest water. If you drop a stone, you could sit there for minutes, listening. And sometimes no sound comes up from the bottom; there's only that voice in the back of your head directing you to that cord of rope descending into the void, that voice telling you what a thrill, what an adventure, it would be to climb down, to seek out. That voice that wonders what alien things may lie at the bottom, out of sight.

A bright moon signals the night and I head off to meet Nikko at his club. The valet in the sparkling white coat and gloves takes my coat at the door and unlike last time he asks for my guns. I don't think anything of it until he directs me away from the game and dining rooms and leads me through a series of disused rooms, their doors flung open, their contents empty, the wallpaper old and peeling. He leads me down into the cellar. At the far wall, he stops in front of a bottle rack, looks over his shoulder to confirm it's only me behind him, then surreptitiously reaches for one of the hundreds of snakebite bottles on the rack and turns it counterclockwise until there's a click from behind the wall. A hidden door swings open. My hands move to find the comfort of my guns, but of course they're not there. I've grown used to going for my guns at the first sign of trouble.

Inside, Nikko stands at the back of the room, smiling but pale. Cloak and his other lieutenants flank him. Cloak's handkerchief is pulled down around his neck, and his jagged, handsome smile puts me ill at ease. It's a small room, with shining gray stone walls. Candles melt on the floor and narrow ledges, throwing cold light onto the walls and ceiling. Two chairs are set around a small square table, like a butcher's block, in the center of the room. The flickering light licks across crimson stains splashed along the top of the table. On one of the chairs sits a closed briefcase, somewhat like a doctor's or snake-oil merchant's traveling valise.

Every muscle in my body is screaming at me to turn tail and run, but when the valet extends his arm, beckoning me to enter, I concede with small, hesitant steps. The secret door ratchets closed behind me. Nikko approaches me from across the room, and hugs me. He doesn't let go for a long time. The air in the small, underground chamber is cold and he trembles slightly. Finally, he pulls away from me and says, "It means a lot, you coming here for me—for us."

Peering over his shoulder, at Cloak and the other gunslingers, darkly dressed with hats pulled low over their eyes, a cold, animal fear grabs me by the heart. Last night I had chickened out when it came to discussing Cloak with Nikko. I wanted to give Nikko the benefit of the doubt. I wanted to believe that no matter how violent or ruthless Cloak made Nikko, that ruthlessness could never reach me. And I hadn't wanted to ruin the night, which had been so good, so much like old times, when the conversation between us had been free and easy. Now, seized with regret, fear in my heart, I look up at Nikko and say, "I need to talk to you. I need to talk to you in private, away from Cloak."

Nikko doesn't seem to hear me, or if he does, he makes no sign of it. He holds my right hand—my stronger shooting hand—in his, running his thumb over the ridges of my knuckles.

"Nikko," I whisper, pulling him close, "please, listen to me. I need to talk to you. Right now. It won't keep."

"It's okay," he says. "We will talk afterwards. I promise." He flashes me a tired smile. He is pale and his eyes are bruised like he hadn't slept all night. "Tattooist," Nikko calls over his shoulder, "we need your expertise."

He leads me by the hand to the table, where he directs me to sit. A bent, spindly man in a smock splattered with dried brown stains, emerges from behind the line of gunslingers. The last of a cigarette dangles from his lips. He holds a half-finished glass of snakebite by the tips of his fingers. If this is the tattooist, I can only hope it's his first drink. He flicks his cigarette onto the floor and shakes my brother's hand. Nikko stands aside and the tattooist takes his seat across from me, moving the valise to the table.

"This part don't hurt a bit, little lady," he says, unlocking his case and flicking open the lid. He takes out a machine that looks like a sadist's pistol, all exposed gears and pumps. On the floor is a tank of compressed air. He attaches one end of a hose to the valve of the tank and the other to the handle of the strange pistol and squeezes the trigger. It lets out a whirring,

221

grinding sound that makes my hands and feet go cold. The tattooist hums to himself as he takes a bottle of black ink from his case and screws it into the top of the device.

He slugs the last of his drink, takes another cigarette from his top pocket, and, lighting it says, "Your hand, darlin'. Your off hand, that is."

Nikko stands at my side and rests his hand on my shoulder. His hand is warm and lends me strength. I look up at him and, trying to smile, say, "You promise we will speak after this?"

"Of course. I promise." Nikko is the only blood I have. I love him. When someone you love asks something of you, how do you say no? Is it not like saying no to love itself? Cloak comes up and stands beside Nikko, looking down on me, like the light of a bad moon. Always, when I feel my love for Nikko overpowering my better judgment, there's Cloak, like a reminder.

I look back at the tattooist with his needle-tipped instrument in one hand and the other hand outstretched, waiting for mine. I make my mind steel and, clenching my jaw, give him my hand. I should have spoken to Nikko last night, but if a tattoo is my punishment for my ambivalence, if this is the tradition that I overheard Nikko and Cloak speaking about yesterday, then it isn't so bad. For me, the tattoo won't be the mark of a gunslinger, but a means to an end. It will be a reminder that the important things can't wait, no matter if they are hard or unpleasant. Next time, I will look at this tattoo and remember to seize my first chance, whenever it comes.

I refuse to flinch when the needle pierces the back of my hand, stenciling out the 'V' of 'VI'. The tattooist finishes the 'I', wipes away the blood, then, despite the snakebite, encloses the numeral in a perfect black circle. Again, he wipes away the ink and blood from my skin. Blood continues seeping from the million tiny pinpricks. He wraps my hand in gauze. My skin burns, like I'm holding it over a fire. But I'm the inflammable girl. The pain isn't so bad, and I'm proud of how well I bear it.

"Fine work, tattooist," Cloak says, picking up my hand, and pulling back the already blood-stained gauze. The gauze peeling off the fresh tattoo sends pain up my arm. I bite my lip to keep from yelping and pull my hand away, carefully replacing the bandage. Cloak's smile is hideous despite his handsome face. "Almost done," he says, stepping back to stand again beside Nikko, who doesn't say anything and will only look at me askew.

"What do you mean?" Fear washes over me.

"One last thing. Something we reserve for our most talented gunslingers. You showed your mettle at Bad Pines. You showed your . . . cunning with your final test. You're a gunslinger not a bullet catcher. This will be a pact between you and me and your brother. This," he says, "is something you've *earned*." Cloak raises his gloved shooting hand. He pulls off the glove with a flourish. His hand is gnarled. Like the man in Los Cazadores who challenged the Bullet Catcher, Cloak's trigger finger has been surgically removed. Everything: the skin, the muscle, the bone, down to the knuckle. In its place, a mechanical finger has been surgically implanted. The 'skin' of the finger is shaped from coiled wire that bends like a compressed spring when he flexes it. His flesh, stripped to the knuckle, is a burned pink color. The skin's been peeled away from the back of his hand and the contents dissected, removed, and replaced. Cloak's hand is misshapen, elephantine.

223

"Terrible, isn't it?" he says, turning his hand over in the candlelight. "But worth it. What any human can do, a machine can do faster, better.

"Of course, for someone without the skill of a gunslinger, such an implement would be worthless. That's why we only offer it to the elite, the gifted."

"If you're offering, I decline," I say, horrified.

Cloak stops admiring his hand and looks at me. "Perhaps offer is the wrong word," he says. "This is something we require of you. This is a tradition. It's something that all great gunslingers must undergo. No exceptions."

"You're deranged!" I yell, jumping out of the chair, but the gunslingers surround me and push me back down. How could I have been so stupid? How could I not have spoken with Nikko last night? Because I was feeling happy and indecisive? And now it's not fear washing through me, but anger. Anger at myself for not being strong enough to tell Nikko exactly what I thought about Cloak.

"Don't worry. We've come a long way since my surgery. We perfected it by the time Nikko elected to have it."

My anger turns to sadness as Nikko unceremoniously raises his hand and takes off his glove. His mechanical trigger finger looks almost natural. The metal folds over the skin of the knuckle, and there's just one long scar running down the back of his hand, where they removed and replaced the bone and tendon.

"We've streamlined the whole thing. Two incisions: one along the back of the hand to allow for the amputation of the bone and musculature, and then another around the circumference of the finger at the knuckle. We've developed a special instrument that removes the whole finger in a single clip. We call it a gunslinger circumcision." One of the gunslingers, still holding me in my chair, guffaws moronically.

"Nikko, please, don't do this to me. I don't want it. Before you let Cloak do this, please, hear me out. Let me speak to you," I plead. I struggle in the gunslingers' grip. I force down panic.

Nikko looks me in the eyes for the first time since sitting me down in the chair. Cloak puts his hand on Nikko's shoulder as though to comfort *him*.

"Nikko, stop listening to him!"

He bends down and cups my cheek in his hand. "Imma, right now it's *you* who needs to listen to *me*. I'm your older brother. I know what's best for you. I'm the leader here. Do you understand? I cannot be easy on you just because I love you. Sometimes being a leader means having to make hard decisions. We will have our entire lives to say everything, but tonight you just need to trust me." He stands and nods at one of the gunslingers, who opens the door for him. He holds my face in his hand for some time, looking at the open door. I press my cheek into his palm, begging him to stay.

"Please. You told me you'd never let anybody hurt me."

He turns his face from mine. "It will only hurt for a moment. I promise." And then he leaves. I scream his name until the door closes behind him. My voice breaks. The tears sting my eyes.

Cloak crouches down and grabs me by my hair and pulls my head back to look at him. I can hear my blood pumping in my ears. I try to shake him off, but the more I thrash, the harder he holds on. There's a fire in his eyes that isn't a reflection of the candlelight. It's madness. I've seen that look before on the faces of people driven crazy by the desert heat.

I throw my weight back, trying to shake Cloak off, but his hands are a vise. He holds me in place as the tattooist, who seems to double as the surgeon, takes a syringe and vial from his case. I want to look away but Cloak won't let me turn my head. When I close my eyes he slaps me over and over, yelling at me to open them, until I relent. The tattooist draws a colorless liquid into the syringe. Another gunslinger pins my arm to the table. Cloak whispers that it will all be over soon. The tattooist inserts the needle into my arm and presses down the plunger. His drugs are strong. The world fades away. I have no more strength to scream.

What would be the use anyway?

Chapter Twenty

I slept, and in my dreams, I was a grain of sand. In the heat of day, I was blasted by the sun and wind. In the dead of night, I was encased in an orb of frost. All around me were other grains of sand. I was pressed up against them, swirled on the wind. But I was alone, carried on the wind over dunes and off the edges of plateaus. Below, I recognized the Bullet Catcher's mountain. I watched our horses galloping along the winding path between the dunes like golden sails. As a speck of sand I passed through the bustling streets of Las Pistolas, the people taking cover as the storm I rode gathered strength. I passed over the homestead of my youth, still on fire after all these years. I watched as a hooded old man, not unlike some unholy version of the Bullet Catcher, kicked in the blackened door and rushed in. On the wind, I screamed out and was blown farther on into the desert. I passed through the iron gates of the orphanage, tarnished and bent now. The windows of the dormitory and church and schoolhouse blown out and the eaves of the roofs caved in. I came to the edge of Sand, my home for so many years. And then the wind died down and the sun came out and baked the sand to glass that encased the town in a perfect, lonely sphere. I melted and came apart, until there was no empty space between the desert and me, until there was no difference between where I had been and where I was going.

I drift back into consciousness on the wind, blowing me out of the desert, back into my body. My head is on fire. The pain transcends pain.

"She's awake," someone says. "Notify Bullet."

I scream out from the pain and the doctor gives me an injection to put me back to sleep. They hold me down on the bed, soaked through with fever sweat, and wait for the drugs to take hold. When it comes, I'm thankful to sleep—no, what I experience is not sleep. Blackness: a thing nearer to death than sleep. There are no dreams this time, just the vacuum of not existing.

When I wake next, Nikko sits on the side of the bed, holding my good hand in his. He strokes the back of my hand with his thumb while paging through a book balanced on his lap. The pain passes over me like rain clouds. When he notices I'm awake, he leans forward and the book tumbles to the floor. He holds my hand in both of his and tells me that there were complications, infection. I've been in the throes of a fever for days. The doctor says my body needs a break from the anesthetic, that each time they inject me I sleep longer, and my breathing becomes weaker.

"Twenty-four hours," he says. "I need you to be strong for twenty-four hours so the anesthetic can work its way out of your body. Then you can sleep."

I try to speak, but my lips don't want to work, my tongue is buried under mounds of sludge, saliva mixed with sand that even in this town, with its machines and electric lights so rare in the Southland, creeps under doorframes and seeps through the cracks in windowpanes, so that if you stay long enough in one place it buries you.

Nikko takes a glass of water from the nightstand. The ice clacks like hail on a tin roof. He directs the straw to my mouth and I manage a couple sips. The water reminds me of the pain. Nikko holds my hand as I twist in my sweat-soaked bed. The look on his face tells me the worst isn't over. I want to spit in his face for what he's done to me. But more than anything, I don't want to be alone, not if I'm going to die. Please, Nikko, don't leave me alone. The hours are interminable and full of pain, but finally the doctor allows me some relief with another dose, and sleep takes me like a mercy.

In my convalescence, my body hasn't felt my own. I am a passenger on a runaway coach, unable to stop, unable to get off. When next I wake, the hallucinations return, worse than before. I feel like I'm floating ceilingward, disembodied. I open my eyes and I'm looking down on myself, still in bed. Nikko, Cloak, and the doctor stand around, talking.

I watch the other me in the throes of fever, screaming at the top my lungs. I've seen others trapped in fever dreams or delirium tremens, I've watched as they drifted farther and farther from reality, carried away by their pains and visions. While they have strength enough, they scream out. Then they grow quiet and die.

"I'm here, Imma," Nikko says, wiping sweat from my forehead.

Pain contorts my face into an inhuman mask. Pain, fear, reveals our animal side. My eyes are dark and wild. My voice is that of a wolf calling to the moon.

"It's me," says Nikko. "I'm right here with you. I love you."

My head falls back onto the pillow, yellow with sweat. And now I'm calling for the Bullet Catcher. Nikko looks at Cloak, and then turns back to me.

"He's not coming," he says soothingly.

"You're a gunslinger now," Cloak says. "He can't come."

I watch myself scream out again in pain, in confusion. Beads of sweat flick off my pallid skin. It takes Nikko and Cloak together to hold me down while the doctor applies the shot to help with the pain. The medicine takes hold. My muscles relax, my eyes unfocus and droop, half-closed. But I'm not asleep, only sated by the drugs. I blink and suddenly I'm back in my body, watching from the bed as Nikko dabs my face and neck with a cool, damp cloth, his eyes shining and red.

"She'll make it," Cloak says, rising to his full height. "She'll live."

A look comes over Nikko, the one I saw on his face the night of the party, when he had that boy killed, a pitiless, unconstrained anger. Standing, he grabs Cloak by his tie and drags him to the far side of the room. He pins Cloak to the wall, holding him by the collar of his shirt. It's easy to forget how strong Nikko is when he wants to be.

"Don't you dare say anything more about my sister!" he yells, bunching Cloak's shirt in his fists and slamming him against the wall. "Dammit, this is your fault!"

Cloak throws up his hands, like a stick-up. "This is no one's fault, Nikko," he says calmly. "I only made a suggestion. You made a decision."

Nikko cocks his arm, readying to punch him.

"Wait," Cloak says, soothingly. "Wait and see. It will all turn out well."

Nikko's voice softens. "How will it?"

"Her fever will break. She will have you to nurse her back to health. She will love you even more for seeing her through this. And her hand will still work. So you see? Everything will work out, yet."

"Her hand is even more mangled than yours!" Nikko seems suddenly exhausted. He drops his arm, lets go of Cloak.

"But it will work!" Cloak says confidently. "It'll be hard for her at first. But she'll have you to see her through that as well. In time, she'll see the benefits, and this will all be a memory of a difficult time that you ferried her through."

The anger goes out of Nikko's eyes. He rests his forehead against Cloak's chest. Forgetting the doctor nervously smoking by the bed, Cloak holds Nikko close, by the back of his head, running his fingers through his hair.

"It will all work out," he soothes.

Cloak whispers a few words into Nikko's ear and departs down the stairs. Exhausted, Nikko drags his feet back to his seat by the bed and waits there until I drift back into unconsciousness.

I wake and the pain has subsided. Or maybe I'm just used to the pain. These fever-filled days have hardened something in me, like scar tissue over a wound. When my parents died, when

231

Nikko left me at the orphanage, I thought I would never get over it. When I had to suture my own wounds after another bullet-catching test, I thought the failure would break me. When Nikko chose Cloak over me, I thought it would shatter my heart. When they mutilated me, I thought I would die. But now I know: I will bend, I will splinter, but I won't break.

I'm the indestructible girl.

Managing to lift my hand, I unwrap the bandages. Ooze from my still unhealed surgery stains the white wrappings a sickly umber. The skin, from my wrist up to the back of my hand, is bluish green. My veins push up to the surface, large and strained from the infection. But the fever has broken before it broke me. Neither Nikko nor Cloak are there when I wake, but the doctor, smoking and lighting cigarette after cigarette, informs me that he's managed to save my hand.

"All said and done, I'd have to call it a success," he says.

I just turn away, wanting to be alone. On the floor are countless rolls of cigarette ash, like gray caterpillars.

"You must be exhausted," he says. He points to my bedside table and says, "We've set up an electric buzzer. You need anything, press the button and someone will come see to you."

He leaves, closing the door behind him. I pull away my blanket. My legs are pale drainpipes of skin and bone. I've been in this bed longer than I thought. Looking at the skin and bone of my legs, I realize how hungry I am.

I press the button and moments later a man knocks and comes through the door. He's tall, with glasses and greased-back hair. He wears the same uniform as the valets at Nikko's club. He takes a step into the room and leans in at the waist, raising his eyebrows, waiting for me to say something. The draft coming through the open door reminds me of my bare legs and I pull the blanket back over myself.

"Food." It's hard to speak.

He smiles, nods and leaves. Sometime later, he returns, carrying a small bed table, heaped with eggs, potatoes, steak, sliced grilled tomato.

When I finish, I push away my blankets. The small act leaves me breathless and panting. A sheen of sweat covers my whole body. My legs are dead things attached to my body. I kick them over the side of the bed and sit there a moment, gathering my strength. Using the headboard as a crutch, I get to my feet, as unsteady as a newborn calf. I take a few knock-kneed steps around the room before collapsing back into bed, my head and my hand throbbing.

The infection has weakened my body, but strengthened my resolve. Over the coming weeks I fall into a routine, reminiscent of my days with the Bullet Catcher. I fall asleep. I wake. I eat my weight in food. Then I lower myself to the floor and start my exercises. I do sit-ups until my stomach burns. I turn onto my stomach and do push-ups until my arms refuse to pump. I sit on my bed, tuck my feet under the light wooden chair and do leg lifts. I've grown bored of waiting to get better.

Nikko visits me every day. I plan my workouts around his visits. When he knocks, I'm sure to be under the sheets, playing the invalid. He looks pained when he sees me still in bed, apparently unable to rise. Let him worry. It's the least he could do.

233

He tries to nurse me, baby me. But I don't give him the satisfaction. I'm tired of sparing Nikko's feelings. I've seen what my consideration for Nikko amounts to.

My only relief comes when Hartright visits. She glugs from her flask and retells the stories I know by heart. Over the long span of my convalescence, she's the only one who doesn't try to make me feel better. She's the only one who brings a smile to my face, the only one who makes me laugh, in spite of myself.

Despite what the doctor said, that they've managed to save my hand, I'm convinced it will never be what it once was. I practice everything with my left hand, the hand that carries the mark of the gunslinger. If my scars are a reminder of my mistakes, then the tattoo is a warning of that darkness that seems to run in my family, from my father to my brother to me. That darkness like the weight of a gun. When I'm strong enough, I do one-handed push-ups with my left hand. The guns Nikko gave me, engraved with my name, sit on my nightstand, waiting for me to take them up again. But I don't. I hide them in a trunk and forget them. I find my old four-barrel in the top drawer of my dresser, under my clothes. I clean it with my good hand, disassembling and putting it back together. I practice spinning it with my left trigger finger, drawing and holstering it, aiming, pulling the trigger, until holding the gun in my left hand feels natural.

The doctor comes by every couple days to check on me and change the wrapping on my hand. After the first month, I don't need bandages anymore. The flesh is mangled and swollen into mounds of pink and purple scars. It still has some healing to do, but it will never look much better than it does now. What's horrifying isn't the ugliness of my hand, but how much it looks like Cloak's. The morning after the doctor removes the wrapping, I ask the valet to bring me a glove when he comes to collect the plates. The one he brings is black leather, just like Nikko's. Just like Cloak's.

For a time, once my hand is unwrapped, my trigger finger is useless. Flexing my fingers, it doesn't obey. Then it occurs to me that it will never *feel* like the rest of my fingers. When I hold the gun in my right hand, my finger feels more a part of the gun than my hand. When I close my eyes, I cannot tell where I end and the gun begins. Then I understand that this new appendage is a machine to be operated, not a part of my body to be felt. And suddenly it obeys.

After two months of hard training, my muscles become tight ropes beneath my skin. The pain is gone. I practice shooting with my unloaded gun. My hand, mangled as it is, flies across the trigger faster than ever. My left hand is faster still and more accurate from practice.

Alone in my room, I've had plenty of time to think, and Nikko has had plenty of opportunities to see Cloak for who he is. My mind is made up.

Gather your things, Bullet Catcher. We're going home.

Chapter Twenty-one

All my clothes, with their familiar scuffs and smells, hang in my wardrobe. I step into my old trousers, wrap my shoulders in my frock coat, and buckle my gun belt around my waist. My holsters hang from my belt, empty. I hadn't expected their absence to feel so heavy. Without my guns, a pearl of fear grows in my stomach. My hand settles over my heart, where I've tucked my old four-shooter into the inner pocket of my coat. I trace the outline of the gun through the wool until my heart slows.

Pulling on my boots, I take a last look in the wardrobe mirror. It's the first time I've seen my refection in a while. The person in the glass looks less like me and more like a woman I used to know. Like a memory of my mother. The skin around my eyes is dark. In my fever, they sheared off my hair so they wouldn't have to wash it. It's just now growing back, short and lopsided. My muscles seemed to have reformed differently than before. My new muscles make me seem somehow taller, older.

Only now, looking at how I've changed, do I feel like I've finally woken from the long nightmare following the surgery.

Running my fingers through my hair, I try to remember how it looked when it was long. I practice expressions in the mirror until I find the one I want, one that makes my darkened eyes look like two stars shining out of the blackness of space. I force the corners of my mouth downward and say to my reflection, "Are you going to stand there all day and worry about how you look?" Slamming closed the wardrobe, I march down the stairs and step out into the street alive with gunslingers.

The streets and boardwalks are a tumult of booze and dancing. Celebratory guns going off in the air. Who knows what they're celebrating? The close of day, or some new misdeed? I have no idea, but I couldn't have asked for better cover. I need to stick to the shadows. And in their dissonance of drinking and yelling, each gunslinger casts a shadow the length of Main Street. I cut a path through the alleys, away from the center of town, until the crowd thins. When I get to the stables they are as dark and deserted as the alleys I took to get there.

Finding No-Name, I press my face against hers and whisper, "I'm here, girl." I saddle her and another horse that's big and dark like the one the Bullet Catcher stole the night we rode out of The Bruise. It could be the same one. Leading them by the reins, they whinny and toss their heads against their bits. I have to stop and settle them, running my hands over the muscles of their cheeks, their bristly coats. When I turn, a figure cuts a deep black shape in the light of the open barn door. My heart seizes in my chest. My hands fall to my holsters and grab nothing but air.

Hartright, looking grave and sober, illuminates her scarred and wrinkled face with the small flame of a match. Her eyes, most days glazed over with snakebite and the memories of old adventures, are sharp, alert. She steps through the doorway and walks across the barn. She rests her weathered hand on No-Name's neck, petting her softly.

"Kinda late for a ride, don't'cha think?" she says, looking at No-Name.

"Just need to clear my head," I say, fixing my eyes on the open barn door.

She leans in conspiratorially, her tattooed hand hanging on No-Name's harness. I follow the line of tattoos running up her arm, to where they disappear under her rolled-up shirtsleeve. She drops her voice to a whisper and says, "I don't know what you're up to, but you're up to something. You have it written all over you."

"I'm not up to anything, Hartright. You've been drinking. You're imagining things."

"Tonight," she says, pulling out a dented flask, "might be the first night in many years that isn't true." She stares at the flask, like she's considering something. She runs her thumb over the scarred metal and sighs. Then she pushes the flask into my hands and says, "No more."

When she looks at me again, her eyes sparkle. "I don't mind telling you, young'un—" Her eyes fall to her flask, still clutched in my hands. I move it to my coat pocket, out of sight. Hartright shakes her head and starts again. "You inspire me, you do. You're planning on facing up to something tonight. I don't know what it is, exactly. Lord knows everyone here has demons that need exorcising. I never doubted you were any different. So I'm facing up to mine too."

She squeezes my shoulder, her eyes are tender and prideful. Hartright's been the closest thing I've had to a friend in this town, but in this moment she could be my grandmother.

"I'll let you get on with it," she says, dropping her hand from my shoulder. "I only followed you to tell you to be careful." She thinks that over for a moment and then says, "But more than being careful, be quick. And more than being quick, be smart. And if you can't be any of those things, be lucky."

I pick up the horses' reins, but my feet are suddenly heavy.

"You knew my father." I stare at the reins in my hand. It feels like everyone knew my father. Everyone but me.

"We rode together, sometimes," she says.

"Was he a good man?"

Hartright pauses for a long time and then says, "He was responsible to his men. He was a strong leader. But no. He wasn't a good man. He had the hellfire inside him."

Nodding, thinking of how much of that hellfire is inside me, how much of it is inside Nikko, I grip the reins tight, until the leather creaks. How is it that we came to be so much like the father we hardly knew?

"At least, that's how he was in the beginning," Hartright says. "When he discovered your mother was pregnant with your brother, everything changed. His anger withered. After you were born, he got soft. He quit us. I think his heart was too full for fighting."

So Hartright knew Nikko and me as babies. She never said. She never talked of my father. It hits me for the first time that I might never see Hartright again, and that I'll miss her. In all my life, there have been so few people I've missed and Hartright might be the least likely of them all. I throw my arms around her and squeeze tight.

When I let her go she winks at me and says, "Go do an old girl proud." And when we part, I don't turn around, for fear of losing my nerve.

The windows of the jail are lit up bright. I stalk through the alleys with the two horses clip-clopping as quietly as they can behind me. I pause in the alley across the street from the jail. I tell myself I'm just gathering my courage, but that's not true.

There's nothing more terrifying than what a gun can do, the lives it can rend apart, the ripples it can send through whole communities, let alone how a bullet can pierce and tear flesh, burst organs, splinter bone. But I'm not afraid—living this life resigns you to the pain. A person who makes a living breaking horses gets thrown plenty. A person who plays with guns gets shot. So it's not courage I'm raising. I'm basking in this last moment before I turn my back on Nikko. Until I cross the threshold of the jail, everything can be put back just how it is at this moment. I can still be my brother's sister. I can still turn around, return the horses to the stables, go to bed, and wake up the next morning and greet Nikko with a hug and a smile. I can still take my place by his side, where he wants me. Closing my eyes, I can see it. The dream is comforting until I think of Cloak.

I step out of the darkness of the alley. Outside the jail, I lay the horses' reins on the post, but I don't tie them. Our getaway will need to be quick.

"Good evening, Ms. Moreno," the deputy says in his slow drawl, tipping his cap as I enter. But his eyes give him away: the surprise that I'm not enfeebled, lying in bed. The jailer looks asleep, his sweat-stained hat resting over his face, his boots up on the desk, but his hands rest on his guns. The bright light of the oil lamps reflects in his eyes peering out from under the brim of his cap. Their card game lies half played on the desk between them. Two cigarettes smolder on the blackened plate they use as an ashtray.

"He's back there," the deputy says with a sardonic grin. "Same as always." He smiles until I draw my gun and duck quickly behind him, so that he's between the jailer and me. I press the muzzle to the back of the deputy's head. When he feels the cold metal against his skin, his body tenses and his hands twitch before moving to the desktop, in plain sight. It all takes less than a second.

The jailer tips back his cap and stares at me hard. He kicks his boots off the desk, and says, "S'pose you want the keys."

"Give them to your friend. He'll unlock the cell."

He does everything deliberately, as though to tell me he's the one in control. But I'm the one with the gun pointed to the deputy's head. The jailer unhooks the ring of keys from his belt and slaps them on the desk.

"Slowly," I growl to the deputy as he reaches for the keys. When he has them, I haul him to his feet by the back of his shirt and steal the shooters from his belt. I tuck my little gun back in my breast pocket and holster one of the deputy's guns. I press the deputy's other gun into his back and say, "Move." I hold him by the back of the collar, keeping him between me and the jailer, who rises to his feet and stares me down as we shuffle across the room.

The Bullet Catcher waits in his cell, his hands hanging through the bars. The look on his face says, 'Where have you been?' The deputy doesn't unlock the cell until I press the gun so hard into his back he winces.

For just a moment, as the lock clicks and the door creaks open that first fraction, my attention drifts from the deputy to the Bullet Catcher. In a flash, the deputy spins on me, grabbing my wrist and pointing the gun toward the ceiling. We grapple for the gun. He hooks me across the face with his off hand. The punch sends me sprawling to the ground, but I still have the gun in my hand. On my back, I take a wild shot at the deputy as he dives back through the door into the jailer's office. My aim is rusty and the shot goes wide. It sends brick dust flying.

The Bullet Catcher helps me to my feet and examines my face.

"Hard to breathe," I say, blood rushing from my nose and down my throat.

"It's broken," he says sagely. Then, without another word, he pinches my nose between his thumb and forefinger and wrenches it back into place. I push away from him, cupping my nose.

"Can you breathe?"

I sniff the air experimentally and smell brick dust and blood. "Just fine," I say. The Bullet Catcher's eyes drop to my gloved hand, and his face tells me he understands everything immediately. All I've been through. Why I've been so long in coming for him.

The deputy, a new shooter in his hand, peeks around the door, and seeing that the Bullet Catcher's back is to him, raises his gun and fires. Without turning, the Bullet Catcher flicks his wrist at the bullet, sending it back the way it came. The bullet ricochets off the doorframe. I let off a flurry of hip shots that send the deputy retreating back into the office.

I hadn't thought I'd hit him, but when we advance to the door and press our backs against the wall, there's a trail of blood leading from the doorway to where the deputy's collapsed, halfway between us and the jailer's desk, upturned for cover. The jailer fires through the open door, chasing us back to cover. Even with the discord of gunfire typical of a Las Pistolas night, it won't be long till our shooting draws reinforcements to the jail. We have precious little time now.

"Help me, boss! Help me!" the deputy calls out from where he lies on the floor. His voice is wet and strangled.

The jailer, ignoring his injured deputy, shouts at us, mockingly, "S'pose you have some plan on getting outta here?"

"No plan, really," I call back. "I just thought I'd kill you and walk out! Easy!"

"We don't need to kill him," the Bullet Catcher says quietly, turning to me. "Covering fire will keep him hunkered down. We can run out the front door."

Why does that set a fire in my chest? There's an anger burning hot inside me that I've never felt before. The deputy's blood runs heavily from his body, spilling through the open door. If he dies, his blood will be on my hands. And I feel nothing. Looking back on my experiences at The Bruise and Bad Pines, I don't feel anything either. My only thought is the jailer, his mocking voice, his black, crow-like eyes, how he ignores his deputy pleading for help. The guns in my hands are hot. My metal finger taps the trigger with a click, eager to squeeze.

243

The Bullet Catcher shakes me. "Ready?"

I nod and the Bullet Catcher bolts through the doorway, deflecting the jailer's first round of bullets into the desk, sending him back behind cover. A half-second later, I dive-roll through the splintered doorway, moving faster than ever before. I take in the room in an instant: the deputy in a red pool, the upturned desk, the top of the jailer's hat sticking above it, the bullet holes in the floor and wall. I see them so clearly I could count them and still have enough time to take out the jailer. The Bullet Catcher lowers his shoulder into the door and barrels through it into the street. The jailer pops up and fires, but he only hits my shadow. I dodge and fire once from the hip, piercing the jailer through the eye. The force lifts him off his feet and sends him tumbling backwards.

For a moment, there's quiet. The puddle of blood around the deputy expands. Fire from the oil lamp, broken in the shooting, spreads up the far wall. The Bullet Catcher runs back in, perhaps thinking I'd been hit. He sees me and stops in the doorway. The smell of blood and smoke fill the air. I holster my guns and approach the desk. The Bullet Catcher follows me with his eyes. I duck to get under the smoke and peer over the upturned desk. The jailer's hands are still on his guns, his fingers on the trigger. His face is caved in where the bullet struck him. Blood bubbles up and spills out across the floor in a bloody halo around his head.

The nausea comes suddenly, doubling me over at the waist. I vomit on the floor. Tears run from my eyes, and I tell myself it's just from throwing up. I wipe my mouth with my sleeve. And I don't know why—maybe to make sure it's real and not some nightmare—but the next thing I know, I'm reaching out, probingly, to touch the jailer. Then the Bullet Catcher is there by my side. He intercepts my hand and holds it in his, until I recognize his bony, scarred hand and look up at him.

"Time to go, Cub," he says, moving between the jailer's corpse and me. He pulls me to the door as the fire grows more intense, casting the deputy's body in orange, ethereal light. Tearing myself away from the Bullet Catcher, I run over to him. He's still breathing. We lift the deputy's arms over our shoulders and pull him out of the burning building.

The night has turned bitter cold and my first strained breath explodes in a puff of steam. Lowering the deputy to the ground, the Bullet Catcher bends to a knee and puts his ear to the man's chest, then he moves his hand in front of his mouth and holds it for a few moments. He stands and says, "Let's go, Cub."

"What about the deputy?" I drop to my knees and lay my ear to his chest, needing to hear for myself.

"He's gone."

All feeling goes out of my limbs, and I can't bring myself to stand, but the Bullet Catcher drags me to my feet. "Cub, this man's troubles are over. Ours are only beginning if we don't leave. Right now." His eyes are soft, but his voice is firm. Is he recalling all the ambivalence he felt when killing was still new to him? How terrible and exciting it was, how the guilt and pain mixed with the feeling of power?

I think of Hartright and—if what Nikko said about her is true—how she was once one of the meanest gunslingers around. I think of her arms, covered in tattoos. I think of all her stories—the ones she could bear to tell—the exaggerated ones, the made-up ones, the ones in which no one died. And now I know why she only told those stories.

"Imma, stop!" Nikko's voice is an electric shock that sharpens my senses. He stands with Cloak a little down the street, before a wall of gunslingers.

Cloak draws his gun and lets it hang from his fingers. "After everything your brother did for you," he says. "He brought you into our family. He taught you to be a gunslinger."

"I loved you," Nikko says, his voice shaking.

I don't even bother going for my guns. "If you love me," I say, "you'll let us go."

"You know I can't." Nikko's shoulders slump, his face distorted between anger and sadness.

"Then come with us!" A look comes across Nikko's face, like he's just stepped out of a darkened hallway into a lighted room. His shoulders rock back, he straightens.

Then he traces the scar on his cheek, the one I gave him, and the light recedes, and he steps back into the shadow.

"Foolishness," Cloak says, tightening the grip on his gun.

Nikko squeezes his eyes shut and when he opens them, his face is a mask. "Get their guns. Lock them up," he says. His eyes flick to the burning jailhouse and he yells to put out the blaze. Cloak and three of his men approach us slowly with their guns drawn at their hips.

"I won't let you go," Nikko says. "And the Bullet Catcher is too dangerous to let run free." He pauses, transfixed by the jailhouse collapsing in on itself, lost to the fire. "I don't think I could live with never seeing you again."

Cloak approaches, holsters his gun and brings out two pairs of cuffs. I look up at the Bullet Catcher, who's the very picture of calm and composure. I grab his scarred hand in my gloved one and squeeze.

"Okay," he says, knowing exactly what I mean to do.

I think about that night in the cave, when I chose my brother over the Bullet Catcher. I remember how I felt I deserved some good fortune after so much rotten luck. But you know what? Fuck that. Life's not about deserving and undeserving. Life can't be divided into the fortunate and unfortunate. You can't go around thinking about what's owed you. Because no one owes you anything. If there is a debt, it's only to oneself.

In a blink of an eye, my gun is in my hand. The gunshot rings out, echoing loudly off the buildings and down the wide street overflowing with drawn guns and boots and snakebitten breath.

Chapter Twenty-two

Folks say time is constant. It's not. Living in the orphanage seemed to last three lifetimes. I was an old woman by the time I left. On the other hand, lying in bed, as fever washed over me, seemed a matter of hours.

Silence follows the gun blast, a silence that feels like minutes, minutes in which my life flashes before my eyes. Running after the Bullet Catcher, turning my back on him in the caves, training with Nikko, my second betrayal. Were all these mistakes? Would everyone have been better off if I'd stayed in Sand, behind Dmitri's washbasin? I can't help but see all the consequences of my poor decisions.

Then everything speeds up. I never have a chance to fire my gun. As the jail burns and collapses with an air of finality, and the gunslingers race to put out the fire spreading to the adjacent buildings, the street erupts in chaos and gunfire. At first, the gunslingers can't tell from where they're being fired on. Some turn on their own posse, thinking they've been double-crossed.

The roofs alight with gunfire. Muzzle flashes illuminate a man's jowly hangdog face, a silvery, foot-long beard, then more faces so full of wrinkles that their eyes and mouths are indistinguishable. Marooned in the middle of the open street, the gunslingers climb and trip over one another to get to the boardwalks, sheltered by the floating boardwalks above them. Nikko dodges the bullets coming down like rain, grabs an injured man by the collar and hauls him to cover. Cloak drops the handcuffs, grabs the man closest to him and pushing him out front, uses him as a shield, running for cover. He drops the man in the dirt, riddled with bullets, dead before hitting the ground, before swinging himself over the boardwalk rail, unscathed.

Out of the alley rushes an ancient figure. "What're you two still doing in the street!" she yells, waving for us to follow her. She shoots into the scrum of gunslingers, giving us covering fire.

"Hartright!" I can hardly believe it. "How—what?" I stammer, reaching the alley out of breath. Behind me, the Bullet Catcher takes backwards steps, the horses' reins in one hand, his other deflecting bullets.

"I'll explain along the way. We need to go."

Hartright leads us down the alley, alongside the one freestanding wall of the jail, then across the street, parallel to the gunfight, and back into the safety of the shadows of the next alley. She pulls me by the arm, half walking, half running.

"There's something you have to understand," she says. "Your brother's a powerful guy, sure. You already know that. But he's not as powerful as you may think. And he's stuck. Anyone with eyes can see what's going on between him and Cloak—"

"That they're lovers?" I say, struggling to keep up.

"No one gives two nickels about who he takes to bed. But ever since Cloak's turned up, Bullet's turned into one mean son-of-a-gun. He got better when you arrived. But it didn't last.

"What I'm trying to say is, believe it or not, Bullet gives more than a damn what you think of him. Between you and Cloak and the powers up north, his head's turned all the way round." Hartright jerks my arm, pulling me suddenly into another alley. We're almost on the other side of town. Guns pop like fireworks in the distance.

"Your brother didn't always call the shots. And there's more dissent in our ranks than you'd think. Us old good-for-nothings, for one, have always been wary of him. He don't think we serve no damn purpose except to drink ourselves silly." She stops to catch her breath and flashes her trickster's smile. "Guess we showed 'em." She sets off again, pressed close to the buildings, darting quickly across streets, the Bullet Catcher and me in tow. "Really, in the grand scheme of things Bullet's just someone to wrangle everyone into the same pen, if you get my drift."

"Wait," I say, grabbing her arm. "What are you talking about?"

"She means," the Bullet Catcher interjects, "that tonight we have all made a much more powerful enemy than Nikko."

Hartright taps the side of her nose, knowingly. "With this little mutiny," she says, "I wouldn't be surprised if the powers that be put a hurtin' on your brother, recall him to the Northland and bring in someone new. They may even put Cloak in charge." Hartright's words buzz between us. My imagination races. What form would these unseen Northlanders' revenge take? And what might happen to Nikko? But there's no use worrying about that now. The battle goes on in the distance. Hartright's breathing is quick and rough from a lifetime of smoking. The horses grumble and shake their muzzles impatiently. Then we set off again.

At the edge of town Hartright presses her back against the side of the building and pokes her head out, looks to the left and right and signals with a wave of her hand that the coast is clear. The flat, dark desert lies before us. The Bullet Catcher steps into the stirrup and swings his leg over his horse. No-Name kicks at the dirt with her hoof, waiting for me.

"Come with us," I say, turning to Hartright. "You can't go back there."

Her face softens, the wrinkles around her eyes turning down at the corners. She looks like she's genuinely considering it. But with the gunfight raging, I know she won't leave her friends behind, the people who, like her, somehow survived youth and made it to old age, the people who she met every morning in the saloon to grumble and reminisce and get drunk with.

The gunshot splits the night in two. Hartright's eyes go wide and then narrow into watery slits. She looks down at her chest, where blood spreads quickly across her shirt. Like oil spurting up from some underground well, the blood is black in the lightlessness. I catch her as she collapses forward. She holds tightly to me and says in a strangled voice, "Don't let me fall, young'un. A person can't die, long as she's on her feet."

The shooter steps forward out of the alley, still pointing the gun toward us. The Bullet Catcher tries to dismount, but Cloak waves the gun at Hartright and me and the Bullet Catcher settles back into the saddle with a grimace.

"Turn around slowly," Cloak says. "I don't want to shoot you in the back."

"A little late for that," Hartright says through clenched teeth.

I move for my gun. Cloak pulls back the hammer of his revolver with a click. "Don't even think about it," he says. "If you weren't Bullet's sister, you'd already be dead."

"Look at me, young'un," Hartright says, her hold tightening around me. "I haven't lived a good life. I've been bad. And when I wasn't bad I was guilty, complacent."

"You're a good person," I say, holding back tears.

She cups my cheek in her ancient hand, rough like the desert sands, and says, "None of us are good. I'm leaving that up to you." She pushes me away, and before I know what's happening there's a hand grabbing my collar and swinging me up into my saddle.

Hartright draws her guns, drops to a knee and spins, moving like someone half her age. She unloads both guns, rolls, and reloads. She's already firing when she gets back to her feet, sending Cloak diving back into the alley.

"Go!" Hartright yells. But I don't. I need to help her. I draw my gun. The Bullet Catcher pulls his big horse around mine, leans over and slaps No-Name on the back. She whinnies, goes up on her hind legs and takes off into the desert. It's all I can do to lean down and hold on tight.

"We need to go back for her!" I yell to the Bullet Catcher galloping by my side. He doesn't acknowledge me. He keeps his eyes straight ahead, his body close to his horse, urging it on faster. He knows the most important thing now is to get as much distance between the town and us. I know it too.

I know it like I know that Hartright is already dead. I kick No-Name with my heels and chase the Bullet Catcher into the night, away from Las Pistolas. In the rush of wind, I let the tears stream from my eyes. I need both hands on the reins, and, besides, it feels wrong to wipe them away. My tears are the only way to show my love for Hartright. She gave me her life. All I can give her in return are these tears. So I give them and feel useless.

For the first few days, I can't stop thinking about Hartright, Nikko, and the mess I left behind. The Bullet Catcher doesn't say a word. He rides ahead of me, hunts small hare for food, and lets me grieve. And I thank him for it.

I was so young when I lost my parents, too young to remember if they were good or bad to me, whether they truly loved me, whether we were happy. What I've learned from losing Hartright, someone who I didn't understand until those last few moments, is that when it comes to those you love, death and separation weigh heavier, hurt more, the older you are. When you're young, there's the feeling that whomever you've lost could someday return. Because 'lost' implies that whoever's gone can be found. But when you're older, death means forever. Only then do I understand what I felt when I killed the jailer. For a moment, my anger, my hate, had made me unfeeling, and in that moment I killed a man. I had not hated him; he had only been the closest person to me that I could justify hurting. But once the anger and hate ebbed away, all that was left was regret for what I'd done. And I thought that if I could only save the deputy it might make up for the life I took. But killing doesn't work that way. There's no making up for it.

Then one night, sitting around the campfire, closing my eyes, I picture myself putting all those thoughts into the fire and watching them burn. The night is long and dark and there are still many hours before first light.

"You've finished grieving," the Bullet Catcher says, poking the fire with a stick, igniting the embers.

Hugging my knees to my chest, I squeeze my eyes closed until thoughts of Hartright and Nikko ebb away. "I have," I say.

"Good. Grief is important, but it has its place. For now, push it down. In the coming days, it will not help us."

Across from me, the contours of the Bullet Catcher's shoulders and hat flicker behind the fire. "Bullet Catcher," I say, making myself look him in the eye. "I'm sorry. I know you will never be able to trust me again. Whatever I can do to make it up to you, I'll do it. I promise."

The Bullet Catcher pokes the fire. The light flickers in his eyes.

"So you are not finished grieving, then?" He looks up at me through the fire, a smile forming on the corner of his lips, making the dimples in his cheek deeper. Or is that just another scar?

Sighing, he leans back on his elbows and props his boots up at the edge of the fire. "Lobo," the Bullet Catcher says.

"What?"

"That's my name. Lobo." He lies back, staring at the night sky that is a colorless, starless canopy over the desert. "You're the only one alive who knows that name." He takes a deep breath and says, "There used to be others."

"Lobo." I turn the name over in my mouth. It seems to fit the Bullet Catcher's weathered face, his eyes that shine in the dark like the animals that roam our mountain.

"When you finish your training, when I am your peer and not your teacher, you may call me by name. Until then you may continue to refer to me as Bullet Catcher."

"Does this mean you forgive me?"

"In Las Pistolas, were you idle? Or did you use your time wisely? Did you learn anything?"

"Too much, I think. I guess I learned a lot about myself. I learned who I am."

"Who you are," the Bullet Catcher says, "is a lifelong lesson." He looks up at the mountains, large and dark in the lightlessness. "There is nothing to forgive, Cub."

I want to jump up and throw my arms around him, but my body feels so heavy, weighed down by the Bullet Catcher's forgiveness.

"We have another three days by horse," the Bullet Catcher says. "Your brother cannot be more than a day behind us. We will need all of that time to prepare."

"Let's ride, then. The quicker we get there, the better."

"And be dead on our feet when Nikko comes for us? Rest is part of preparation." He lies back down and says, "And do not bother to dream, Cub. Dreaming wastes energy. We will need all of it for what is to come."

I sit by the dying fire and watch the Bullet Catcher until he drifts to sleep. Getting up, I walk around the fire and lay in the dirt beside him. Closing my eyes, I clear my mind, not wanting to waste energy. But one thought persists: Lobo, the

255

name of the Bullet Catcher. And suddenly I understand the nickname he gave me. He is Lobo, the wolf, and I am Imma, his cub.

The night is dark and cold, but the light is coming. I feel it readying to rise over the horizon to melt the frost that lies over the desert basin like a shroud.

Chapter Twenty-three

Except for the layer of dirt covering everything, our mountain camp is largely how we left it: a picture of easier times. After the long ride, all I want is to lie down on my thin cot and sleep. But there's no time. We have a day. Maybe.

When I trained with the Bullet Catcher, he would lead me running through the paths and switchbacks that cut across the mountain. The Bullet Catcher showed me how to set traps, track game. He made me memorize every hiding place and path. It never crossed my mind that he was teaching me more than how to hunt. He was teaching me to defend our home.

Now we rig the steep slopes with pitfalls and snares. We stack boulders, secured on hair triggers, attached to trip wire. We build walls by stacking whatever we can: logs, rocks, clotted dirt. We pry apart bullets and gather their powder in satchels that we spread over our makeshift walls. If the gunslingers break the perimeter, we'll set the walls on fire. I get the feeling that this time the Bullet Catcher doesn't plan on going quietly. There's no plan B. No accounting for getting captured.

"With only two people this place is indefensible," the Bullet Catcher says, stripped to his white, collared shirt, the sleeves rolled up, the collar open and sweated through. "So we must at least give the impression that it's well defended."

"Why don't we run?" I ask, heaving another rock atop the makeshift wall.

"To where? The gunslingers have eyes in every town. Here, we have the high ground, if not the numbers."

The camp sits in a high valley between two peaks. It's protected by a sheer rock face on the desert side. On the other, by the lake. There are places, dense with trees, where the slope is less acute, but the going would be slow and exhausting. The narrow path through the high boulders that I first followed the Bullet Catcher through, so long ago, is the easiest way up. With our walls and traps, we've made a bottleneck, so that the narrow path—the most defensible point—will be the gunslingers' best approach.

Standing atop one of the tall boulders, overlooking the path, we make stacks of large stones to hurl down on the gunslingers.

"What if Nikko sends the whole town down on us? We'll never be able to defend against that many people."

"He can't send the whole town. First, there aren't enough horses. Secondly, he cannot afford to send everyone to hunt down two people, no matter who those people are. Think of the gunslingers as a machine. If there's nobody behind the controls it will stall and break down. And Nikko has people to answer to. As much as he can't afford to look weak by letting us go, he can't afford to let everything go to hell either."

"How are stones going to bring down a whole posse?"

"Stones have brought down larger foes than that." Finishing another small pyramid of stones, he puts his hands on his hips and stretches his back, standing straight and tall in the sun. His shirt hangs off his torso like wet laundry on the line. He shields his eyes with his hand and peers down at the desert below. "There," he says, pointing.

On the edge of the horizon, dust blooms from the hooves of galloping horses. Gunslingers.

"I count twenty . . . maybe more. We have only hours now. There is no more time for idle chat."

We stand at the edge of the clearing. The Bullet Catcher points across it to a thin, white tree with brittle, peeling bark.

"Can you hit that tree from here?" he asks.

"Of course."

"Can you hit it without aiming?"

Without turning to the tree, I draw my gun and shoot from the hip. The dry bark explodes.

The Bullet Catcher stares at the tree for a time and says, "Your brother is a good teacher."

I holster my gun and click the strap closed.

"Will you be using your guns today?" he says.

"What do you think I should do?" The Bullet Catcher only stares at the tree with half its trunk splintered away, creaking, threatening to fall over. After he doesn't answer, I say, "I haven't thought about it."

"What have you been thinking about?"

I shrug. The tree cracks and collapses.

Now he looks at me, with that look old people get in regards to the young, like the age difference makes them another species. "You should always be thinking," he says. "Always."

"What about meditating? What about clearing your mind?"

"We are not monks, Cub. Do I look like a peaceful man? Bullet Catchers don't meditate. We obsess. We clear our minds of everything but a single thought. We focus on that thought, so as to understand it like a painter understands every facet of painting: the colors of his paints and how those colors combine to make new colors. A painter knows every bristle of his brush, every knick in his paint knife, every fiber of his canvas. When he paints, he thinks of his mentor who taught him, he thinks of all of the painters who came before him. He understands all these things as one thing, one thought. He is thinking of painting and nothing else. *That* is how we will meditate."

"The gunslingers will be here in hours. We don't have time to meditate."

"So, now you know more than your teacher?"

"But what if they arrive and we're not ready? They'll kill us."

"Then it will be a good final lesson."

He turns and walks down the path to the lake, overgrown in the months we've been gone. What I would give for a bath right now. I might die today and never have a bath again. In the face of death, eating, bathing, the small daily things suddenly seem the most important. I long to do everything one last time.

"Your thoughts are scattered," the Bullet Catcher says, sitting cross-legged on the lakeshore. He stares out across the water, at the sun falling toward the mirrored plane, the mountain range rising like rusty saw teeth.

"How could you tell?"

"Because I know you, Cub. You are one who is always looking over their shoulder, to the past. And that is good. The past can tell you much about what is to come. But the past is only a lesson. The present is where we apply those lessons." He pats the cold dirt beside him. Evening is coming and the air is already growing cool. A shiver runs through me as I sit.

The Bullet Catcher says, "Meditate on warmth and you will not be cold." He closes his eyes and says nothing more.

The sun dips below the rim of the mountains and the fiery reflection on the water turns dark and disappears. Beside me, the Bullet Catcher takes long, deep breaths, a look of calm on his face. His back is straight, his shoulders relaxed. His silence is the same as when he sleeps, the same silence as the dead. It is difficult not to think of Nikko, of what the coming hours might bring. But the Bullet Catcher told me not to worry and I do my best to trust him.

Only when the cold is unbearable and I can't stop my teeth chattering do I close my eyes and think about warmth. Nothing else. And I don't know why, perhaps because she took me in from the cold and saved my life, or maybe because the Bullet Catcher is right when he says I'm always looking toward the past, but in my mind I picture an empty shack. Endd's shack. Inside is empty except for the table. And on the table there is a lamp.

The lamp glows bright and white, like the air on a hot, clear day. It lights the room completely so that there are no shadows, not even under the table. I am not in the shack. I am the shack, and I have emptied myself of everything except for the lamp that is warmth.

Then the Bullet Catcher is there, standing on the other side of the table, cupping his hands around the lamp, looking into it like he does the fire on cold nights in the desert. Now I'm in the room too. I watch myself walk over to the table and cup my hands around the lamp, mirroring the Bullet Catcher.

"Warmth is a form of energy," the Bullet Catcher says. "And energy is power." He sighs and takes a seat in the chair that wasn't there a moment ago. He points to the empty chair beside me and I sit. "Do you understand?" he asks.

"I don't think so."

"What is a gun?"

"Power."

The Bullet Catcher says nothing. I stare into the lamp, trying to untangle his words.

"Let me put the question differently," the Bullet Catcher says. "When you are afraid, how do you comfort yourself?"

My hand instinctively reaches for my shooter, but it's not there.

"We are all afraid, Cub. Dying is frightening. Living? Even more so. Like a gunslinger, when you are afraid you reach for your gun. Fear makes you feel weak. A gun makes you feel strong. A gun is a defense against fear."

"So, what does a bullet catcher reach for when they're afraid?"

The Bullet Catcher smiles and holds out his scarred, empty hands. "Nothing," he says. "Gunslingers hold power in their hands, but they don't understand the greater power within all of us. A gunslinger aims to conquer fear. But a bullet catcher knows the power of fear. A bullet catcher knows that there is no courage without first being afraid. A bullet catcher doesn't try to beat their fear. They resolve to understand it."

The Bullet Catcher's eyes fall to my gloved hand. I look down and pull off the glove. I examine my hand, turning it over in the warmth of the light. The metal of my trigger finger begins to spread across the back of my hand. My skin turns silver and peels back like the top of a tin can, revealing my tendons turned to wire, my bones turned to a mast of steel, my blood thick and black, like oil. And somehow it reminds me of the lesions covering Endd's skin, and the Bullet Catcher's, covered in scars.

"It is a bad scar," the Bullet Catcher says, shaking his head.

The metal crawls up my wrist and over my arm, across my shoulder and into my body. I feel my ribs turning to a cold cage for my heart, straining to pump the thick, black oil through my body. The lamp in the room flickers and dims. The pump in my chest that used to be my heart grinds gears, pumps pistons. It revolves like the chambers of a gun. I scream and my voice is the report of a gun.

Then, when my fear is most pitched, I reach out in the darkness, not for my gun, but the lamp. My strength is the memory of my parents, of Nikko as a boy, Hartright, and the Bullet Catcher, all the people I've loved, and who have loved me in return. And suddenly everything goes dark, disappears, like a sudden wind blowing through an open window, snuffing out the lamplight.

"It is time," the Bullet Catcher says, gently shaking my shoulders.

Slowly, I wake from the dream and open my eyes and I do not feel like my gunslinger father's winter child, my sunny brother's cold sister. I feel reborn as the Bullet Catcher's autumn child, warmed by a light from within. The Bullet Catcher crouches

263

in front of me, his eyes familiar, understanding, compassionate. Beyond him, the moon has risen high in the night sky, casting silver light across the lake.

"You were in my head," I say dreamily. "How did you do that?"

"I did nothing," he says, smiling. "Though I'm flattered you think me so powerful. If you saw me, you only saw yourself. In your dreams, you are all things.

"Come. The night grows late, and your brother will not delay for us," the Bullet Catcher says, before heading back up the path to camp.

Standing, I gaze out at the lake. I click open the straps on my holsters and draw my guns, the guns I stole from the dead deputy. His blood stains the steel. I draw my arm back to throw them into the lake, but instead I holster them, clicking closed the strap. Waking from my meditation, I felt strong and confident, but already the feeling begins to fade, replaced by old fears. I'm afraid of dying. But more so, I'm afraid of letting the Bullet Catcher down. I'm afraid to lose him, like I've lost everyone else.

Turning, I run after the Bullet Catcher, ready for the fight.

Chapter Twenty-four

The moon is high and bright, like a second daylight. The Bullet Catcher and I perch up on the boulders on either side of the narrow path leading up the mountainside toward camp. I grip my guns. My body is heavy with exhaustion and the weight of the bandoliers making an X across my chest. We listen for twigs breaking, voices whispering, traps going off.

There's no sign of the gunslingers down below in the basin, their tracks whipped away by the desert wind. If they were patient they'd wait for a night when the moon wasn't so full, when it didn't cast its cool light over everything. But the gunslingers aren't patient. Enrage a hive of bees and they don't stay put, gather their forces, plot revenge. They swarm; they attack.

Could Nikko kill me? Would he? Or would he shoot out my arms and legs, bind my wrists and ankles, sling me over his shoulder, and carry me back to Las Pistolas?

And could I kill him?

After the jailer, I don't know if I could take another life. Though Nikko never taught me how, I'm a good enough shot to disable someone without killing them. I can shatter the tiny bones in a hand. If given enough time to aim, I could take off a trigger finger. But what then?

The Bullet Catcher whistles a bird call, the song of the sage sparrow. He points to his eyes and then down to the path below. The sound of boots echo off the walls of the narrow pass. The Bullet Catcher drops to his stomach, a heavy stone in his throwing hand. I make myself flat against the rock. The gunslingers emerge from the darkness, walking in a slow crouch, two at a time. I count six of them, three groups of two. Where are the others? I don't see Nikko or Cloak.

When they're right below us, the Bullet Catcher rains rocks on the gunslinger's heads. He connects with his first throw and the lead gunslinger collapses in a heap. He gets off a few more throws before the gunslingers open fire. The Bullet Catcher's already ducked away and is lobbing rocks from a different position. He moves and throws. A gunslinger finds him in the darkness, aims, fires, and gets his own bullet between the eyes, bent back by the Bullet Catcher.

With the Bullet Catcher drawing fire, I have plenty of time to aim. Holding my gun in both hands, I steady myself by lying on my stomach and propping my arms on the smooth boulder beneath me. The darkness and the gunslinger's frantic movements make it difficult and I waste a few shots trying to hit fingers and the flashing glints of gunmetal. Emptying my lungs, I still my body and hit three of the four remaining gunslingers in the knees and feet. The last gunslinger turns my way and fires wildly. Ducking behind the rock, I peer across to see the Bullet Catcher stand to his full height, from his perch on the boulder. In the dreamy, silver light of the moon, he looks ten feet tall. He leaps down on the gunslinger. All I hear is the sound of the gunslinger's body collapsing beneath the Bullet Catcher's weight, a strangled scream, the sound of a neck snapping. Then silence.

The six gunslingers are strewn across the ground like tumbleweeds turned to shrapnel under wagon wheels. The Bullet Catcher stands over the crumpled body of the last man, breathing steam. He senses me, finds my eyes in the darkness, and points up the path in the direction of our campsite, signaling that he'll meet me there.

When we meet at the line of trees around the clearing, the Bullet Catcher's eyes shine in the moonlight as he checks me over for bullet wounds. I grab his hands and squeeze them tight.

"I'm okay," I say. "I'm fine."

He raises his hand to stop me speaking. The sound of dry brush snapping underfoot comes from the woods. He pricks his ears, and waits for more sounds. Is it an animal or the gunslingers? I close my eyes and do the same, listening to the sounds of the mountain. The footsteps are quiet, trained. They'd be imperceptible to anyone not used to hunting these trails and switchbacks.

We run at full speed through the woods, toward the sound. Our footsteps are silent. We know every fallen tree, every trap, every dry patch of ground that could crackle underfoot. We traced these paths earlier in the day. We repeated our steps in that obsessive, methodical way of the Bullet Catcher's that turns every action into second nature.

We stop at a line of trees. Shadows move up the mountain, clawing at the dry brush with their hands, struggling to pull themselves up. The lead gunslinger can't be more than ten yards away. His breath is hoarse and tired. In the darkness he could be Nikko. He's about the right height and size. The gunslinger grabs a low tree branch and heaves himself up a few more feet. Five yards away now—so close I can see by the shape of his nose and lips that he's not Nikko. Only a few steps away, the gunslinger's close enough to reach out and grab me if he saw me, but he doesn't. I'm the unnoticeable girl. The ground begins to level out and he straightens his back, grabs a small sapling to help pull himself up the last incline and falls headlong into one of the camouflaged pits we'd dug all across the mountain to hunt boar and big cats and wolves.

The others, a short distance behind, hear the scream, but in the darkness they don't see what happened. One moment he was there, the next: gone. They rush to where they lost sight of him. Their fear of the dark, their fear of the Bullet Catcher, makes them move without thinking. More shadows appear farther down the slope, emerging from the darkness.

The traps detonate in quick succession. One of the gunslingers steps in a snare and is yanked high into the canopy. Another stumbles across a trip line, releasing boulders and logs, tumbling down the mountain. The gunslingers let out terrible breathless screams. They try in vain to get out of the way. Most never know what hit them.

The sound of screams, of rumbling boulders and logs, glides off down the mountain and is replaced by silence, uninterrupted by birdsong or wolf howl or any other sound typical of the night.

The mountain holds its breath.

A dull moaning rises from the pit. Calmly, the Bullet Catcher picks up a large stone, lifts it over his head, waits for a moment, then lets the rock fly. There's a soft, wet sound, like the rock hitting muddy earth, then silence again.

The ensnared gunslinger, hanging upside down from the tree, swings back and forth, struggling to free herself. Drawing my pistol, I steady it on my forearm, and fire. The line snaps and the gunslinger plummets to the ground.

Silence falls again over the woods.

The Bullet Catcher taps his ear and points down the mountain. Pricking my ears, I hear a faint creaking sound, coming from just out of sight. As it draws closer, the creaking is joined by the sound of ropes stretched taut, and gunslingers grunting and wheezing.

A shape emerges from the shadows, flanked by more gunslingers. The mysterious object sits on a pair of metal wagon wheels that creak as they turn over rock and brush, moving inch by dogged inch up the mountain. The object is vaguely the shape of a cannon, but with a hundred barrels instead of one. It's huge and heavy-looking, and slow as their progress is, I can't fathom how the gunslingers manage to roll it up the steep incline. Then I see it. The gunslingers pull ropes, strung through metal loops that have been screwed into the trees and hammered into boulders farther up the mountain face. Those first gunslingers weren't trying to flank us. They were anchoring the ropes to use as leverage. But I can sever the rope with one well-placed bullet. Straining my eyes in the darkness, I take a step out of cover. A twig snaps under my foot.

Everything stops: the creaking wheels, the straining ropes, the sound of the gunslingers' breathing.

"Load!" one of them yells.

Without time to aim, and with the Bullet Catcher pulling me back up the mountain to better cover, I let out a flurry of bullets, shredding one of the trees anchoring the ropes. The tree shudders, groans, and snaps. The taut rope whips back down the mountain, but the weapon stands fast. They've already chocked the wheels.

"Move!" the Bullet Catcher yells in my ear. He pushes me in front of him, up the mountain, before overtaking me and diving behind one of our low, makeshift walls. The weapon makes a terrible clicking, whirling noise as its barrels start spinning. Lowering my head, I sprint for cover. I lunge over the rocks and the Bullet Catcher pulls me down and jumps on top of me, pushing me into the cold dirt. Bullets sing through the night. The wall chips away under the gunfire, hailing us with rock and wood shrapnel. The trees around and behind us sever at the middle and come crashing down, as though buzz-sawed.

When the gun stops, I try to lift my head, but the Bullet Catcher pushes me back down, flat against the ground, and growls into my ear, "Wait."

"Reload!" one of the gunslingers calls and a moment later the gun starts up again.

Finally, the gunfire ceases and the Bullet Catcher rolls off me. His skin tightens around his mouth and eyes as he pushes down pain. Lying on his side, he tears at the earth with his long, scarred fingers. The back of his coat is shredded, and he's bleeding from countless bullet grazes that have torn through his clothes and ripped his skin like slash marks from a whip. His back is streaked with blood. I reach out to touch him and he grabs me roughly by the wrist and holds my hand tightly.

The look in his eyes is hurt and wild. The muscles in his cheek twitch as he grits through the pain.

"I'm fine, Cub," he says, peeling the shredded clothes from his torso.

"We need to bandage you up," I say, trying not to let the fear of his wounds creep into my voice.

"Later, when there's time." On his belly, he pulls himself on top of the wall and peers down at the gunslingers below. We watch as they dismantle their weapon and start carrying it up, in pieces, on their backs. Other gunslingers flank the carriers with their guns drawn.

I take aim at one of the gunslingers. A bullet ricochets off the rock near my head, sending dirt into my eyes, and I duck back into cover. To the left and right of our position is only open ground. We'd be gunned down in moments if we tried to cross to different cover.

"We can only retreat," the Bullet Catcher says through gritted teeth. He pulls out the box of matches he uses to light his pipe, strikes a match and tosses it into the dried sticks and brush. The gunpowder we'd spread earlier ignites and sets the wall on fire, a burning barrier between us and the gunslingers. It'll only buy us a few minutes, but it's better than nothing.

"C'mon," I say, pulling the Bullet Catcher's arm over my shoulder. We keep low until we pass out of range of the gunslingers. The Bullet Catcher stops and catches his breath, using a tree to bear his weight.

He waves me away when I try to help him. "We need to double back to camp," he says. "On flat ground, we can come at them from two directions. They won't know where to aim their machine gun." The side of his face, squeezed tight against the pain, alights in the bronze colors of the fires burning on the mountainside. The other side lingers in shadow.

"You've lost a lot of blood," I say, not knowing what to do.

"True enough, Cub," he says, making his voice calm and even. "But the wounds aren't deep." He lurches away from the tree, and we head toward camp.

We break through the woods into the clearing. I don't hear the hammer click or the report of the gun, all those things I've been trained so well to notice and react to. The force of the shot spins the Bullet Catcher around. He lurches in the dirt, clutching his shoulder.

Nikko and Cloak, with his still smoking gun in hand, stand at the edge of the clearing. They approach us slowly, Cloak never taking his gun off us. Nikko's shooters stay holstered. He wears his bronze and chrome bullet-catching glove over his left hand. Cloak wears his sharp smile, the one that makes me want to break all his teeth.

Nikko's expression is a shadow. He rests his hands on his guns and says, "I wonder, old man, do you remember the last thing you said to me when first we parted ways?"

The Bullet Catcher, clutching his shoulder, looks directly into Nikko's eyes. Spasms pass violently through the Bullet Catcher's muscles. He spits a glob of blood at Nikko's feet. "I said I was disappointed in you."

Cloak's smile widens like a slash across his face. "It's you who disappoints, Bullet Catcher. You were beaten so easily," he says. "Obviously, Nikko has no more need for teachers."

"Only fools believe they have nothing left to learn."

Cloak tenses, his finger trembling just above the trigger. Nikko holds out his hand, staying Cloak for the moment.

"You told me he abandoned you," I say, working up the courage to speak.

Nikko's shoulders drop, and he looks off to the woods, where the sounds of the gunslingers grow closer. "I told you what you needed to hear," he says, unable to look at me.

"You told me what you wanted me to believe."

With Nikko looking off to the woods, I drop to a knee to check the Bullet Catcher's wounds, and, fast as I dare, slide my hand to my holster.

"Don't even think about it," Cloak says, shaking his gun at me. "Take your shooters out slowly and throw them on the ground."

I draw them out, pointed up. I watch Cloak the whole time, hoping for a flinch, a momentary distraction. Anything. If I drop my guns it's all over.

Cloak's eyes flick to Nikko. The moon is a cold, silver lantern, looming in the night, lighting up the open meadow, and Nikko's eyes are bright and wet. Too late, Cloak sees me. He shoots. But he's too slow. I dive and fire. Cloak howls and his gun goes flying. With whatever strength he has left, the Bullet Catcher lunges at Nikko, tackling him to the ground. The Bullet Catcher, on top of him, punches him again and again.

I can hear the gunslingers running up the mountainside, behind the veil of trees. Cloak is gathering himself in the dirt, squeezing off the blood running from his forearm. Nikko can't throw the Bullet Catcher off. The first of the gunslingers comes running into the clearing, gun drawn. I fire two quick shots at her knees, and she falls head first into the dirt.

I pull the Bullet Catcher off Nikko and yell into his ear, "We need to find cover!" His eyes are wild. He seems to only half understand, but he lets me help him to his feet. I only have time to spare Nikko a look. Blood runs from his mouth and his broken nose. The state of him, inside and out, breaks my heart, and I have to fight the urge to grab him too and take him with us.

Behind us, Nikko is back on his feet and yelling orders to the gunslingers emerging from the woods, who are carrying the machine gun in pieces. As we retreat, I bombard them with covering fire, slowing them down.

At the lake, I pull the Bullet Catcher behind one of the large boulders and, pressing our backs against the cool rock, we struggle to catch our breaths.

The Bullet Catcher stares off into the middle distance, across the lake. His breath is wet and ragged. He turns to me, his chin resting on his shoulder, and says, wearily, "Run, Cub. Run."

My mind flashes back to Hartright, sacrificing herself for my sake, the sound of gunshots receding as the Bullet Catcher and I rode away.

"Are you kidding?" I say, forcing myself to smile. "We got them right where we want them."

The Bullet Catcher's eyes slide half closed and he smiles. Blood runs from the corner of his mouth. I let him lean against me as I check my ammo. Three bullets in my left gun. Two in my right. My bandoliers are empty. I load all five bullets into one gun and drop the other in the mud. I shrug off my empty bandoliers and, taking off my coat, rip the long sleeves from my shirt, then rip the sleeves into strips that I tie around the Bullet Catcher's shoulder. He doesn't flinch when I put pressure on his wounds.

"Imma. It's not too late!" Nikko calls from the mouth of the path, farther up the lakeshore. There's a new edge in his voice. "The old man is beaten. Save yourself. Join me. You're a gunslinger, like me. Like father!"

The Bullet Catcher looks at me with eyes that tell me to do the smart thing. His eyes tell me the fight is over.

"Not on your life," I say.

"You're being foolish, Cub," he wheezes.

"I've had a lot of foolish teachers."

He smiles at that. Straining, he gathers himself to his full height. I pull my coat back on, and with my gun in my hand, my metal trigger finger ready to fire my last five bullets, we share one last moment of quiet before the end. Together, we limp out from behind the rocks to face Nikko and Cloak and the gunslingers.

The night's grown long and the moon's completed its arc, dipping toward the mountains at our backs. This moment before dawn is cold, pitched, and colorless. Nikko and Cloak stand side by side with what's left of their posse behind them. Less than I thought: five gunslingers, standing astride their machine gun, reassembled and pointed meaningfully toward us. Even if my aim were perfect, I don't have enough bullets.

"It's over, Imma," Nikko says, his face smeared with blood. "For my sake, step away from the old man."

The Bullet Catcher loosens himself from my grip and pushes away from me.

"Don't give up," I say, holding tightly to him.

"One thing at a time, Cub." he says, prying my fingers from his arm. "Give me room."

I do what he says and let him slip away. We're pinned down between the gunslingers and the lake. I'm fast, but not as fast as their machine gun. Nikko waves his hand toward the Bullet Catcher and Cloak draws his pistol and progresses down the muddy beach. Cloak holds one of his hands between the buttons of his jacket in a makeshift sling. Blood trickles from his arm, where I shot him.

Cloak slugs the Bullet Catcher across the face with the broadside of his gun, dropping him to his knees. "I shouldn't make a habit of this," he says, looking down at him. "I'm going to get a reputation for killing old people." He looks at me, winks, and says, "Don't worry, Imma, your friend Hartright didn't suffer long."

Cloak points his gun down at the Bullet Catcher's head and pulls back the hammer. "Last words?"

The Bullet Catcher looks dazed from Cloak's blow and doesn't seem to hear him.

"And to think," Cloak says to me, "you chose him over us." He squeezes the trigger. And just then, the Bullet Catcher cups his hands around the end of the barrel. An explosion erupts from Cloak's revolver. The air around the two men sets on fire. The oxygen itself seems to burn, vibrate, and burst. The gun backfires, exploding Cloak's hand. The force of the blast sends the Bullet Catcher sprawling backward. I hit the ground and taste mud. When I look up, Cloak is still on his feet, in shock, gripping the mangled flesh that was, a moment ago, his shooting hand. His mouth is agape as though to scream, but no sound comes out. Seizing on the moment of confusion, I draw my gun and send five bullets into the shocked gunslingers, lingering by the machine gun. They hit the ground, howling at their ruined hands and burst kneecaps.

I point my gun at Nikko, but only because he's the last man standing. I risk a glance at the Bullet Catcher. He lies on his back, unmoving. The lip of the water kisses the top of his head, wetting his hair. I don't know if he's alive or dead.

Nikko rushes to Cloak's side and catches him as his legs go out from underneath him. I remember the first thing Nikko taught me about fighting bullet catchers: 'Press the barrel to the skin. All a bullet catcher needs is an inch and a moment.'

"Nikko . . ." Cloak squeezes from his shocked, airless lungs.

Nikko falls to his knees, cradling Cloak in his arms. Tears stream over his bloodied cheeks and spill onto Cloak's face and shirt. Cloak's lips are colorless and trembling. Nikko holds him tightly to his body, grasping, clutching at his clothes that slip through his fingers with Cloak's weight. Nikko touches his forehead to Cloak's. His lips move quickly, whispering something too softly for me to hear. He wipes the dirt and sweat from Cloak's face with his shirtsleeve and suddenly, almost unexpectedly, Cloak goes limp in his arms. Nikko holds the back of Cloak's head in his hand, like a newborn baby, squeezing the dark strands of hair between his fingers.

Keeping my gun trained on Nikko, I sidestep to the Bullet Catcher, and check his pulse. It's faint, but there. I can't see any new wounds. The blast must have just knocked him out.

Nikko doesn't look at me. He holds onto Cloak, cupping his cheek in his palm, and says, "I know if there was a sixth bullet in that gun you'd already have used it."

The gun goes limp in my hand. I let it hang from my finger by the trigger guard, before letting it fall in the dirt.

"I wouldn't," I say.

"You killed him," Nikko says, almost to himself. "You killed him."

"Not me," I say, trembling, equally sorry and afraid. When he looks up at me, his eyes are bloodshot.

"Not you," he says, sliding Cloak's body from his lap and standing. "Do you think any of this would have happened without you?" He draws his gun and holds it at his side, gripping it so hard his fingers turn white. "Is it so easy for you to shirk blame?"

"Nikko . . ." I speak his name without knowing what to say after. "Nikko, please. Can't you see what he was turning you into? You're not this person."

"And how do *you* know what kind of person I am? You hardly know me." He points his gun at Cloak's body and says, "He knew me. He knew me better than anybody. He loved me." He stares at the ground between us, tapping the gun on his hip. "And what about you, Imma? Do you love me? Are you even capable of that?"

"You're my brother. I love you no matter what," I say, my voice nearly a whisper.

"You're a liar." He looks up at me, his eyes red from holding back tears, but calm. He raises his chin in the direction of the Bullet Catcher and says, "You chose him over me. Over blood. No, I was wrong. You're not a liar. You're a monster."

The Bullet Catcher lies on his back behind me. Gunslingers litter the forest floor like so many autumn leaves. The soft ground soaks up their blood.

And then I'm reaching into my breast pocket and drawing my tiny single shooter. Why? Perhaps because I am the monster Nikko thinks I am. Or maybe because Nikko has his gun drawn and I don't and that terrifies me, makes me feel naked and defenseless.

Nikko stares at me, a look of disbelief on his face. "Well, that settles it," he says. "You'd shoot your own brother? Do it, then."

"We can make this right. We can fix this." I just want to hold him, tell him I'm sorry, tell him everything will be okay. Couldn't it be that simple?

"No," he says. "We can't." He raises his gun, not at me but at the Bullet Catcher, lying on the ground, defenseless.

I don't think, I react. I pull the trigger. I don't know what Nikko was going to do, if he was going to shoot the Bullet Catcher or if he was just giving *me* a reason to shoot. After all, he was right. I had made my decision. I had chosen the Bullet Catcher over him. Maybe Nikko was making his own choice. I didn't wait to find out. I shot first.

Nikko flicks the air with his gloved hand and pain blooms in my gut. I drop my gun and fold my arms over my midsection. I stagger, trying to keep my balance, and drop to my knees. Hartright's voice is in my head: 'Don't let me fall, young'un. A person can't die, long as she's on her feet.'

When I look up at Nikko he seems very far away, as though he and the rest of the world are receding. Or maybe it's me who's on her way out. "I'm sorry," he says. And then, "But you did that. It was your gun. Your bullet. You've killed yourself."

My hands are sticky and covered in blood when I lift them from my stomach. Panicked, I can only cup my hands and scoop the blood back up toward the wound, trying to push it back in. It's useless. I let the blood down, suddenly exhausted, wanting for nothing but sleep. I crawl on my hands and knees toward the Bullet Catcher. I rest my head on his chest. Nikko watches, his face white, his body trembling, as though, despite what he said, if he's to have a hand in my death, the least he can do is face it, to not turn away in the final outcome.

"I'm ready," I say to no one. I close my eyes and rest my ear to the Bullet Catcher's chest and wait, suddenly impatient for death, like a consolation prize.

Behind my eyes, the lamp inside Endd's shack appears. When I focus on it, the flickering lamp ignites in a gas fire, burning warmly, brightly. The lamp emits a ragged, but fiery pulse. The pulse emits a low, uneven sound: my heart beating. But unlike before, my light is not alone in the room. There is another lamp burning beside it, like a mirror image. The lamp is the Bullet Catcher's. I am not alone, because I am not just me. I transcend the body lying here, bleeding out, dying. I fill Endd's shack with the Bullet Catcher—Lobo—with Hartright, with Nikko as a boy.

"Where does your power lie?" the Bullet Catcher asks. The lamp grows brighter until it envelops everything in warmth and light.

And when I open my eyes the world is set on fire by the dawn bursting through the line of trees. I get to my feet. My skin is desiccated, my muscles are stone, my bones are hollow. But I get to my feet. I'm covered in blood and cold like the dead, but I am alive.

Nikko looks like when we were children at the orphanage, when one of the Brothers or Sisters would beat him. He'd make his face stone. He wouldn't let them see how much it hurt.

"It didn't have to be this way," he says. "We were family."

"We are family," I say, half turning to him, spreading my stance, ready.

He's impossible to read in this moment and I think that perhaps he was right when he said that I didn't know him. He looks back at Cloak, turning cold on the ground, and perhaps he's again thinking of me as a monster, someone who deserves to die. Or maybe he's only thinking that he's already come so far, and already lost so much, that he needs to see things through. Whatever he's thinking, when he turns back to face me, he raises his gun and fires.

Never has the world moved so slow, never have I been so quick. I accept the bullet into my palm and, closing my hands around it, I feel its warmth, its energy, radiating in all directions. I spin, cradling the bullet, curving it around me as I turn. I spin all the way around, shifting my feet in the soft mud, my stance strong and firm, the way the Bullet Catcher taught me, and when I'm facing Nikko again I straighten my arms and open my hands, letting the bullet go, not so much aiming, but guiding it home.

Nikko dives out of the way, but I anticipated it all before he did. I know his movements. I know he favors to dodge one way and not the other. I know he extends one arm out for balance and pivots with his left foot. As he desperately tries to dodge the bullet, Nikko's hand, gloved in that husk of metal, explodes in a shower of sparks. Dropping his gun, he falls to his knees, grasping his hand, the metal glove twisted and exploded into shrapnel.

Staggering over to him, one hand pressed to my belly where the blood has slowed to a trickle, I bend down and pick up his gun. I don't aim it at him. I just hold it at my side, pointed at the ground. It's too heavy to lift anyway, but he doesn't know that.

"We are family," I say. "You're right. It doesn't have to be this way. It's not too late."

He looks up at me, eyes squinted in pain, his body curled over his crippled hand. His face twists, his broken, askew nose casts a jagged shadow across half his face, his lips curl, his brow furrows. "I hate you," he says, and he spits at my feet.

Nikko got to his feet, staggered to Cloak's body, and tried to lift him with his good hand. He dragged him a few feet before he gave up. He turned, kissed Cloak's lips once and rose. He spared me one more terrible look and walked back up the path.

I had a long time to call him back, to try one last time to make things right. I had a long time to put a bullet in his back. I knew if he lived he would keep coming for me. I looked at my palm and traced the circle of the bullet-catching scar. I turned my hand over and traced the circle of the gunslinger tattoo and remembered my promise to myself, to seize my opportunities when they showed themselves. But I just stood there and watched him go, wondering if it was the last time I'd ever see him. And despite what it meant, I hoped it wasn't.

Then he was gone, lost against the sun and the pine. The sound of his footsteps crunching on the frost-webbed path went on for a few seconds more and faded into the quiet and the twittering of birds signaling morning.

I wanted only to lie on the ground and let sleep take me. But I heard Hartright in my head again, telling me to stay on my feet. And I did. Because there's a power in me, a burning light that refuses to go out.

Epilogue

Removing the bullet from my gut was the hard part. Simply heating the knife and finding a strap of leather to bite down on was bad enough. But it needed to be done. If it would kill me, removing the bullet, it would still be better than the slow death brought on by infection or blood loss. The bullet had passed through Hartright's flask, but had been slowed down enough to save my life. It wasn't so deep and had missed my organs. After it was done, and my shaking hand had threaded the last stitch, I passed out and didn't wake until the next day. I propped Hartright's flask up on the storage chest in my tent, like a photograph, and thanked her for saving my life a second time.

The pain was terrible. But it did not kill me. What was worse was watching the Bullet Catcher, swathed in bandages that were bled through moments after I wrapped them, as he battled back from the brink of death, struggling, gritting his teeth, his skin cold and covered in sweat. I sat by his bedside with my hand in his, whispering I-don't-know-what, just to let him know I was still there, to give him a direction back. And if he was to die, I wanted him to know he wouldn't have to be alone. After doing all I could to coax him back to life, it was

284

the only way I had left to help him. Because he would have died alone if I had never followed him out of Sand. Whatever my being here was worth, it had to be enough. I told myself that over and over until it started to feel true.

The gunslingers, too wounded to make it back to their horses, let alone to town, wandered into camp. As they approached, I kept my hand on Nikko's gun, but there was no fight in them, and when they collapsed or threw themselves on the ground in the clearing, I could do nothing else but help them. When they were well enough, I sent them on their way. But I kept their guns. I added them to the Bullet Catcher's trove.

When I was strong enough, I walked through the woods to find the dead. When I found a body, I dug a hole and buried it. The ones who died at the bottom of the pitfalls were easy. They were already in their graves. I just filled them in.

Lastly, I made my way down to the lakeshore, where Cloak lay, half buried in the mud and sand from the tide sweeping over him. His good-looking face was shriveled, the color of water stone: gray and green. His skin had shrunk around his jaw, drawing back his lips and making the hairs of his beard look long and wiry.

I buried him facing west, looking out toward the water. I knew so little of him and understood even less. The things I did know I didn't like, save for that one stolen moment, when I saw him with Nikko. I thought of Nikko's face in that moment, his smile when they kissed, so warm and loving. Cloak gave that to my brother, he inspired that love in him. I thought about that when I said the few words I had energy enough to spare

Cloak. Then I rolled him into his shallow grave, and pushed the cold earth on top of him. I marked his grave with a simple marker, made from lashed together sticks. I hung his gun belt and handkerchief from it, gave it a final look and forgot him. There are some people worth keeping in your memories. Others are only worth forgetting.

By spring, the grave was covered with new heathery grass, bright green and soft. The marker was broken, and the belt and handkerchief had been blown away by the wind or carried off by some animal.

When the Bullet Catcher finally woke, there was a dangerous gleam in his eye. At first, he didn't understand that the fighting was over. But when he saw me trying to keep him still, afraid he'd pop one of his sutures, he calmed.

"So, we beat them, then?"

"No sweat," I said.

"I was never worried, Cub. Not for a moment."

He wasn't fond of the sling I'd fashioned for his arm, or the sutures, but after he checked himself over, all the time wearing a dissatisfied look, he nodded his head and seemed proud of the work.

"You've done well, Cub." All the same, he tried to untie the sling, but when he felt the full weight of his arm in his wounded shoulder, he groaned and looked like he saw stars. He didn't fiddle with it after that.

When the Bullet Catcher was well enough, we set to putting the camp back together. We moved slowly but surely, our strength returning. One night, after the camp was fixed up and the blood had been washed out of the dirt and grass by rains, we sat around the fire, with fresh meat roasting over the flame, filling the air with a delicious gamey smell. We were both finally well enough to eat something substantial. Everything was finally back to normal, but even then, I knew it couldn't last. Nikko and the gunslingers were still out there and we couldn't afford to wait for them to return.

The next morning I woke to find the Bullet Catcher already up and about, his horse kneading the dirt with his hoof, the saddlebags packed. No-Name watched me emerge from my tent with an impatient expression, she too loaded up with saddlebags.

"Let's go," the Bullet Catcher said.

I packed the few things I had—Hartright's flask, my tiny one-shooter, some clothes—and we set off. We rode down the mountain, through the brush and trees. We came out onto the burning plane of the desert in a plume of sand and dust. I looked out over the golden expanse and the piercing blue sky overhead and thought of how empty it all was, and how full. And we rode on.

Acknowledgments

There were many people who played integral roles in this book's creation and it is a great pleasure to thank them for their help, but it's an even greater pleasure to take credit for their hard work. Unless you disliked the book, in which case it was entirely their fault, I assure you.

Thank you to June Saraceno, my first teacher, who made everything I wrote afterwards possible, who taught me my first writing lessons, the bedrock on which my writing is still built; who taught the first classes I ever looked forward to attending, who pointed me towards great writing and gave me courage to find the beginnings of my own style—though I already knew then I would never be an even adequate poet.

Thank you to Carol Anshaw and Jim McManus, who gave so many hours to read, critique, and discuss my awful, earnest, fledgling stories; whose notes and comments I strained over and complained about; whose patience and wisdom made me into a writer.

Thank you to Masie Cochran, who first told me to write this story one cold Portland evening, hunkered down in a bar over warm drinks. I'd never have written it in the first place without her encouragement.

Thank you to my great friends and first readers, Mary Breadon, Kait Heacock, and Tyler Samson, who because of their intelligence and skill, and because our friendships are too invested to ever derail, pointed out every mistake, cliché, and poor decision I made.

Thank you to Jennifer Erskine and Steve Waterman, who were the first people to read the early manuscript and—to my astonishment—enjoy it. And more than that, who then put it in front of others who could help nurture it to publication. Without them not only would that manuscript still be sitting in a drawer in my desk, but my life would be headed on a wholly different course than the one it's on now.

Thank you to my agent, Jessie Botterill, who was this book's greatest champion, who not only worked tirelessly to find a home for it but whose keen editorial eye helped shape its story.

Thank you to Brenda Gardner, Jenny Jacoby, Jennie Roman, and everyone at Hot Key Books, who, even after the help of everyone I've already thanked were still given a half-formed thing, and who managed to help make it whole.

Thank you, Douglas Adams, for making me laugh when it otherwise seemed impossible. Thank you, Ray Bradbury, whose books got me through my youth. It is a pleasure to burn.

Thank you to Dan Gurska, who I have always leaned on in the hardest times, and without whom I'd never have made it this far. And thank you to all my friends, for the support and love, especially in those times I've been incapable of returning it in kind.

Thank you to my family, my brother and sister, against whose characters I am forever comparing my own, and for whom I always want to improve. And thank you to my mother and father, who gave me the only two things I'd ever need, the only things anyone truly needs—love and time.

Joaquin
Portland—Brooklyn—Mill Valley
2013—2014—2015

Joaquin Lowe

Joaquin Lowe grew up in the San Francisco Bay Area, and
has lived in New York, Chicago, Portland, and London.
He was educated at Sierra Nevada College and the School
of the Art Institute of Chicago. *The Bullet Catcher* is his first
novel. Say hello on twitter @JoaquinLowe

Thank you for choosing a Hot Key book.

If you want to know more about our authors
and what we publish, you can find us online.

You can start at our website

www.hotkeybooks.com

And you can also find us on:

We hope to see you soon!